The Spanish Steps

BRUCE BAIN

The Spanish Steps
Bruce Bain

© Copyright 2018 Bruce Bain
All rights reserved.

Bruce Bain
Salt Lake City, Utah
www.bruceobain.com   facebook.com/bruceobain   twitter.com/bruceobain1

BookWise Publishing, New York City, NY
BookWisePublishing.com

Cover illustration: Amber McRae
Cover design: Melissa Lowe
Interior design: Karen K Christoffersen

Library of Congress Cataloging-in-Publication Data
Bain, Bruce.
The Spanish Steps: a love story from a man's point of view about the important women in his life / Bruce Bain. — 1st ed.
ISBN 978-1-60645-225-7 (pb) 978-1-60645-226-4 (eb)
1. Romance. 2. Relationships. 3. Title.
LOC 2018948479

10 9 8 7 6 5 4 3 2 1
Printed in the USA

9/10/2018

Dedication

To Mom and Dad,

who instilled in me a profound love for words and music.

Introduction

THEY SAY TIMING IS EVERYTHING IN LIFE. This especially rings true in the arena of love. When I think of all my swings and misses, stops and starts, catching someone on the rebound, or it being *too soon*, the times I've bounced off other souls, lost chances I might not have even realized, like ships passing in the night, *my head swims.*

They also say you can't choose with whom you fall in love. If that's true, then you can't choose *when* it happens either. Love finds us in its own sweet time. It's a difficult enough proposition with impeccable timing, the perfect alignment of the stars, and the blessing of the Universe. It seems downright hopeless without those *lucky* components on your side.

My story is one of love and timing, and because of the inherent heartache felt when those don't magically synchronize, it is also a story of pain, healing, and growth; a tale of rebirth, hope, faith, and second chances.

This adventure will explore the *seemingly* never-ending battle raging between ego and soul; for when we finally discover the difference between wanting and needing someone, we realize that peace may be an even greater gift than love.

The Spanish Steps abounds with the lessons that love has taught me about living one day at a time, even one *moment* at a time. I liken *living in the moment* to not looking down while on this tightrope we call life, lest we see the perilous chasm below. Love has taught me that it's wise to take one careful step at a time; to not think too much about the difficulty of getting to the other side.

But, then again, love has also taught me that sometimes it's even better to toss caution to the wind and take a huge leap of faith.

Prologue

Feeling that my internal clock had adjusted to the time change, I awoke refreshed and anxious to start my day. After a quick shower and a breakfast of fruit and juice, I hit the streets just after dawn. I walked briskly past sights that would normally snare the less focused, but I had just one place on my mind this morning, the Spanish Steps of Rome.

I made my way up the gentle incline of *Via del Corso* as the Eternal City slowly embraced what would be a bustling, summer day. I turned right on *Via Condotti* and caught my first glimpse of the Steps rising from *Piazza di Spagna*. They had taken on an almost mythical quality in my mind since becoming the featured setting in my song, written over two years ago. So, it felt a bit surreal as I entered the square.

I blew right past the charming *Fontana della Barcaccia*, where the more famous son learned his craft at the feet of his father. With all due respect to the Bernini family, my business was at the top of the Steps, not the bottom. My pace finally slowed as I began my ascent of one of Rome's most beloved sights. Gone were the azaleas that adorn the stairway in April and May, but the setting was beautiful nonetheless.

I had hoped to have the place to myself at this early hour, and I did. As I continued to climb past the first terrace, my mind drifted back in time to when I wrote the lyrics and the thoughts and emotions that went into those words; the hope, the promise, the romantic notion, all of it. But the very reason that brought me to this place now collided with the reality that I had no business being here at all. Yet *here* I was; so on I climbed.

I neared the top of the Steps, and now my mind wandered forward a day and a half, to the following night. I pictured the sun on the other side of the sky, setting instead of rising. I took the final steps through *her* eyes, as I would surely have arrived first, waiting at the top. *What will she feel when she sees me here? What is in her heart after so much time? Will she even show up at all? Would she cover that final distance of her two-year journey?*

I stood on the top terrace, below la *Chiesa della Trinita dei Monti*, and looked this time through my own eyes. I envisioned her finding me among the throngs gathered for sunset. *What would I feel inside? Would there be a rekindling of a spark that had since gone cold? Did I ultimately even want to feel anything for her? Did I not have everything I wanted as I held someone else in my arms just three nights ago?*

I gazed over the awakening city and felt a very real sense of panic. The clock was ticking, and I still had so much to figure out in such a short time. Rome would soon be alive, busy, and noisy. I turned and strode toward the one nearby place I knew I could find some peace and begin to sort things out: the gardens of *Pincian Hill*.

Chapter 1

Oh, mirror in the sky what is love?
Can the child within my heart rise above?
Can I sail through the changing ocean tides?
Can I handle the seasons of my life?

Landslide—Fleetwood Mac

October 2014

"Wow! Girl, you definitely need to take a couple laps around the universe."

I spoke loudly enough to be heard above the decent cover band playing classic rock but softly enough that those seated at the nearest table weren't privy to our life stories being shared over sips of bourbon.

Staring into Kate's glittering brown eyes, I was conflicted. I knew the words I'd just spoken were true, but something deep in my heart, in the place where sparks ignite into flames, I wished desperately I were dead wrong.

But our story doesn't begin on that snowy December night in *A Bar Named Sue*, where we would later celebrate our first kiss in the parking lot, but rather a few months earlier, on an otherwise uneventful workday in October.

"Jamison? Charles is on line one for you."

"Thanks, Pat," I replied as I walked past the front desk into my office and picked up the phone.

"Hey, Chuck, what's up, my friend?"

"Jamison, meet Kate. Kate, meet Jamison. She's got a project coming up that we need your help on as we're slammed. I've got to scoot into a meeting. I just wanted to connect the two of you, and I'll let you both take it from here. Take good care of her, buddy. See ya!"

I heard Kate's phone come off speaker mode as she picked up the handset.

"Hi. Sorry that introduction was so quick."

"No worries, Chuck is a busy boy. What can we do for you?"

I worked in sales and marketing for a small video production company, and Charles and Kate were employed at an advertising agency, both companies located in Salt Lake City. Charles and I went back at least fifteen years, and while I knew of Kate, we'd never officially met.

"We've got an event coming up for one of my clients and can't quite handle everything internally. It's a multi-camera production, and Charles tells me that's right in your wheelhouse."

"Absolutely. Let's talk dates and specifics, and I'll check the availability of the guys."

We spent about fifteen minutes going over the project. Kate impressed me right away as being quite competent and pleasant. I found out later that I gave a similar impression.

After we hung up, I spent a moment before snapping into action on her project, thinking she sounded quite nice and cute—if that kind of thing can be transmitted over the phone. *I wonder what her story is?*

Over the next few weeks, we exchanged several emails and a few phone calls leading up to her event, and my team completed the project flawlessly. We'd built a solid and warm professional relationship during the process, but it hadn't been necessary for us to chat face-to-face. After one of the shoot days, our lead videographer on the project, Denny, dropped a hard drive of the footage on my desk and asked if I'd ever met Kate.

"Nope, I've just been dealing with her over the phone so far."

"She's cute; just a little thing, only about five feet tall."

"Hmm, maybe I'll see her when I drop off the drive. Great work on her project, by the way. Thanks!"

I didn't meet her this time around, but I had a strong impression we would soon. It was difficult to explain, but I felt some sort of connection with her. There was an indescribable energy I was in tune with that told me she would have a role in my life. In many ways, the planets were aligning for me to be open to some good things to come from the Universe; but to fully explain that, I must go back a couple years to a time when I wasn't fond at all of what the Universe was handing me.

You already know my name is Jamison. Jamison Barrick. If that is spoken with a Sean Connery accent, it almost sounds James Bond-ish. No, I'm not named after Irish whiskey (different spelling), but I do have some Irish in me, as well as Scottish, British, and a bit of German. I'm basically a nice guy, or at least I hope people describe me that way. I'm in my mid-fifties. There's no need to get too specific after one reaches a certain age or maturity. Early, mid, late—if it's all in the same decade, I figure it's close enough. I'm youthful in spirit, if not in actual time spent on the planet.

As for the visual description, I'm somewhere in the middle of the spectrum between ruggedly handsome and hideous-looking.

I'm bald, so instead of fighting that gift of heredity, I shave my head twice a week or more frequently if something fancy comes up. I'm over six feet tall, and I diligently attempt to keep the label of *athletic build*, but a love of food, winter inactivity, changing metabolism, and the ravages of time all take turns threatening that. I have blue eyes that sometimes lose their brilliance when I'm stressed or sad. And I wear a goatee (probably to hide a less than prominent upper lip), which has gone gray with time.

I'm far more creative than analytical. I couldn't help my two daughters with math homework from the time they were fifth-graders but could assist them with writing papers and more right-brained assignments. I love music. I took up the guitar a few years ago, about four decades later than I should have, and have been able to combine two loves, writing and music, to create songs. I've even performed them live—playing, not singing (think of a bad *American Idol* audition to understand why)—and I would enjoy recording some of them. I did begin writing lyrics those four decades ago, never calling them poems, however, as I always had a tune in my head as I wrote. On the side, I've been attempting to monetize this passion, even hiring an agent with connections in Nashville.

I'm also what I'd like to call a *hopeful romantic;* so many of the songs I've written are about love. They're personal and reflect my life and reveal my patterns. I tend to keep coming back for more despite love's many setbacks along the way. I haven't learned to be completely cynical yet. I suppose that isn't such a bad thing. *Or is it?*

Chapter 2

It used to be all I'd want to learn
Was wisdom, trust, and truth;
But now all I really want to learn
Is forgiveness for you.

Forgiveness—Collective Soul

Now that I've taken care of the introduction, here's the story.

I was coming out of my second marriage, but first, the back story. *Damn! Do I sound like Elizabeth Taylor?* My first wife, Carrie, and I remained great friends and partners in raising our daughters after our split. The simplest way to describe our demise would be to say that I gave up on us too easily and too soon when we encountered rough seas. It would be quite the understatement to say I was lacking in the maturity department when it came to appreciating what I had and comprehending what love really was at the time. But two wonderful daughters came from our union, and I will be forever grateful for their amazing mother and one of my most enduring friendships.

After several years of being a single, soccer dad/coach, and not really dating much, I embraced the idea of friends lining me up. This was before the free swiping apps of today but shortly after pay sites like *Match* and *eHarmony* started popping up. I suppose I was simply being cheap by leaving the fate of my love life in the capable hands of well-meaning friends. They seemed to have a handle on who would be *just perfect* for me anyway. One such attempt at playing Cupid led to a name and phone number on a Post-it note, a couple of phone calls, and me pulling my car into a dark driveway on a cold January night for a true blind date. There were no profile pictures to stalk back in that day.

Anna opened the door, and I did a kind of Tiger Woods' fist pump on the inside. Her hair was dark, she had olive skin, gorgeous brown eyes, and an exotic look that attracted me instantly. There was also a childlike innocence about her which would have reincarnationists suspecting she was on her first or second life. The intel I had going in was: mother of two kids, going through a divorce, separated for a few months, her soon-to-be ex was a jerk, and she was pretty. While the first few items were indeed facts, the last part of the report was opinion, and I concurred. We had a wonderful first date at a friend's house playing Texas Hold 'em. Another date followed, then many more. Meanwhile, she wrapped up a rather lengthy and nasty divorce, and we were married a little more than three years later.

Earlier, I mentioned the need for Kate to take a few laps around the universe. You will soon learn why she needed that, but the wisdom behind my words was hard earned, and its roots can be directly traced to my years spent with Anna. This is not a tale of Jamison and Anna, but some context is essential in understanding what makes me tick and how difficult lessons learned impacted the relationships I will share.

If anyone ever needed to circle the galaxies for an extended period after splitting with her husband, it was Anna. Of course, at the time, I lacked the foresight and astuteness to see that. I came to learn she had never truly been alone and was always in some form of a relationship since her adolescence. In my humble opinion, she lacked the wisdom gained from the soul searching that is done during those valuable voids between lovers. So much growth comes from those long, dark, and painful nights when it all comes crashing down; but Anna chose a pattern of avoiding that process by moving directly to the pleasantness of a fresh relationship.

As we dated and eventually were married, she was busy trying to *find herself* at the same time as attempting to grow closer to me and establish a solid foundation for marriage. This is certainly not the ideal recipe for success, but it partially explains why she sometimes seemed checked-out and not fully engaged in us. Add into the mix my nature at the time to want to fix everything for the one I loved. It all made for a very unhealthy cocktail. Initially, I saw a struggling, single mom, escaping the dominant rule of an emotionally abusive ex, and I saw my role as one riding in on a white horse to save the day.

After we married, I assumed the troubles with her ex were behind her, and I struggled to understand why she was, at times, emotionally unavailable to me. My instincts were to try even harder to fix everything. When I perceived that my partner seemed to lack the capacity to appreciate me for all I so gallantly brought to the table, I allowed resentment to fester, which led to even more withdrawal on her part and created quite a vicious cycle. Little did I know, but Anna was fighting a battle inside that would eventually make all the marital stuff seem quite trivial in hindsight.

The following years were extremely difficult as our marriage eroded before my eyes. I was living with a woman who was, for some reason, very much lost, while I was under the smug and mistaken impression that I had my own shit completely together. The reality was that through the experience we shared, *I found myself*. I was a significantly better man at the end than at the beginning.

While she sought to figure out some very fundamental and deep-seated things about *herself*, the search was, unfortunately, accompanied by some ugly baggage which is all too typical in such situations—betrayal, pain, guilt, resentment and, eventually, resignation and complete surrender. But those feelings did not define us. Time is the great healer, and they were replaced by sincere remorse, forgiveness, compassion, and, yes, love.

Anna is now remarried, and we are dear friends. I am still close to her two kids, Jade and Nate. She happens to be happily married to a *woman*, the love of her life. And I couldn't be more thrilled for her. She is very much at peace with who she is and how far she has come as a person. She is truly the very best version of herself she has ever been since I've known her. Everything I'd hoped was inside her when she answered my knock on her door on that long-ago chilly, winter night has come to fruition. That it didn't come while she was with me is irrelevant. That it did happen is everything.

There were some very dark days during this time, but I probably learned more about myself and what I'm made of than at any other time in my life, and I took these lessons with me going forward. When I add up the personal growth I experienced in the process, I must admit, even knowing the outcome and the toll it exacted from me to get through everything relatively intact, I'd probably do it all over again. As a wise, Italian woman would one day teach me, despite how it might feel in the moment, love is not a matter of life or death.

———♡———

A few months after all of this, a letter arrived in my mailbox on a hot August afternoon in 2013. Through the mail, the Third District Court of the great State of Utah informed me, in a rather anticlimactic way, that my divorce with Anna was final.

Chapter 3

I can't find the right romantic line,
But see me once, and see the way I feel.
Don't discard me just because you think I mean you harm;
But these cuts I have, they need love to help them heal.

Don't Let the Sun Go Down on Me—Elton John

ANNA BOUGHT ME OUT OF MY SHARE of the house we'd purchased in 2008. That year might ring a bell as the start of the housing market crash and the economic downturn. We had purchased high, then I was forced to sell low, meaning I took quite a beating financially. But I had just enough for a decent down payment to get into a modest townhouse in a condo complex. My youngest daughter, Bailey, helped me pick out something that wouldn't feel too much like a huge step backward at that point in my life. She totally nailed it.

I enjoyed the swimming pool on the property, long bike rides, (I got my athletic build back that summer) the abundance of *me time*, entertaining friends and family, and just the right amount of gardening without having to mow a lawn. I was happy and at peace.

I'd chosen a part of town not too far from my mother's house. My dad had passed away in January 2012, and Mom became my project of sorts. With my daughters now grown and on their own, taking care of Mom became an important mission to me. Our routine included a weeknight dinner date and shopping on Sundays.

I didn't really date much. I was taking my own advice of getting in touch with me—sorting everything out that I'd been through with Anna, taking inventory of the damage, and determining what remained inside me. I had trust issues and was determined to proceed cautiously with the female species.

By November 2013, I was feeling good about things, because I finally accepted another line-up. *Facebook* was huge, so by the time the big day arrived, I'd seen pictures of a woman, and I had several chats back and forth on the app. She scored points by liking sushi, so I picked my favorite restaurant for our first date.

Her name and features are totally irrelevant here. The only reason I bring her up is to offer some context to my state of mind and heart by the time I met Kate. I admit, I kind of fell for this lady. The rush of possibilities was enticing; add to that the ego stroke of someone being interested in *me*. Ultimately, it was all a mirage, as she was someone desperately trying to figure out many things in *her* life, and she appeared to be a serial dater. This experience would foreshadow the sorry state of dating at my age. There are a lot of damaged people out there, some more so than others. We were finished by early January.

As was my custom, I tried to find meaning from the brief affair, to glean some sort of lesson from the experience. Suffice it to say, I realized I completely lacked proper perspective in evaluating a potential partner. I had emerged from the desert after a long, thirsty adventure with Anna, and the first person who offered me some water looked damned wonderful. I clearly didn't know how to even recognize wonderful. Lesson learned.

Something good, other than additional wisdom, came from the breakup. Shortly after, I bought a guitar and started taking lessons. I didn't know it at the time, but that first guitar was merely the gateway drug. There would be more.

One of the other great benefits of my newfound freedom was the expansion of my horizons and my enjoyment of various types of relationships. Whether it was subconscious or not, I gravitated toward the safe harbor of platonic friendships. I could enjoy female companionship, doing the things I liked, without any added pressure of commitment, intimacy, or wondering why they didn't call or text. A couple of these friendships were with women several years younger than me, all but assuring things would remain in the friend zone.

My sushi buddy was Courtney. I could satisfy my raw fish cravings monthly with her and catch up on life. We'd met in a fitness class at my local gym and hit it off. I assumed I served a similar role in her life as she did in mine; someone of the opposite gender with whom to enjoy an evening out and offer a different perspective on life and love. Courtney's dating life was often the subject of our discussions, while she knew all the stories from my recent dates, my last marriage and divorce. We even covered *rebound girl*, as Courtney labeled her.

Abbey was my concert buddy. Our platonic status was forever cemented from the time she wondered out loud if her mom and I would be a good match. She was a vivacious blonde, her hair usually in a ponytail. She wore glasses and had a cute, cartoon character-like voice. We could cross a true legend off our wish list when we saw Sir Elton John together. That was the first of many concerts we'd attend. Though she was many years younger (again, no need to do the math), she'd been raised well and had an appreciation for the recording artists of my era. She was, in fact, named after a rather fine *Beatles* album. Abbey worked in the advertising industry, so our paths had crossed often. She had branched off into event planning and was very helpful when my oldest daughter, Kiara, was preparing for her early October wedding, offering her wealth of expertise to ease the concerns of the bride-to-be.

We got together for dinner in November as an opportunity for me to thank her since the wedding and reception went off without a hitch. Abbey picked Courtney's favorite sushi restaurant, *Takashi*. I almost felt I was cheating, but the rolls and appetizers were far superior to anywhere else in the city. I'd simply beg for forgiveness if I chose to confess my transgression or, heaven forbid, get caught in the act. I gave Abbey a detailed accounting of the wedding, as detailed as I could. I was in a daze that night, focusing on not losing it too much during my toast to the bride and groom.

In between eating edamame, cucumber salad, and various tasty rolls of salmon, yellowtail, and albacore, plus sipping sake, we caught up on work stuff, talking about projects on which we both worked. In addition to Abbey's own business, she still took on contract work with a couple of ad agencies in Salt Lake. She was in the middle of a nice stretch, professionally.

"I was hired for some freelance work for *Omnia Communications*. I'll be producing some Utah tourism spots for Charles. I have ten days booked this month for location scouting and shooting."

"That's great! We did a project for *Omnia* last month, a couple days of multi-camera shooting," I responded.

"Were you working with Charles?"

"No, it was for Kate's French client, *PathoLogique*. You worked together a few years back at *Latitude*, right? What's her story? I may have met her once. She might have been part of a group in an edit bay viewing finished spots."

Abbey was speechless and just looking at me with wide eyes.

"What?" I was puzzled by her expression.

"You would be perfect for each other!" she blurted out excitedly.

"Really? She's not married? How old is she?" I figured they were close in age.

"She's now single and a few years older than me, but you kind of skew younger," she offered a little wink.

I took that as a compliment before wondering if my maturity went into her assessment.

"Why do you think we'd be perfect together?"

Abbey gave an answer that hit home and stayed with me for the next several weeks, until the night I finally met Kate.

"Because you both occupy the same space in my heart. You are kind of the same person."

"Wow, that's pretty cool."

My words didn't make it to the intended ears as I saw the excitement in Abbey's eyes vanish almost as quickly as it had arrived.

"Uh, oh. I don't like that look."

"The timing might not be very good," she sighed. "She filed for divorce recently. He moved out in September, I think."

"Oh, boy. I've experienced that scenario before. Once in a lifetime is plenty."

I felt the wind leave my sails. We'd gone from perfect match to a cul-de-sac in a heartbeat. But for some reason, I didn't completely throw in the towel then and there. The intrigue surrounding Kate was overcoming my doubt. *Whoa, boy! Let's not be speeding past those red flags, again!*

Maybe she was feeding off my energy, but Abbey seemed to get a second breath of optimism.

"She did date a guy for a while last month, so maybe she got her rebound out of the way," she shrugged. "She's kind of deep, like you. Always posting stuff from *Elephant Journal* on *Facebook* and talking about her journey." Abbey's eyes rolled. I don't think she was harshly judging her friend but was just more pragmatic about matters of the heart.

"So maybe she's been processing things for a while. I know their split had been a long time coming. Kate and Jeff are very different. Maybe she's already moved on. We're meeting for lunch next Tuesday. I'll get a feel for where she is on that journey of hers." The event planner/matchmaker was in her groove. "I hope you saved room for some *panna cotta*."

For the remainder of our dinner, I was trying to process the two distinctly different and contradictory signals coming from my heart and my brain. By now you can probably guess which part of me was winning that internal tug-of-war.

Chapter 4

I can see the sunset in your eyes,
Brown and gray, blue besides.
Clouds are stalking islands in the sun.
I wish I could buy one, out of season.

Baby, I Love Your Way—Peter Frampton

I HAD A GREATER SENSE OF URGENCY TO LEARN all about Abbey's lunch with Kate than my concert buddy had to share with me. Tuesday afternoon went by without a call or text. I wasn't sure if no news was bad, indifferent, or simply no news. I hit the gym after work, and my *Guts & Butts* fitness class did a fine job of pushing it out of my head for fifty-five minutes. Wednesday came and went; a busy day at work which had me out of the office for a good chunk of the day on a shoot, trying to keep a nervous client happy. I was halfway through my Thursday when I finally gave in and texted Abbey

So . . . how did lunch go with Kate?

Can we chat after work?

Sure.

I hate the word *sure*. It is nothing more than a reluctant *yes*, a resignation of sorts. *Can we schedule your root canal for this Friday morning? Sure.*

I just assumed Kate had shown little or no interest in me when Abbey brought up the subject of her grand epiphany. My mood was already rather sour for the remainder of the day, as my main task for the afternoon was emailing clients to inquire why their payments were so overdue.

I was on the way to my mom's house to take her to dinner when Abbey called.

"Hi, Abbey." I tried to sound as cool as possible.

"Hey, sorry I couldn't text you back. I was in a casting session."

"No worries at all." I kept up the facade, despite dying to know how things went.

"She canceled on me Tuesday. We had dinner last night instead." I think she was taking great joy in dragging this out. "Good news. You made a nice impression on her when you were handling the *PathoLogique* project. I believe she used the word *intrigued*. She thought you were nice and was wondering about your story."

Okay, and now for the bad news, I thought. But I didn't come clean with my doubt.

"Cool! That *is* good news." *Now, let that other shoe drop.*

"She's super busy right now, but she sounded open to meeting you. My advice would be to play it cool, and let this happen when it's supposed to."

I wondered if Abbey were shielding me and if there was more to the story. This was her first attempt at playing Cupid for me, so I honestly didn't know how to read her. I decided to take her at her word.

"Sounds good. Thanks for mentioning me to her. I appreciate it. Hey, I'm pulling into my mom's driveway, so I better scoot."

"What's on the menu this week?"

"She picked *Wendy's*, so I can get a salad and escape relatively unscathed."

"Have fun, and we'll talk soon."

"Bye."

I sat for a moment in the driveway and felt all the needless nervousness of the past few days completely dissipate. Instead, calm enveloped me, making me a much more attentive dinner date.

November gave way to December, and the winter snows began to blanket the landscape of northern Utah. The air had a cold bite to it. I stayed busy at work. It was client Christmas gift season, I had year-end billing to get out, and our company party, also known as the *Renegade Productions Winter Solstice Luau*, was coming up.

Outside of work, I kept up with my efforts to master the guitar, although I dropped the formal lessons and went the *YouTube* route to learn new songs. I eased my guilty conscience by taking Courtney to *Takashi* early in the month, and I burned those pesky December calories a few nights a week working out at my gym. Life was good, and I really was content. It's usually at those times in our lives, when we aren't looking for anything at all, when things find us.

I was playing guitar to the glow of my Christmas tree one night in mid-December, when I decided to give my sore fingers a little break. I grabbed my phone, and out of habit, I fired up *Facebook*. I had a notification, a friend request from none other than Kate Campania. I'd recently read an article about the dangers of social media on kids, how receiving *Likes* and getting *Friend* requests weren't unlike the effects of the high one feels from dopamine. Let's just say that those feelings aren't exclusive to society's youth. I felt an immediate jolt. The notification was 35 minutes old. I set the phone down to play it coy by not responding too eagerly.

Feeling pathetic, a mere fifteen minutes later, I answered her request. Our potential budding relationship now had the blessing of *Facebook*. And, yes, I did spend several minutes that night stalking her photos on the popular app.

A day or two later, I received a text from Abbey.

Should I invite Kate to the Solstice Party?

Before I hit SEND, my *Hell, yes!* was toned down a bit.
Splendid idea!

The *Winter Solstice Luau* was my brainchild, and I have taken it with me on my journey through a few of the prominent video production companies in the Salt Lake Valley. I am a creature of light, and I mourn the days getting shorter after the Summer Solstice and celebrate the longer days ushered in by the winter version. Even though there are several weeks remaining of cold and snow, at least it gets gradually lighter with each passing day. So, we don our Hawaiian shirts, wear our leis, invite friends and clients to our office, and eat massive amounts of food, courtesy of a potluck provided by the team. I am the bartender and have been told that my margarita recipe rivals anything in town.

I thought Kate would fit in seamlessly with the mix of the *Renegade* team, our clients, and neighbors in the building, who seem to look forward to our party. This year it was slated for December 19th, the closest Friday to the actual day of the Solstice, which usually falls on the 21st. Our crew is a fun one. Kate had already met Denny, a camera and audio guy and CJ ran another camera on her project. Dave May is our editor, who has been a great supporter of my efforts to learn guitar. He was smart enough to start playing in the 7th grade. Luke, Alan, Koji, and Patrice made up the rest of the team. Poor Patrice, the only female in the group, must feel as if she were swimming in a sea of testosterone some days. Our company rose from the ashes of a corporate downsizing move. We were lean, nimble, and not missing the corporate oversight at all, hence our company name.

I was incredibly busy the day of the luau; preparing food, stirring crock pots, greeting clients, friends, and freelancers we hired for bigger projects, and documenting the day for social media. We did our usual lunch session, then re-racked for the after-work crowd. I started up the blender about 3 p.m., since it was 5 p.m. on the east coast.

Abbey and Kate were planning on coming together around 5:30 for drinks. I was feeling a buzz about their impending visit and the overdue meeting with Kate, and maybe a little from my drink. I had the blender churning out my renowned margaritas, which were being eagerly devoured by our guests, but I opted instead for my old standby, Woodford Reserve bourbon.

We had our usual late rush of people dropping by on their way home from work. I was in our back lobby socializing when I heard Abbey's voice among the crowd. I turned to greet her, but she was as good as invisible as I caught my first glimpse of Kate. Had our paths crossed before, I'm certain I'd have remembered. She was, as Denny described, just a little thing, about five feet tall with shoulder-length, dark brown hair and friendly and vibrant brown eyes. I recall vaguely what she was wearing—boots, a knee-length skirt, and a sweater—but I was completely focused on her beautiful face and confident smile.

"Hi, I'm Kate."

"You certainly are." I cringed over my reply in the moment, but in hindsight, it was smooth for me.

"I'm Jamison." I extended my hand rather awkwardly, feeling like it was the 8th grade all over again.

"I'm Italian. We hug." She leaned in, and we embraced.

Well then, ciao bella! I felt warmth engulf me, and the bourbon had nothing to do with this sensation.

Chapter 5

Maybe I'm wrong.
Won't you tell me if I'm coming on too strong.
This heart of mine has been hurt before.
This time I wanna be sure.

Waiting for a Girl Like You—Foreigner

I OFFERED OUR NEW GUESTS A DRINK. Abbey chose a margarita, while Kate pointed to the amber-colored beverage in my cup and indicated a preference for that spirit.

"I think I'll have what you're drinking. I'm not really a tequila fan."

"Ah, a bourbon girl," I said approvingly. "I keep the good stuff hidden. Let me go pour you some." *Very impressive!*

We settled into one of our edit bays. Dave was there, already entertaining a pair of clients that Abbey knew. I didn't feel bad about focusing on Kate after everyone was introduced.

"So, you're Italian. Do you speak the language?"

"No. I'm three generations removed from the old country, but I'm actually taking some online lessons before I go to Rome for my birthday in February."

"That'll be great for you. My birthday is in February, too, the 2nd. Groundhog Day."

"No kidding? Mine's on the 4th."

"Wow, almost birthday twins; a few years apart, that is. By the way, I speak Italian."

"No kidding?"

"No kidding. I studied abroad there in college, in a city called *Perugia* and in Rome. My minor was in Italian."

"Maybe you can be my Italian tutor. The online course has its limitations."

"Va bene," I smiled at the idea. "Have you been to Rome before? What a great birthday present."

"No, this will be my first time. Seems like the perfect place to turn forty and start a new chapter in my life."

"Assolutamente perfetto." I began our first lesson.

We were quickly corralled back into conversation with the others, who seemed to magically appear out of thin air. I could have sworn Kate and I had the room to ourselves. I made a deliberate attempt to not fawn too much over her, but I liked what I'd seen so far. I had to excuse myself a few times to refill cups with my frozen concoction, greet newcomers to the party, and say my goodbyes to those leaving. Each time, I returned to my seat next to Kate and was greeted with a warm smile. *Damn, she's pretty!*

The party eventually started to wrap up. We were down to just a handful of guests. We must be getting older because this bash used to go on well into the evening. Abbey and Kate purposely hadn't partaken of our varied spread and were planning on going out to eat after.

"Do you want to join us?" Kate offered out of the blue.

"Sure!" (*Okay, this was the one exception of my disdain for the 'sure' word. I stated it in exuberance in response to a surprise offer. I'm glad I've cleared that up!*) "Where are we going?"

"We were thinking *Morelia*," Abbey responded.

I had been grazing on our offerings since about noon, so I wasn't terribly hungry; but I wasn't going to sit this one out. I'd just pass on the chips and salsa.

"Let me see if Alan will handle cleanup."

"We'll help," both said in unison.

"No, you're the clients. Alan owes me anyway."

Alan didn't owe me a thing, but he saw that I had two lovely ladies waiting for me, so he graciously said he'd finish cleaning up. *Now* I owed him.

We took Abbey's SUV to the family-owned Mexican restaurant just a mile from the office. I picked the seat across the table from my dinner companions so I could engage them both. It seemed appropriate to order a round of margaritas, obviously not the first choice for Kate and me, but they were tasty. Abbey declared my recipe to be better, scoring valuable points, although after her suggestion to bring Kate to our party, her total couldn't possibly be any higher.

Our conversation was generic, focusing mainly on work. I had no way of knowing where this could lead, if anywhere, but there was an immediate comfort level that I felt with Kate, as if we'd known each other a long time. Nothing earth-shattering was revealed during the meal, but we continued to discover more things we had in common.

We wrapped up our dinner, and I picked up the tab, or more accurately, *Renegade Productions* did, as a thank you for the *PathoLogique* project and hope for more work from Kate's agency.

We drove back to the office and said our goodbyes. Abbey gave me a hug and a wink and drove off, strategically leaving me and Kate alone in the dark parking lot. Butterflies filled my stomach.

"It was great to finally meet you. I'm glad you could make it tonight."

"Same here. Abbey has said a lot of nice things about you. All true, I might add."

"Thanks and likewise." I could have used a big dose of smooth just then. "Would you like to grab some Italian food together soon?"

"That would be nice, but I've got a better idea. How about I have you over and cook for you? I've got a few family recipes up my sleeve."

"That sounds *perfect*." I had no way of knowing it at the time, but I would be using the word perfect quite a lot over the coming months.

"My dad is visiting for Christmas and things are kind of crazy, so maybe we can plan it for after he goes back to Boston."

"Sounds great. Did you grow up back there?"

"Yes, I grew up near Baaahstun," she overemphasized the New England accent.

"Are you a Red Sox fan?"

"Of course. You better not be a Yankees' fan," she said sternly, as if it were a deal-breaker.

"Nope, the Yankees suck. I've been a Sox fan since I was a little kid."

"Whew! I'm glad we got that out of the way," she said tartly. "I'd better get going."

She gave me a very warm embrace that lingered just the perfect amount of time to let me know that she liked what she'd seen so far as much as I did.

"I hope to see you soon."

"You will," she said as she looked back before getting in her car.

I watched her drive away, noticing that the butterflies had been replaced by another somewhat familiar sensation that was responsible for the wide smile on my face. I was sure glad she wasn't a Yankees' fan!

As I started my car and let it warm up a bit, I checked my phone for any texts or missed calls. There was a text from Abbey that she must have sent before pulling out of the parking lot.

So, what do you think of our little friend?

I didn't want to sound nearly as exuberant as I felt.

She's okay . . . :-) Thank you! I just might owe you one.

The following week kept me busy between tying up loose ends at work before the holidays and final Christmas preparations. I've had my girls on Christmas Eve ever since my divorce from Carrie, and this year was no different. Of course, their men were included; one now owning the title of husband, and the other would soon, I suspected.

We had a wonderful evening. I savored this new phase when my adult children had become my dear friends and were simply fine human beings. I grilled teriyaki-seasoned flank steak, as requested, on the back deck of my condo as a light snow was falling. We sipped red wine, ate dinner, then exchanged gifts. I give them a few vinyl records every year to add to their collections, so they provided the background music while we celebrated. My small home overflowed with love.

After everyone left, the warm atmosphere remained. I put a record on the turntable and sat on my couch, enjoying the solitude. *Steely Dan* isn't exactly Christmas music, but their album, *Asia*, went down nicely and complemented the Basil Hayden bourbon; a gift from the boys. They were keepers in my book, worthy of my precious daughters. The only illumination came from the Christmas tree with my gifts from the kids sprawled underneath. There was also a shiny, new guitar; a gift to myself. I justified the purchase as a reward for my slow but steady improvement. I felt complete contentment, but I did allow myself to wonder if Kate had enjoyed her Christmas Eve as much as I had enjoyed mine.

The Saturday after Christmas, I had to attend my sister-in-law's birthday party in downtown Salt Lake at the residence of one of her friends. I'd asked Abbey if she would go with me, as there would be many unfamiliar faces, and I really didn't want to go solo. She had been invited to join some friends to hear a local band play in a bar in the south part of the valley on the same night. We struck a deal to go to the birthday party together, make an early exit, and then see the band play.

I was glad to leave the party when we did. I love my brother and his wife, but their crowd really isn't mine. On the drive to *A Bar Named Sue*, in the suburb of Sandy, Abbey was texting a good portion of the way there.

"Kate might join us," she said abruptly.

"Really?"

"Yeah. She was skiing with her son and her dad today and said she might like to sneak away for a little while."

"Does she know I'll be there?"

Abbey gave me a look that said, "Duh! That's kind of the whole idea." She schooled me in the ways of matchmaking.

"Your drinks are on me tonight, darlin'."

I was introduced to Abbey's friends, some of whom I'd met

before, as well as most of the band members setting up. I had a bit of guitar-envy as I checked out their gear.

"I fully expect you and Kate to ditch me when she gets here. I've got plenty of company so don't worry."

"You are a fine human. What are you drinking?"

Sweet Home Alabama started the set, and these guys weren't bad at all. *Don't Look Back*, a *Boston* hit, followed, and it was apparent that classic rock was on the menu for the night, which was fine by me. My seat faced the entrance to the bar so I could spot Kate as she came in. Right on cue, she walked in during the middle of *Foreigner's* mega-hit, *Waiting for a Girl Like You*.

I might have been a little biased already, but she seemed to light up the place as she approached our cluster of tables. She greeted Abbey's friends that she knew, then Abbey, and finally made her way to me. We hugged, and I spoke into her ear to be heard above the music.

"I wasn't expecting to see you so soon. This is a surprise."

"I hope it's a pleasant one," she said, her lips almost touching my ear.

Duh! "Yes, most definitely."

Chapter 6

In a noisy bar in Avalon,
I tried to call you;
But on a midnight watch, I realized
Why twice you ran away.

Southern Cross—Crosby, Stills & Nash

KATE ACCEPTED MY OFFER OF A DRINK and chose High West Campfire Whiskey, a local selection. I'd waited to order until her arrival, so I went with the same. We did, indeed, ditch Abbey, taking our seats at a small table for two on the edge of the section that our group had claimed.

"How was skiing today?"

"It was cold up on top; and windy. We didn't last the entire day. Dad got kind of tired, and my son got a little bored."

"How old is he?"

"He's 68," she said, laughing at her own humor. "But my son is 13 going on 21."

"That's a fun age." It was my turn for some sarcasm, as I remembered my awkward teenage years. *Had I ever truly grown out of that phase?*

"Yeah, so much fun that I needed to get out of the house before I committed manslaughter."

"Win, win then. He gets to live, and I get to see you."

"Cheers to that!" We clinked our glasses together. Her smile was making the rest of the bar and the other people disappear. *Not a bad line for a song,* I thought.

"So, what brings a pretty girl like you to a bar in Sandy, Utah on a snowy December night, other than your regard for the sanctity of life?"

"The band, of course; and maybe a cute guy." I may have met my witty match.

"Of course, it's a pretty good band, but I haven't really noticed if there are any cute guys here."

She gave me a very cute eye roll. Her face was quite animated. I assumed she couldn't hide her emotions well and was a genuine person who preferred not to, anyway. I ended up being spot on with my assumptions.

"What is your story, Kate? I've only heard bits and pieces from Abbey."

"How far back do you want me to go?"

"Whatever you think is pertinent."

I clearly heard every word she would speak in the next hour. The band playing didn't muffle even one. In fact, I will be able to recall practically the entire conversation years from now. I was both intelligent and wise enough to accurately interpret their meaning and understand the ramifications of completely ignoring them. My brain was fully capable of processing the data it received and acting accordingly. But my heart was calling the shots. Even in hindsight, I'd have it no other way.

"I grew up in Newton, Mass. Dad was a philosophy professor at Lasell College. My parents divorced when I was in Jr. High; I lived with my dad after the split. Competitive gymnastics consumed me, and my club was my life; so when my mom moved, I stayed. She passed away a year after my son, Sean, was born, but never met him. We were a bit estranged."

"I'm sorry on both counts," I offered.

"Thanks. It was hard to lose her; maybe even harder because we weren't very close. A lot of regret involved."

Kate seemed incredibly self-aware and knew exactly what was pertinent in her story. She was well prepared to share her tale. I just listened.

"I didn't really date at all in high school. Gymnastics dominated my life completely. Looking back, I wish I'd had more balance, but while in the thick of things, it's hard to see the effects of being so one-dimensional. Like thousands of other girls, I had Olympic aspirations. I fell way short of that dream, but I got my college education paid from it.

"I was offered several scholarships, made a few campus visits, and totally chose to break out of my comfort zone and leave the east coast behind. I ended up at the University of Texas."

"Wow. I'm in the presence of greatness! I ran college track but was just a walk-on at Utah. No offers or campus visits for me." I did a mock pout.

"Did you eventually earn a scholarship?"

"I did, after that first semester, and books, too."

"You got your education paid for. That's all that counts."

"True. Keep going, but I do want to hear all about Austin later. I hear it's a great place."

"It is a great town. So, during my freshman year, fall semester, I met Jeff, my soon-to-be ex. He was one of the trainers assigned to the gymnastics team. He was going into physical therapy but soon changed direction and went into a somewhat related field—bio-medical engineering. He now designs artificial knees and hips for ex-athletes with too many miles on them. I can't even picture him going any further than he did in physical therapy. He's a much more analytical type than a people person. His bedside manner actually kind of sucked."

"His charms apparently worked on you," I interjected.

"We'll, let's just say I was kind of gullible at the time. Like I said, I hadn't really dated before, so it didn't take much to become smitten by the guy wrapping my ankles and giving me ice bags. He was so different back then." Her voice trailed off, and she stared wistfully off in the direction of the band. Her wounds were obviously still quite fresh.

"It was a whirlwind romance. Things happened so fast, but I had no context as to what constituted fast. I met his parents, who lived in Dallas. My dad met Jeff when he flew out for President's Day weekend. Everyone hit it off, and before I knew it, we were engaged and planning a late summer wedding.

"It was kind of stressful competing, going to school, and being married. That first year was rough, but we managed. I was doing okay in the meets, but my scores were never good enough for my coach or me. Floor was my favorite in the rotation, and beam. I was one of the best on the team on beam. Most of the girls hated it, but I loved it for some reason. Late in my sophomore season, I was on vault in practice and way under-rotated. I came down hard and crashed, tearing my ACL, PCL, *and* MCL in my left knee. Maybe if you play your cards right, I'll show you my scars someday," she smiled, and I had to laugh.

"That sounds pretty horrific. I'm guessing months of rehab."

"Yeah, it was devastating. I knew my gymnastics career was over the second I hit the mat. Rehab was a beast after the surgery. My timing was good, though, I had surgery after finals and had all summer in therapy.

Jeff was actually very sweet and took great care of me. I just focused on school for my final two years at the U. They honored my scholarship and took care of the medical expenses. I was an undergraduate assistant, which kept me close to the sport and my team. I got my degree in marketing and advertising and graduated a year ahead of Jeff, since he'd changed majors. I found a marketing job right out of college with the *Round Rock Express*, the AAA farm club of the Texas Rangers."

"That would be fun, combining sports and work. What brought you to Utah?" I asked.

"Jeff got a job offer from a startup bio-med company out here, so we moved soon after he graduated. His timing was perfect. A couple of their products were very successful, and he was on the ground floor of a lot of growth. We did well, traveled a lot, and had some great years together. I got a job at *Latitude Advertising*. That's where I met Abbey. Seems like forever ago. Then I became pregnant with Sean after a few years of just the two of us."

We took a small break from her story, and I ordered another round of the whiskey with an interesting smoky finish. The band took a break and, after mingling with their small fan club, they started the second half of their set. Abbey seemed to be doing just fine without us, so Kate continued.

"After Sean was born, things really changed between me and Jeff. He was traveling a lot, training the sales team, and schmoozing doctors all around the country, and a little bit internationally. He seemed to withdraw from us. I was consumed with Sean, so we started growing apart. Mom passed away, and I didn't feel much support at all from Jeff, which made things even worse. I wondered what was causing his disconnect. Was he was cheating on me or did he have a substance abuse problem?"

I didn't delve into those issues. I'd let her reveal her various layers on her schedule.

"I talked myself into being content that we were just roommates. Otherwise, we had a sweet life, a nice home in Olympus Cove. We took trips to the Caymans, Europe, and Maui. I sold the relationship I'd always wanted for a lifestyle I enjoyed."

I was beginning to realize that Kate might be a bit out of my league, but I did empathize with her for enduring a loveless marriage. Her all-too-familiar story made me sad for both of us.

"But I realized how empty my life had become, how unfulfilled and unhappy I was. A Caribbean beach is nice, but without a zeal for life, it was all pretty hollow. We didn't fight at all; there wasn't even enough passion between us to do that. So, Sean never saw any conflict. But he was growing up with a pretty warped perspective on love.

"This past year, I tried so hard to shake Jeff out of his malaise, but nothing worked. I finally gave up in September and told him I wanted a divorce. It was so unreal. He basically said okay and moved out. He didn't even fight for us, for me. He didn't show any emotion at all, like it was a business decision."

Her eyes welled up with tears. I instinctively reached my hand across the table and grasped her's in mine. She gave a tiny squeeze in response. It didn't help that the band was in the middle of belting out the *Journey* ballad, *Faithfully*.

"I'm sorry you've gone through all that. It must still feel so raw."

"It was a long time coming, but yes, it still hurts. Even though I made the decision to end things, I still feel rejected." She paused and took a sip of her drink. "So, that's my story. I've basically been in love with only one man in my life. I've spent the past twenty years with him and have no idea how to do this single thing. I've never really dated. There are so many experiences I've never had, and yet I'm about to turn forty. I'm just trying to find my way in this new world of mine."

"You definitely need to take a couple laps around the universe," I said, stating the obvious. Still holding her hand, I slowly released it to reach for my glass of whiskey and take a long sip. My mind raced back to that sushi dinner with Abbey, when she first concocted the idea of Jamison and Kate, and how she quickly retreated from her scheme. My thoughts drifted even further back to Anna and the mistake she made of not taking some time to figure things out. I reluctantly realized that Kate and I were doomed from the start by horrible timing. She confirmed this with the following words.

"So, I'm pretty much damaged goods and not exactly relationship material. Someone would have to be crazy to fall in love with me right now," she summed up the current state of the heart.

That fact couldn't have been clearer had it been spelled out in neon lights, like the large beer signs adorning the walls of the bar. Yet, I was about to go completely insane.

Chapter 7

You've awakened something
Deep inside my soul,
And every moment, every breath,
I feel it more.

Kiss Me Softly—Journey

"THAT'S GOOD TO KNOW," WAS THE CLEVEREST RESPONSE I could come up with, trying to hide the fact that the wind had been knocked out of me. Nothing about Kate looked damaged on the outside, and her body language and enticing eyes didn't exactly say, "Run like hell, Jamison!" So, I wasn't completely overcome by a sense of dread. *Silly boy!*

"Now it's your turn," she leaned back, able to relax a bit after sharing the trauma of her story.

"Well, it sounds like I'm a couple years ahead of you." I began my tale in the present before dipping into the past.

I gave her the *Reader's Digest* version of the string of events that led me to this point in my life as a single, middle—aged male. It contained my marriages, my kids, and a few funny dating stories.

My lesbian ex-wife chapter was the only part of the story that seemed to surprise her.

"So, that's pretty much my story in a nutshell." I ended just as the band finished its set with a very fine rendition of *Hotel California.*

"You sound like a great guy who tries to learn from life's experiences without holding onto any bitterness."

"I try," I said honestly, appreciating her compliment and solid observation.

"Wow, they were great! Did you two even notice?" Abbey had approached our table with a smile on her face, obviously proud of her matchmaking abilities and not even a little bit perturbed that we had been in our own world most of the night. We both just smirked at her.

"I'm getting a ride home with Christie. I'm right on her way, so take your time, kids."

"I've got to get going anyway, back to the boys. My son is safe from harm now," Kate said, looking at her phone to check the time.

"I'm still going with Christie." Abbey winked at me as she hugged Kate goodnight before embracing me.

"Thanks," I whispered in her ear.

Abbey and most of the group filed out of the bar as Kate and I had our final sips of water.

"Are you good to drive?" I asked her.

"Totally." We'd shifted to water a while ago, being responsible adults. "Hey, I don't have your phone number," she added.

"I don't know. Next, you'll be wanting to keep a toothbrush at my place," I deadpanned as I dug my phone out of my coat pocket.

"I'd add pajamas, but I sleep in the nude," she said with a feigned look of innocence. *Yay, finally someone to match my warped sense of humor!*

We swapped numbers and punched them into our iPhones. I helped her on with her puffy, down parka, and we made our way to the door and out to the parking lot. I was oblivious to the chill in the air, but Kate noticed.

"Let me start my car to warm it up." She reached in, started it, and turned on the heater without getting in. She closed the door and stood close to me.

"What are you doing on the night of New Year's Day?"

"I don't have any plans yet."

"Good, don't make any. I take my dad to the airport in the morning. Would you like to come over for that home-cooked Italian dinner in the evening? Sean will be with Jeff."

"That sounds wonderful." *What an understatement.*

"Maybe we can start those Italian lessons."

"Perfetto."

She drew even closer to me. I didn't suspect it was because she was cold. My usual Jr. High jitters were, for some reason, completely absent.

"Can I ask you something?" I realized my question would require a follow up question.

"Sure." *Okay, maybe that word isn't so bad. She made it sound quite sincere.*

"Is this considered our first date?"

"Why do you ask?" She chuckled at my odd query.

"Because I have never kissed anyone on the first date. That's always seemed so presumptuous on the guy's part. Kind of a dumb policy of mine."

"Hmm," Kate was measuring her response. "Then I'd have to say no, this is definitely not our first date. We'll count the Solstice party."

"I was hoping you'd say that." My words stopped as our lips met.

When that first, long, and passionate kiss had ended, I was sure that her car was plenty warm, and her windows well-defrosted.

We reluctantly pulled away from each other.

"Will you please text me that you made it home safely?" *Chivalry is not dead.*

"I will."

"Thanks for sneaking away."

"The pleasure was mine."

I opened her car door. I was right, a blast of warm air escaped as she took her seat.

"Here's a vocabulary word for you: *Baci*," I said with a crisp Italian accent.

"I know that one. Kisses," she smiled. She looked away for a moment before turning to me and closing her door. "Dammit, you just had to be a good kisser, didn't you?"

"Sorry." Perhaps I should have said thanks.

"I'm not." She was beaming.

She drove away but didn't take any of the warmth with her. I was standing there in a snowy parking lot, a huge grin on my face, trying to figure out what had just transpired. If Kate was trying to scare me off, she was doing a pretty poor job of it. If there were mixed signals being sent my way, only one was getting through.

My drive home was a blur. I was still floating when a text came in on my phone.

Home safe. It was so nice getting to know you. *Grazie per i deliziosi baci!* (I cheated and used an app)

I figured I would respond in Italian now that she had the app to translate.

Grazie a te per una notte perfetta. (See you next week.)

Her response was as perfect as the night had been.

Can't wait!

I got undressed and laid in bed, but it was impossible to wind down and fall asleep. I kept replaying the wonderful night in my mind. I was conveniently splicing out the part where she warned me in advance not to fall in love with her. That section was replaced by the kissing scene in the parking lot. In my line of work, I can appreciate the magic of good editing. It was almost midnight on Saturday. I couldn't wait for Thursday night.

Thankfully, the days flew by. I took Mom for errands on Sunday, and on Monday, after a busy day of year-end billing at work, I had a dinner date with my stepdaughter, Jade. Even though her mom, Anna, is an ex, Jade will never be. It's another silly rule of mine. The label 'ex' doesn't apply to kids, or nieces and nephews, for that matter. I know that sounds complicated, and in a perfect world everyone stays together, but it's a far from perfect world.

Jade was a beautiful, soon-to-be 15-year-old girl going on at least 21. She inherited her mom's olive skin and brown eyes. She was way too pretty for her own good and for my protective nature. We had remained close even through the divorce, or maybe I should say because of it. She'd gone through quite a bit of change in her home with my leaving and the surprise entrance in her life of her mom's girlfriend, who eventually became another stepparent. Add the simple fact that at the time, she was entering the hellish world of Jr. High, and I figured that I could offer some sort of anchor for her. I adored the girl and had no intention of losing her in my life. Thankfully her mom was one hundred percent supportive of my wishes.

We tried to grab dinner as a chance to catch up every couple of months and were long overdue when I picked her up and drove toward her favorite soup and salad restaurant. We talked about the young hormonal lads chasing her. I reminded her boys have cooties and don't outgrow them until they're in their late thirties, just to be safe. Thank goodness, her ever-swinging pendulum of estrogen-driven emotions was drifting more to the cootie end of the spectrum. At the time of our last dinner, she'd seen stars in her eyes about a certain boy. They apparently were now ancient history.

"So, what about you, J1? Any news to report on your love life?" she asked as our salads arrived.

"Well, J2, there is a new lady I barely started seeing." We still used our nicknames for each other. She must have seen a sparkle in my eyes because she pounced on it.

"Oh, J1! Tell me about her!"

"We haven't seen each other much yet. I kind of like her, but it's early," I clumsily summarized.

"That's awesome!" she squealed. "You haven't been excited about anyone for a long time. What's her name?"

"Kate." I couldn't help but smile as I said her name.

"Kate and Jamison—that has a nice ring to it." She was already carving our initials together on a tree. "I could see it in your eyes when you said her name. You're falling in love!" She always enjoyed teasing me.

"It's still way too early for that, J2, and I'm going to take this really slow. But I might have one more left in me."

As I mentioned earlier, math was never my strong suit, and that kind of miscalculation can get a man in trouble.

Chapter 8

Well my time went so quickly,
I went lickety-splitly out to my old '55.
As I drove away slowly, feeling so holy,
God knows, I was feeling alive.

Ol' 55—The Eagles

OVER THE YEARS, I'VE CONCLUDED THAT NEW YEAR'S EVE is an overrated holiday, so I typically leave it to the young and less wise to do the partying for me. I prefer a quiet night of music and contemplation, usually alone, or I'm not at all opposed to a mellow celebration with a small group of friends. This particular evening, I shared with a couple of guitars and some wonderful vinyl records.

I was enthusiastic for what the coming year would bring. After the customary reflection that comes with changing of the calendar, I concluded I was at a pretty good place in my life. I was safely beyond the rebound phase after my divorce, a good eighteen months in the rearview mirror, quite content and open to what life had in store for me. And I was particularly excited about my date with Kate the following night. I would wait until then to truly celebrate the start of 2015.

We had exchanged several texts since our night at the bar. She confessed to stalking me on *Facebook* and being particularly fond of a photo of me in a tux, while I admitted to being impatient with the amount of days I had to endure before I would see her again. I'd asked her what I could bring to dinner, and she insisted that I just bring myself. The gentleman in me wouldn't accept that arrangement, so I bought a decent Italian red wine I hoped would pair with whatever she was preparing. I also purchased a small bouquet of flowers in a vase to add some color and aroma to our evening.

Kate lived in an upscale neighborhood, nestled high on the east side of the Salt Lake Valley, in the shadow of the very prominent Mt. Olympus. Her home was not far from where my rich aunt and uncle lived while I was growing up. Kids from this and nearby neighborhoods fed into the more affluent schools in the valley. As I pulled into her steep and snowy driveway and saw her spacious house, I again felt that *I'm not in her league* sensation in the pit of my stomach. It disappeared quickly upon her opening the door.

She looked even more radiant than she had when she lit up the bar. I was greeted with a hello, a smile, and a warm embrace. We had some unfinished business from the parking lot because, without words, the hug segued into a kiss. She deftly reached past me to push the door closed without breaking contact, to keep out the cold and also deny the neighbors a show. A minute may have passed before the kiss ended. I wasn't sure. Time tends to stand still in such moments.

"Sorry, I'd been waiting almost a week to do that again," she confessed with a mischievous ear-to-ear grin.

"I'm sure I can find it in my heart to forgive you," I played along. I presented her with the flowers and wine, which she had not noticed until then.

"Thank you! They're beautiful, and the wine looks tasty."

She led me into the kitchen and set the flowers and wine on a large island covered in marble. The spicy aroma of the tomato sauce simmering on the stove filled the room, making me salivate in anticipation. The main floor of her home was well lit, inviting, nicely appointed, and quite lovely. I did notice that very little art hung on her walls, which she would later attribute to her 'commitment issues.' She had several candles burning in both the kitchen and the living room and music playing from overhead speakers. It was a very inviting and romantic setting. She had me open the wine, and we caught up on the week that had passed. I'd worked, but Kate's agency closed between Christmas and New Year's, and she'd been busy entertaining her dad and her son, who was out of school for the holiday break.

We sat by the fireplace to sip the wine before dinner. Our conversation never waned, nor would it all night. We seemed to have so much in common: the related industries in which we worked, many friends and acquaintances, music, various authors, Italy, and the similar way we both approached life. Neither of us was content to simply live life, but we each felt the need to feel it, first and foremost, for better or for worse. Abbey had been right; Kate and I were very similar souls. Our glasses, now empty, we moved into the kitchen for dinner.

"Thanks for having me over for dinner. The sauce smells fantastic."

"Of course! There are meatballs, too. It's a family recipe I learned from my Italian grandmother on my dad's side."

I refilled our glasses while she served the meatballs and sauce over fresh fettuccine pasta she had quickly cooked to a perfect *al dente*. Eggplant *parmagiana* rounded out the wonderful meal. We took our places at the table, illuminated by candlelight, with a soft rock singer/songwriter mix playing overhead. My new favorite Italian word, *perfetta*, came to mind. It simply was perfect— the company, the conversation, the romantic setting, the food and wine and, especially, the warm feeling that filled my heart. Everything felt so right and so engaging.

Kate revealed more about herself through her honest words and with each layer she peeled away, I became even more enchanted. She had such a zest for life and a soul that was very much alive and aching to soar. But her wings had been severely clipped the past several years. She described Jeff and their relationship in detail. She'd lived with a man who was more a roommate than a partner fully engaged in building a life together. As I sat in the beautiful house they had shared, it was clear I could not match Jeff's wealth on a material level, but he wasn't even close to my level in terms of being emotionally present. I was everything he wasn't in so many ways.

I helped Kate wash the pots and pans and load the dishwasher with the plates and utensils. I quite liked the closeness, working side by side in the kitchen, often rubbing shoulders and elbows. Anna and I used to joke that we did some of our best work in the kitchen. *Am I one of the few males out there that has discovered that chopping veggies and washing dishes together constitute foreplay? Now the secret is out!* We'd emptied the bottle of wine, but she had another Italian red teed up, ready to open and pour.

With our cleanup chores completed, we sat on the stools at the island and sipped and chatted some more. A song by the group Bread played: *Baby, I'm a Want You*.

"I love this song!" Kate's eyes lit up as the guitar chords progressed and the vocals began.

"Then let's dance." I took her glass and set it down, led her by the hand to the space between the island and the table, and we shared a wonderful slow dance, our bodies pressed tightly against each other. I would have felt her heart beating had my own pulse not been so strong.

The song went by much too fast for both of us. Thankfully, James Taylor came to the rescue with *Something in the Way She Moves* to extend our bliss.

"I can't even remember the last time I danced in this kitchen, much less anywhere," she said softly into my ear. Then, apologetically, she added, "I need to stop talking about Jeff, especially in these amazing, romantic moments with you. I'm sorry." I could hear both sorrow and hope in her voice.

"No need to be sorry at all. I totally understand what you're feeling. I've been there."

"Thank you for being so understanding. You're pretty awesome, Mr. Barrick."

"I happen to think you are *awesomer*, Ms. Campania."

We took our dance to the couch, along with our wine. I cannot recall the rest of the soundtrack that played for us that night as we kissed, talked, kissed, laughed, and held each other tightly. I felt intoxicated and not from the wine. I recognized the very specific emotion I was feeling, one that had been buried inside me far too long, the sensation you wish could be bottled up and saved for eternity. The sparks that flew between us were so strong that they could have powered a small city if that magic could be harnessed.

Neither of us was hesitant to try to articulate the waves of euphoria that were washing over us. Not that we were exceptionally eloquent with our words. Often it came down to a simple *wow* between kisses. We both marveled at our many similarities and our very few differences, despite being from different parts of the country and coming from very dissimilar backgrounds.

We talked about her impending trip to Italy. She had always hoped to visit Rome with her husband, but it had never worked out. She took this as a sign that her trip was to be a very meaningful and important part of her growth and healing, as she turned forty, and started a new chapter in her life. I told her of several sights in Rome that were essential to see. I'd been back just once since my college days but remembered the city well enough to make solid recommendations.

"I've got several books at home about the city and the language. I'll dig them out and bring them next time I see you. Assuming there will be a next time, of course. I don't ever want to be presumptuous."

"I don't know about that," she deadpanned. "It's not like we hit it off very well tonight. I think we totally lack chemistry. What do you think?"

"It's been borderline torture. I'll just ship the books to your workplace." We both chuckled.

"It's very tempting to want you to experience Rome with me as my tour guide and translator."

"As wonderful as that sounds, this seems like one trip you should take solo. I might have to book a birthday trip myself to somewhere warm, like Hawaii, so I won't be tempted to hop a flight and join you."

"You're probably right." She laid her head on my shoulder.

"I don't want to, but I should get going." I could barely see the hands of the clock on the wall in the dim light from the fireplace, and they revealed that it was shortly after 1 a.m. The night had flown by.

"There's not a single part of me that wants you to leave." Kate looked at me, her eyes revealing a myriad of emotions.

"The wise gentleman inside is the only part of me keeping me from staying," I said, trying to convince myself that in this moment I possessed any wisdom whatsoever.

"We can wait, although it would feel quite right and natural, even now."

"I hate it that you are as rational as I am. I look forward to the moment when neither of us is, or has to be." We kissed one long, last time, giving each other a little something to remember until we were together again.

I reluctantly walked to my car and glanced back to see her standing on the doorstep, still watching me. I always look back. I was glad that she was of a like mind, though that hardly surprised me. I flew home in my car, which had somehow sprouted wings again. If there were any red flags along my route, I didn't see them. Had there been an elephant in the room back at Kate's house I didn't sense it. We see and feel exactly what we want. Sometimes we don't control the events in our lives, but rather they control us. I was now past the point of no return. No amount of sound logic or prior words of warning from Kate could possibly stop me from recklessly running toward her.

Chapter 9

After you've seen and done it all,
And it's time to find your home,
Meet me there, at the very top
Of the Spanish Steps of Rome.

The Spanish Steps—Jamison Barrick

THE NEXT MORNING I WAS AWAKENED BY THE FAMILIAR BEEP of my phone announcing an incoming text. I felt slow and groggy and didn't immediately reach for the device, giving myself a few moments to transition from dreamland to a lucid state. I didn't get a lot of sleep the night before as I was completely unable to wind down and turn off my mind from reliving such a wonderful night. There was nothing to edit out this time. I savored each moment over and over. I finally grabbed my phone, wondering if the text was from the person who owned my final thought as I drifted off to sleep, as well as the first one to come to mind upon awakening.

> Could hardly sleep . . . couldn't stop thinking about you, and when I did sleep, I was dreaming about you. Can't wait to be with you again.

I let her words sink in for a moment before responding. What a way to start my day with a dose of warm, liquid sunshine flooding my heart.

I'm beginning to think you are a mythical creature, like a unicorn that somehow fell out of the sky. That or I had the most incredible dream. Either way, you can't possibly be real . . .

That was the most eloquent way I could express that this all seemed too good to be true.

I am very much real, Mr. Barrick. Hope you are!

Whew! Just checking! Yes, I am, too. And for the record, I don't slow dance to Bread with just anyone . . ..

This would begin a wonderful thread of texts between us that described what would become a beautiful love affair in our own words and told this sweet story better than any gifted author ever could. I wouldn't delete the hundreds of texts until several months after they served any practical purpose. But I'm getting ahead of myself.

I felt as if I were floating on a lofty cloud the rest of the day. With both Christmas and New Year's Day falling on a Thursday this year, I took both Fridays off, along with the rest of the working world. I concluded this was a good day to hit the gym to burn some holiday calories and take my tree down, along with the other Christmas decorations. I waited until it was mid-morning in Hawaii before calling my favorite cousin, Barbara. *Please don't tell the others.*

"Aloha, Jamison!"

"Happy New Year, Barb!"

We exchanged pleasantries before I got down to the business of my call.

"You know how you've been suggesting I come visit you for a while?"

"Yeah, are you finally going to accept my invitation?"

"Yes, if you're going to be around later this month or early February."

"I'm not going anywhere. What made you decide to finally get your butt over here? Winter blues setting in?"

"Actually, it's to keep me from going to Italy. Long story. I'll tell you all about it when I get there."

"You've got me intrigued! I can't wait to hear this story. Book your flight. I'll plan on picking you up whenever you get in. I'm totally flexible."

"Thanks, Barb. I'll get online today and book it and let you know! Love and aloha!"

This was a smart, preemptive move to avoid all temptation to join Kate in Rome. I was still very much aware of her need to take those laps around the universe and that trip started in the Eternal City. Who knew where this thing might lead, but I felt it prudent that I should give her a very wide berth to go through all the healing and growing she desired.

Kate and I texted back and forth a lot over the next few days. She had her son for the remainder of the weekend and indicated that, while she would love to chat with me over the phone, she wanted to keep her dating life on the down low with Sean. He was already dealing with the transition of his dad moving out, and she wanted to minimize the challenges he faced. That made perfect sense as I'd experienced the same ones with Kiara and Bailey. We were trying to figure out the next time we could get together and chose lunch the following Tuesday. Even though only four days, it seemed like an eternity. In the meantime, absence was making my heart grow fonder.

Tuesday finally arrived, and lunchtime came not a minute too soon. I had zero focus at work during the interminable morning.

Kate admitted to having a similar issue. We met at a quaint restaurant, Cafe Madrid, located about halfway between her downtown agency and my office in the suburbs; they specialized in tapas.

Our embrace in the parking lot was punctuated with a quick kiss, by our standards anyway. She was glowing. *How is it possible that she gets prettier every time we meet?* I had packed a couple books with me, as promised. One was a pocket-sized Rome tour guide, and the other was an Italian tutorial that covered the basics for a traveler to the country. I presented her with the books once we were seated.

"These books will have to suffice because I definitely won't be going with you to Rome. I'm going to visit my cousin on Oahu around the same time. We will be eleven hours apart, practically half a world away." That had a poetic ring to it.

"You were serious about not being tempted!" I saw mostly appreciation in her eyes, along with a bit of disappointment.

"Well, if you promise to show me the scars on your knee, maybe one day I'll take you there."

She smiled. "That sounds incredible. The showing you my scars part." We both laughed at that insinuation.

"Do me a favor while you're there. Catch the sunset at the top of the Spanish Steps or walk to an overlook of the city called *il Pincio*. That area is one of my favorite parts with *Piazza Navona* being a close second. It's a beautiful square but lacks the wonderful view of the city."

"I'll definitely plan to go there some evening for sunset, perhaps on your birthday. I'm so excited."

"I'm so jealous, but being able to get in some body surfing will console me."

This was one of Kate's favorite restaurants. She knew the owners, who stopped to say hello. She ordered for us and chose well: crispy, glazed Brussels sprouts, meatballs, a cheese platter, and calamari.

"Are you busy Friday? Sean is with his dad this weekend."

"I am now," I smiled. I was doing a lot of that lately.

"I'd actually love to hang with you all weekend, but I'm trying to resist that temptation and schedule some friend time and me time, too. Keep a good balance. You know what I mean?"

"Absolutely. I read those articles from *Elephant Journal* you post on *Facebook*," I joked. *For the record, I really did glance at the articles to gain insight as to what made this woman tick.*

"Oh great, not you, too! Abbey gives me so much crap about that."

"Really?" I played dumb.

"I'm just trying to figure this out as I go along. It's all new territory for me."

I appreciated her self-awareness and desire to navigate the immense changes in her life as best she could. That introspection was completely lacking for Anna at the very time she needed it most. I was, fortunately, more self-aware than at any other time in my life, although I paid dearly to get to this point. I was hearing what Kate said, not simply what I wanted to hear. I was determined not to get caught up in wanting to fix her, although on the surface it didn't appear she needed fixing. I wasn't attempting, in any way, to try to ease the pain from her split with Jeff or speed up the healing process. We were both extremely cognizant of exactly where she was on her life's path, despite the incredible chemistry that sizzled between us. Whatever this was, or would become, it had *Proceed with Caution* written all over it.

The lunch hour flew by. I would soon become aware that this would be a familiar phenomenon over the next couple of months. Time spent with her had its own clock, and it ran at warp speed compared to the time spent away from her. We discovered another strange chain of events. The flowers I would bring to her would wither and die at an amazingly slow rate.

We reluctantly walked to the parking lot, hugged, and kissed goodbye.

"You make my heart smile," she said, sliding into her car.

I had a moment to respond before she shut her door.

"You are extraordinary, Kate."

She blew me a kiss and drove away; me knowing full well I would be worthless the rest of the day at work. I looked at the sky before getting in my car. Salt Lake City was squarely in January's gray and cold grip, yet I hadn't even felt the chill this season. I had a source of heat inside of me that winter couldn't touch.

I ended up being correct. I didn't have a productive afternoon back at the office. I was daydreaming like a smitten schoolboy. I couldn't stop thinking about Kate, and I didn't have any desire to, either. I thought about her trip to Rome, her journey, her fragile yet smiling heart, and her eyes that seemed to be a gateway to her soul. Some song lyrics started floating through my mind. I quickly pushed that aside and tried to buckle down and get my work done. I would fully embrace the song when I got home to a more creative setting.

I was not yet to the point where I could write music to go with my lyrics. I would get there soon, and that combination would prove to be a magical turning point in my life. But for now, I wrote what others would classify as poetry, though I could never bring myself to use that word.

Before I sat down to write, a small glass of Woodford in hand, I had to shake off the absurdity of writing a love song for and about someone I'd, technically, only met eighteen days ago, and I'd seen four times. *Too much, too soon* was one of my favorite lines from the movie *Slap Shot*, and I chuckled to myself when I connected an old sports comedy to my current love life.

It was probably too soon in the game to be feeling the way I did, yet Kate was matching me stride for stride. *Just don't fight it and start writing,* I thought. It's not like she would know I'd written a love song, or poem, for her barely in the infancy of our relationship, or whatever we decide to label it. We had packed a lot in those eighteen days. Why not celebrate them? The pen hit the notebook, and within thirty minutes, I'd written a song. *It's a song, dammit!*

It ended up being a one-take wonder. The first draft would be the final version. I would never revise a single word. I included a line in Italian that translates, "We will discover only through living, my love." I read the lyrics over and over, amazed by what I'd just written. I loved the symmetry of the song, the shape of it, like an elegant haiku. I loved the words, their meaning, and the emotion behind them, as well as the astute foreshadowing revealed in the chorus.

It was impossible to know the impact this song would have on my life over the next two-and-a-half years. It would take on an almost mythical quality in my world, and it would promise love—but also threaten it. I could not imagine when I wrote these words that they would send me flying off to Rome, searching for answers on a quest of my own, every bit as pivotal as the one on which Kate was about to embark. The title was simple, and the destination it described would become a powerful and irresistible magnet for me.

The Spanish Steps

You shared with me your journey
In a noisy, crowded bar.
Your words made
The band all but disappear.
I saw it there, in your eyes;
Your soul, about to soar;
The passion within you
Finding sweet release.
Our worlds collided
With that first kiss.

(Chorus)
I hope you see and do it all
And leave no stone unturned;
That you find answers
To all your questions
Until there's nothing left to learn.

First stop, the Eternal City . . .
Flying solo, finding you.
By touching your roots,
You will surely grow.

Together we spoke the language
Swept away by sweet songs.
Lo scopriremo solo vivendo,
Mi amore.
Our souls overlapped
With that first dance.

(Chorus)
After you've seen and done it all,
And it's time to find your home,
Meet me there, at the very top
Of the Spanish Steps of Rome.

(Bridge)
I hope your journey
Brings you back to me
Where you are is where
I wish to be.

(Repeat Chorus)
After you've seen and done it all,
And it's time to find your home,
Meet me there, at the very top
Of the Spanish Steps of Rome.

Chapter 10

There's a bit of thunder pounding in my heart;
A little uncertainty that's been there from the start.
Don't tell me all the looks you gave were the ones that I misread,
Cause all I hear now is a voice inside my head.

Could This Be Love—Toto

THE REMAINDER OF THE WEEK PREDICTABLY WENT BY at a pace that would bore even a glacier. Kate and I shared several sweet texts back and forth that reinforced my belief in the power of the written word.

She would text me at random moments. Sometimes just knowing that she was thinking of me was as meaningful as the message sent. I was drying off from my shower Friday morning, the day of our next date, when I noticed a new text.

I love feeling this way! This is who I am at my core. Thank you!

She's thanking me? I did my best to respond as eloquently.

I'm rapidly running out of superlatives for you . . . I can't wait to see you tonight!

I debated whether to show her *The Spanish Steps* later that evening. I printed it out at work just in case I was feeling brave.

I honestly didn't think that presenting her with a love song so soon would seem out of step with all the romance that had already rapidly transpired. I folded the song, placed it in an envelope, and tucked it in my coat pocket as I left work.

A light snow was falling as I made one stop on the way to Kate's house. I chose a dozen pale, pink roses at a floral shop. *Really? It's too soon for red roses, but you've already written a song!*

Once again, there was an incredible burst of energy unleashed when Kate opened her door. I was getting very fond of her home's entryway, along with the kitchen and living room, inhabited by a very happy woman who greeted me, hugged me eagerly, and kissed me enthusiastically. We seemed to pick up each time where we'd left off. I presented her with the flowers.

"They're gorgeous. That's incredibly sweet of you, but the last flowers you brought are still fresh."

Indeed, they were looking as beautiful as they had over a week ago. I helped Kate trim the roses. She smiled while inhaling the sweet aroma once they were arranged in their new vase.

That reaction is why men give women flowers. Sadly, that had never been part of the repertoire between me and Anna. Her ex-husband often gave her roses to apologize for his many verbally abusive outbursts. She equated roses with pain and could never quite disconnect from the past, even with a different, well-meaning man giving her the flowers.

I was glad Kate had no such issues. From what I knew so far, Jeff didn't strike me as a dozen roses kind of guy. Maybe he started out that way. It's tragic that humans can wilt away, just like an old, listless, dead bouquet.

When I previously asked what Kate wanted to do on this evening, she suggested we just wing it. That ended up meaning we would spend a good half hour on her couch chatting and, yes, kissing. We'd both been deprived of that simple act of human connection. When we finally came up for air, we realized we were hungry for food, as well. We picked a brewpub that was just a short distance down the hill from her house.

"Would it be okay if we walked?" she suggested on that cold, winter night. Given the fact that I was suddenly impervious to the chill of winter, thanks to a certain, pretty lady, I agreed.

The partially obscured full moon cast a pink glow over the newly fallen snow as we strode, gloved hands clasped, down the gentle slope toward the restaurant that was part of a shopping center. The upstanding folks of Olympus Cove would *never* use the term *strip mall*. The snow crunched under our feet, and we could see our breath. It was a perfect moment.

She broke the silence. "In all the years we lived here, we never walked down together. Even on a warm summer night. Thanks for being flexible."

"Of course." I was trying to grasp just how caged her soul had been for such a long time. So simple. A short walk with the one you love. *How hard is it to simply be present?* I was happy Kate was coming back to life, and I had a small role in her resurrection.

I ordered the ahi tuna spring roll salad, while Kate went for the *margherita* pizza, perhaps prepping for her trip to Rome. We shared a pitcher of a house-brewed, amber ale. Our conversation drifted back to her relationship with Jeff. She tearfully described a couple of instances of infidelity on his part that were uncovered with a minimal amount of sleuthing: credit card receipts in pockets, online phone bills that showed all the activity, a text popping up on one of the rare times he allowed the phone to escape his grip. Sadly, I could relate all too well.

"He was so careless, like he wanted to get caught." I just listened. "And the thing I don't get is how he had so little passion for life, yet he could muster up the energy for an affair or two. Who knows, maybe more?"

I offered what little insight I could, recalling a book I'd read, *The Four Agreements*. "The important thing is to not take anything he did personally. Whatever Jeff did had nothing to do with you. He's responsible for his demons, not you."

"That sounds like something right out of *Elephant Journal*." A smile returned to her face.

She apologized several times for making her soon to be ex-husband the theme of the night. I reassured her I understood and that this is exactly what comes with the territory of caring for someone. I could have said loving someone, as that is what I felt inside, but I wasn't quite ready to spring that word on her. Instead, I decided to let other words express my growing and very deep feelings for her. I dug the envelope out of my coat pocket.

"Remember how I mentioned on New Year's Day that I write songs?" She nodded. "Well, I wrote one the other night. It's about you, Rome, us . . . .. Just read it."

She unfolded the paper and silently scanned the heartfelt words. When she finished the last verse, she looked up at me, her eyes once again wet.

"This is so beautiful. You are beautiful. No one has ever written a song for me. If you keep this up, I'm going to end up falling in love with you." She reached across the table and took my hand in hers.

"Oh, good. That's my master plan." I winked at her, knowing full well that I was already there.

The words on the paper would also affect her, years later, beyond the joy she felt on this night.

This time I left before 1 a.m., just barely, and time again flew by swiftly before my departure. After dinner and the walk home, we talked a little more about Jeff before she declared the subject off limits. We got out her Italian books and looked at the sights of Rome and went over some useful vocabulary. Just before I went home, she made an important declaration.

"I think I'd like you to meet Sean. I'm not sure when or how, but I'd like him to know the reason I seem to be smiling all the time."

I was touched by her offer and knew full well the magnitude of her wanting to introduce me into her son's life at such a delicate stage for him.

"I'm truly honored that you'd consider such a thing. It means a lot to me," I replied humbly.

"He's a tough kid and seems to be adapting well. And besides, Jeff already has a girlfriend. They may have gotten a bit of a head start."

"Ouch," was the first response out of my mouth, and the insinuation of pain was with Kate in mind, not her son.

"Yeah," she sighed. "This isn't about getting back at him or anything. I just want Sean to know that life goes on, and I'll be just fine."

"However you want to proceed, I'm with you one hundred percent."

"Thanks. I'm so grateful I met you." She wrapped her arms around me tightly.

"*Anch'io* means 'me, too.'" We held each other tight for several minutes, not a word was spoken, both of us basking in the mutual gratitude.

"Did you know there are two ways to say, 'I love you' in Italian?" I broke the silence.

"I did learn one way, even though I don't think I'll need it on my trip," she smiled.

"You never know. You might meet a good-looking Italian man at the top of the Spanish Steps. But anyway, there is a mild form of 'I love you' used between siblings, parents or good friends. That's *ti voglio bene*, which I believe translates as, 'I want good for you.' Then there is the romantic or passionate way to say it that is more reserved for lovers, and that's *ti amo*."

"I do know that version. Italian is such a beautiful language. I want to be fluent someday."

We sat in the quiet glow of candlelight for a few more precious minutes.

"I better get going. You said you've got a 9a.m.yoga class," I reluctantly came back to earth.

"I kind of wish I didn't, or I'd just have you stay the night. And we'd sleep in and then eventually get around to making breakfast together."

"Mmm, that sounds amazing—the breakfast part." I tried to keep a straight face.

She slugged me playfully.

"Just for that I'm kicking you out now!"

As we tasted our final kiss goodnight at my new favorite place in her house, the entryway, she held me close and put her lips to my ear.

"*Ti amo*, Jamison Barrick. I really do," her voice cracked with emotion, and I felt her tears on my cheek.

"I love you, too, Kate. *Ti amo tantissimo, cara.*" I held her even tighter. "Why are you crying?"

"Because my heart is literally overflowing," she replied, gazing deeply into my eyes. I thoroughly believed her.

If her heart was spilling over, mine was absolutely bursting.

Chapter 11

I'm just a realistic man,
A bottle filled with shells and sand;
Afraid to love beyond what I can lose
When it comes to you.

Chances—Five for Fighting

LOVE HAS GOT TO BE THE BIGGEST ENDORPHIN RUSH possible. I've experienced a runner's high on many occasions, certainly during my college track days and even more recently on bike rides and workouts. Those activities release but a trickle of the chemical compared to the jolt received from both loving and being loved. Suffice it to say I was close to overdosing all weekend long.

Kate had indicated that this would be a weekend for friends and me time so I planned accordingly. On Sunday I caught a matinée basketball game at the University of Utah with my oldest daughter, Kiara. She taught high school biology and was a happy newlywed who married her best friend and adventure buddy, Tyler. He was busy skiing the fresh Utah powder with friends on this bright and sunny, yet cold January day, which allowed for some nice father-daughter time that I cherished.

I'm obviously biased, but I think both my daughters are beautiful, kind, young women. Kiara still has her lean and athletic soccer build and stands five feet, seven inches tall. Her hair is naturally dishwater blonde, but lately she's been going with reddish brown and a cut with cute bangs. Her eyes are a unique and pretty mix of brown, green, and a tiny bit of blue. She's my shy daughter, once pleading with her little sister to go up and ask for a spork at KFC, yet she entertains a classroom full of high school students six periods a day.

We grabbed a bite to eat before the game so we could chat. My dating life happened to come up, and Kiara seemed surprised that I'd met someone I liked after a series of lineups that had all been less than an ideal match. I gave her the basic details of my budding relationship with Kate and painted an accurate picture of the woman who currently owned a huge piece of my heart.

"She sounds pretty normal. Dad, I won't lie, that last one about a year ago was kind of weird," referring to *Rebound Girl*. It was sweet to see how the shoe was now on the other foot, with my daughter feeling protective of her father. I had to laugh that being normal was the minimum threshold. Not a bad place to start, come to think of it.

"I think you'd like her. She's very normal. And she's a Red Sox fan." Kiara and Bailey were big sports fans. I'd coached them both in soccer since they were little girls.

My daughters were very intelligent and possessed outstanding intuition. I'd come to trust their ability to accurately judge character and their disapproval would probably be a deal breaker, right up there with the woman being a Yankees' fan. They saw the Anna train wreck coming a mile away, as opposed to me seeing it right before the derailment. And they had correctly pegged *Rebound Girl*. It was reassuring they had my back on matters of the heart.

Utah was routing Washington State by halftime. I checked my phone while Kiara was on a bathroom break. Kate had texted a couple of times.

Hey, what are you doing tonight? I know I said I needed some me time. But I'd rather have some YOU time.

I should have shown some wisdom and insisted she stick to her original plan to spend some time alone. But at this point, I was like a moth to the flame.

At the U hoops game with Kiara. Done in about an hour or so

Come on over after, if you'd like. Bring a guitar!

This would not be the last time she would change plans and pick me over her solitude. She was new at being by herself, while I had already mastered the art of living alone without feeling lonely. In hindsight, I probably should have been stronger and made myself less available. But I highly doubt that it would have changed the eventual outcome in the slightest. Even then, while floating in a warm, tranquil sea of love-induced endorphins, I felt deep down that there was an unseen storm just over the horizon and I was living on borrowed time. I didn't completely ignore the foreboding feeling. I simply chose not to swim toward the shore and seek shelter.

After the Utah victory, I dropped Kiara off at her house, located near Salt Lake's lovely Liberty Park. I played for a moment with her sweet black lab, Mia, then swung by my place, picked up my Christmas guitar, and raced toward Kate's home, my car knowing the way there by now. No flowers were involved this time, which was fine. The others still looked fresh.

We enjoyed another amazing evening getting to know each other better. With each layer that was revealed, we seemed to fall for the other even deeper.

Talking came so easy, usually accentuated by abundant laughter, and the moments where we sat in silence, looking at the fire dance, her head on my shoulder, lacked for nothing.

We made a quick dash to grab some fresh-Mex takeout, and after dinner I pulled out the guitar. Of the songs that I'd been learning on YouTube by printing out the chords, Eric Clapton's *Wonderful Tonight* sounded like a good one to spring on her. The lyrics were included with the chords and Kate started singing along. She had an amazing voice, her vocal skills eclipsing those of mine working a six-string acoustic guitar.

As it was a work night, I left just before 10 p.m. We were becoming downright responsible grown-ups. Our goodbye at the entryway did take fifteen minutes, so maybe I spoke too soon. Part of it was spent talking, however.

"Would you like to meet Sean next weekend?"

"That would be nice. I'd like that." I was touched that she was that comfortable with us.

"I'm glad. It would be on Friday night. We're going to southern Utah Saturday morning. He's out of school on Monday, and I'm off for Martin Luther King Day."

"I'd love to meet him."

"I love you," she said as she kissed me a final time.

"Ti amo, cara." I opened the door and walked toward my car, turning back to say, "We better get cranking on the Italian. It's just a few short weeks before you go."

"Va bene. Buona notte, bello." She watched me back down her driveway and speed off before closing her door.

Of course, we couldn't wait nearly a week to see each other again. We had been chatting on the phone each night before bedtime. Apparently, the Jamison cat was out of the bag with her son. On Wednesday, she surprised me with a call, asking what kind of Subway sandwich I liked and if it would be okay if she surprised me by coming to my office for lunch.

It had been unseasonably warm and sunny the past few days so we decided to eat outside in the sun on a bench, normally spoken for by the few people in my three-story office building who needed a smoke break.

"I'm loving this surprise. Thanks for bringing me lunch. But just seeing you would have been more than enough."

"You're very welcome. I didn't like the idea of not seeing you before Friday. Speaking of, are you up for an auto show that night? Sean loves two things, cars and music."

"That sounds great. Does he know I drive a Camry?" I assumed his taste was geared to more of a high-performance car than mine.

"He'll find out soon enough. He's going to like you," she smiled confidently.

"I sure hope so. I'm a little nervous about that. What makes you think he will?"

"Because you make his mom very happy. He mentioned that he's noticed a difference in me."

"My coworkers have detected an extra skip in my step, too. Thanks to you."

"This is awesome, isn't it? Even if we are kind of crazy," she slightly alluded to the elephant on the bench with us.

"If being crazy feels this good, I'm not sure I want to be sane."

She planted a huge kiss on me before getting up to leave. I had a permanent grin on my face for the remainder of the day.

I washed and vacuumed my Camry before picking them up on Friday night. My boring, yet dependable sedan was, at least, going to be clean. We had a more subdued than usual greeting at the door, given the fact we had an audience and spent a few minutes in the kitchen with introductions and small talk. I wasn't aware of how tall Jeff was, but I suspected Sean got his height, or lack of, from his mother's side. He had a slight build, short brown hair, and was very polite, if not a little on the shy side. We hit if off right out of the gate and would eventually enjoy a fun, even sarcastic, relationship. He even ranked my car above the Accord and Altima. The $8 trip to the car wash had paid off.

The car show was fun, as fun as lusting after things I could never afford could be. Sean was in heaven, taking the driver's seat in well over a dozen of the shiny vehicles on display. I was careful to take any affectionate cues from Kate. I can still remember a date shortly after my divorce when the woman was all over me the first time we did something with my girls. Bailey was younger and oblivious, but I'll never forget the look on Kiara's face. I would defer to Kate on such things. She took my hand in hers while strolling through the convention showroom. *All righty then!*

We went to a nearby restaurant that served Indian food. I was a novice with this cuisine so I let the pros order. I was thoroughly enjoying the company. Jokes and laughter abounded. We looked every bit like a happy family. I suppose in a perfect world, on paper, I would have chosen a fellow empty nester. I did my share of helping to raise another's children with Anna. While I loved them dearly, the experience wasn't without challenges. I'd concluded that if one truly loved another, acceptance of all that came with the package was part of the deal. I've always disliked the term baggage.

Back at the house, Sean politely said goodnight and disappeared to his bedroom upstairs, giving Kate and me some privacy before I went home.

"He really likes you, I could tell," she had a look of pure contentment on her face as we sat together on the couch.

"He's a very sweet kid. I'm relieved he approves. My daughters' blessing on such matters is huge to me, so I get it."

"I hope I pass their test, too," she said hopefully.

"I have no doubt you will. They are very big on normal so unless there is a hidden side of you I don't know about, I think you are golden."

"What you see is what you get."

"And I see an incredibly beautiful woman." Her body melted into mine as we sat in silence.

They had an early departure time in the morning, and Kate had not finished packing, so I didn't linger. Again, we said a long, reluctant goodbye in the entryway.

"This was a perfect night. Thanks for joining us." Her words were packed with emotion. "You might not fully understand this, but it meant the world to me to be with the two people I love the most in this world."

I looked at her, speechless for a moment.

"Just when I think I can't possibly love you any more than I already do, you say something like that."

In that moment my heart ached, but in the most exquisite way possible. It was simply growing, further expanding its capacity to love.

Chapter 12

Oh, when our bodies touched
On that burning beach,
I could have sworn that heaven
Was within our reach.

Dip Your Wings—Peter Cetera

MY TRIP TO HAWAII WAS RAPIDLY APPROACHING, but I wasn't nearly as excited as I should have been, given the chance to escape the cold Utah winter for some quality beach time. My reasoning for the vacation was a bit flawed, which was something I'd repeat two and a half years in the future. Kate was heading east, to one of my favorite places on the planet, so what did I do? I chose to travel west about the same distance, to be practically on the opposite side of the world from her. And why? First, I chose this path to avoid the temptation to join her on her much-needed escape, and secondly, to distract myself while she was away, rather than be sitting around in the January snow and freezing temperatures. So, the intrinsic value of a tropical vacation for my birthday was a distant third in the equation. Memo to myself: *start doing things for the right reason!*

I got a little taste of life without Kate over the weekend that she took Sean to Zion National Park for some sightseeing and hiking. My kids all hit the road for the holiday weekend and my sushi buddy had recently found love, so it was a solitary weekend for me. By the time I went back to work on Tuesday, I was glad I'd made the decision to bolt for the island of Oahu while Kate would be walking the streets of the Eternal City.

We did text each other several times while she was in southern Utah. She sent some photos of her doing yoga poses on the red rock and Sean climbing boulders, along with our usual mushy stuff. We got in a lovely date night after she returned, driving up to the ski town of Park City, enjoying tasty but overpriced sushi before catching a screening of one of the movies playing as part of the Sundance Film Festival. On this date, I learned a very important lesson the hard way. Twizzlers are far superior to the Red Vines I purchased in the concession line. I immediately went back and remedied my mistake. We jokingly labeled this as our first fight, and I called her high maintenance for a good week after the incident. We made up almost immediately as we held hands while driving down the dark canyon before entering the Salt Lake Valley. She provided the soundtrack during the drive with songs from her phone.

Kate had Sean at home for the upcoming weekend, as the following one would be spent in Rome. She invited me over for dinner with the two of them on Saturday night. We both were scheming up additional ways to see each other as much as possible before we departed for our separate destinations. I didn't have her flight details when I made my reservation, just the departure and arrival dates. I decided to fly out the same day but return a couple of days before she did. Amazingly, our outbound flights ended up being within an hour of each other, so I suggested I take her to the airport and pick her up when she returned.

It was decided we would celebrate our February birthdays together at a nice restaurant the night before we were to fly out. Kate picked *Flemings*, a high-end steakhouse downtown, where my sister-in law, Angie, worked as a manager. We were talking on the phone before bedtime the Sunday night prior to our departure, trying to iron out the logistics for both dinner and the airport.

"I've got an idea," she spoke with a mischievous tone. "It might make sense to just have you spend the night after dinner. That way you don't have to go home, then drive right back, early in the morning." She ended her sentence with an inflection that made it sound more like an enticing offer than a statement.

"I don't want to say goodnight at the front door the night before I leave for Rome."

I didn't attempt to hide my giddiness over her offer.

"I'd love to spend every possible moment with you before we find ourselves apart. I'm really going to miss you, especially knowing the wonderful sights you'll be seeing."

"I'll miss you, too. It'll be weird not being able to communicate daily," she responded.

Kate decided not to transfer her cell phone plan with her to Europe but rather rely simply on email for our communication, using the Wi-Fi at her VRBO apartment. I would be on the dark side of the moon, so to speak, on the other side of the world. In addition to knowing I would miss her dearly due to the time and distance apart and the lack of communication, I had some trepidation regarding her trip to Rome. I knew a big part of her purpose for going was to do some soul searching, to process her impending divorce, and to create a new starting point in her life while celebrating her fortieth trip around the sun. I legitimately wondered where I would fit into this equation. Would she have her *'holy shit, what am I doing?'* moment while sitting on a bench in *Piazza Navona*? She really had no business falling in love so quickly and we both knew it. I knew full well I would be holding my breath for most of my trip to the Hawaiian Islands.

The next evening while packing, I received a text from Kate.

My divorce was final today. I hope you aren't going to run now that I'm a single woman ;)

I didn't know what to say. Congratulations or I'm sorry. I chose something in between.

Are you doing okay? I know from experience how you must feel, emotions all over the place. I'm not going anywhere. I love you and wish I could give you a big hug right now.

You can give me more than a hug tomorrow night. Can't wait . . .

Me, too. Whew! I'm so relieved that I won't be sleeping with a married woman! How would I explain that to my mom?

Glad I could help maintain your purity! Thanks for making me smile, like always. Ti amo!

The next day I did my best to stay focused enough to tie up all the loose ends at work and at 5 p.m. sharp, I said goodbye to my jealous coworkers. I went home and quickly freshened up, threw my suitcase in my car and drove to Kate's with a little more urgency than normal. After the usual electric greeting at the door, we drove downtown to *Flemings*, located across the street from the arena that is home to the Utah Jazz. Thankfully, there was not a home game on the schedule, making parking a breeze on a Wednesday night.

I'd called Angie earlier in the week to reserve a table, and she promised to take good care of us, given we were celebrating dual birthdays. She stopped by our table to say hi and to get properly introduced to my girlfriend. The two of them hit it off nicely. Angie was in the hospitality business and was incredibly outgoing so it would have shocked me had they not. And Kate seemed to be universally loved. The appetizers and small plate options looked incredible so we went that route, choosing the seared ahi tuna, sliced filet mignon, *burrata caprese*, and we split the famous Flemings' potatoes and house salad. We got Kate off to a head start on what would be her go-to beverage while in Italy, opting for a bottle of red wine from Tuscany.

"Happy birthday, Mr. Barrick," she said as we clinked our glasses together.

"Buon compleanno, Ms. Campania."

My birthday would be the following Monday, the day after the Super Bowl. Kate would celebrate hers in exactly a week, on her final day in Rome. We were fifteen years apart and yes, I often worried about that age discrepancy, even as youthful as I felt and acted. So far love had been blind and unconcerned with the math, but would it eventually become a factor? That was completely out of my control so I couldn't let it keep me up at night. Kate's unaddressed need to experience the single life for the first time in her adult life did that already.

"I've got something for you." I reached into my coat pocket and pulled out three items.

"We agreed that this dinner was our gift to each other," she protested.

"I kept to the rules, these are just little things. This is a birthday card, to be opened on your birthday. This second one is to be opened at the top of the Spanish Steps." I handed her a blue, then yellow envelope, both of Hallmark proportions. Then I gave her a simple, white, letter-sized envelope. "This one you can open on the plane during your New York to Rome leg and not a moment sooner."

I had gone back through all our hundreds of old texts, which were duplicated on my iPad and cut and pasted the very best and sweetest words that we shared together, and printed out almost five full pages of our romantic exchanges and sealed them in the envelope. Written on those pages, in our own words, was our incredible love story, barely a month old but nonetheless powerful and poignant. I really couldn't wait for her to relive the beautiful emotions that inspired our words. It had been a delightful experience for me to read our poetry again and then compile it all together for her.

"I've changed my mind. You can open it somewhere over Kansas or maybe even Nebraska."

"Deal. Well, I have something for you too, all within the rules," she smiled as she dug out a small box and a card from her purse. "You have to wait for your birthday to open them."

"Deal." I agreed to her terms. "I hope you know that you are the greatest gift I could possibly ever receive. *Ti amo,* Kate." We were holding hands across the table, staring into each other's eyes, completely oblivious to the other humans in the restaurant. If they were paying any attention to us, they would be certain to feel the pangs of jealousy.

"I love you, too. I still don't know what I did to deserve you, but I'm incredibly grateful that you came into my life."

We drove back to her house, mostly in silence, her hand caressing mine, quietly soaking in the palpable love that flowed between us. There was also an unspoken anticipation in knowing that we would be lying together when it came time to say goodnight, not to mention what would transpire before that moment. We had done well to wait for this night as long as we had, considering the love and passion that simmered just below the boiling point ever since that first, romantic, slow dance we'd shared in her kitchen.

When we walked into her house there was neither a wild explosion of passion nor a mad dash to her bedroom. Instead she gently took me by the hand and led me upstairs, one slow step at a time. Not a single word was spoken but the look of love and contentment in her eyes spoke volumes. And my return gaze revealed to her, a deep appreciation for everything we were about to share and the wonderful expression of love we would experience together.

I think I will now do what they used to do in the movies, simply let the scene fade to black, leaving some things to the audience's imagination and keep the intimate details of that special night between Kate and me. I will add, simply because I'm a guy and am biologically compelled to share at least some information, that everything was as wonderful as I had envisioned it would be. And that is a colossal understatement.

Chapter 13

You went to a strange land searching
For a truth you felt was wrong.
That's when the heartache started.
Though you're where you want to be,
You're not where you belong.

Better Days—Graham Nash

IT'S SUCH A SIMPLE PLEASURE, waking up next to the one you love. Yet it's something that is easily taken for granted, unless you've gone long, barren stretches of time without experiencing the underrated delight. I will forever consider such tender moments as the precious gifts they are. Those were the thoughts that swirled in my mind as I admired the woman lying beside me, still sound asleep, with the faint light of a winter's dawn gently illuminating her serene face.

She began to stir, her movement perhaps triggered by that extra sense we humans possess when someone is watching us. Her eyes opened and were greeted by the smiling face of a man hopelessly in love with her. She smiled, a look of pure contentment filling her countenance.

I articulated with great exuberance the first thing that popped into my brain. "Hi!"

Kate started chuckling.

"What?" I asked. Was it something I said?

"It just takes me a little while to get going so early. I can see you're a morning person," she assumed.

"Not necessarily. I'm just a *you* person."

She kissed me, appreciatively, on the forehead.

Our flights weren't too brutally early but we had to get moving. We showered and dressed quickly and were on the road in thirty minutes. We decided we'd grab a bite to eat in the interval between getting through security and boarding. We parked in the long-term lot and our timing was perfect as a shuttle pulled up within minutes. We both got off at the Delta terminal, even though I was flying Alaska Airlines, with gates in the other terminal. Kate had TSA Precheck, so she planned to go ahead and buy us coffee and something to eat while I snaked my way through the longer lines with other *infrequent* fliers.

Our timing was, again, impeccable as she walked up bearing breakfast while I was putting my belt and shoes back on. We sat sipping coffee and eating muffins without saying much. We were both dreading the goodbye.

"I suppose it's too late to talk you into coming with me." Her eyes exuded sadness.

"Considering I've packed mostly shorts and flip flops, I better stick to the plan. Besides, two is a crowd when you've got some soul-searching to do."

"I know. It's just a lovely thought. You've probably got a big wave with your name on it to catch, anyway." She was smiling now. "Well, we better get going to our gates. I'll miss you."

We stood and shared a final kiss and embrace.

"*Ti amo,* Kate. I hope no one else says those words to you until I pick you up next week," I winked, injecting some humor into the moment, mostly for my sake.

"*Ti amo,* Jamison." Her eyes were misting.

She started walking toward her gate while I made my way toward Terminal 1. Of course, we looked back, twice. She blew a kiss my way on the second glance back, before disappearing in the crowd of hurried travelers.

I had a short flight to San Francisco and a brief layover before boarding a larger plane, bound for Honolulu. I was warming up to the idea of a tropical vacation, with warm being the operative word. I could not remember the last time I'd felt the hot rays of the sun heat my body. It had probably been since last October. Except for the upcoming weekend, my cousin Barbara would be working. So, I was looking forward to some solitary beach time, soaking up enough vitamin D to get me through the remaining weeks of winter and the typically colder and stormy early spring of Utah.

My thoughts drifted east to Kate flying somewhere over America's heartland. She would have opened the envelope and read our love texts by now. I hoped she had experienced half as much joy in reading them as I did while compiling them. We figured we'd have about a thirty-minute window, after I landed on Oahu and before she departed JFK, to have one final conversation over the phone before going to radio silence, if our flights cooperated, that is. I settled in to watch a movie, looking forward to hearing her voice one last time. A second film was required to kill time on the long flight over the Pacific.

I've always enjoyed that first breath of warm, humid air any time I've landed somewhere tropical. I inhaled deeply as I walked up the sky bridge toward the terminal. I live in the second driest state in the country, so any humidity is pleasant to me. Back in the day, it would make my surfer boy blond hair go curly, clearly not an issues these days. Once I got inside the terminal and had a little privacy, I immediately tried Kate on the phone and, luckily, we connected a few moments before she boarded her flight to Italy.

"Thank you for printing up all of our sweet texts. I actually cried on the plane reading them!"

"I'm glad you liked the gift, but sorry for the tears. It was fun putting it all together."

"It was perfect. Thank you. How is it there?"

"Sunny and warm with a lot of palm trees. Are you getting excited?"

"Yes! I've already heard Italian being spoken while we've been waiting. Hold on a sec. Sounds like my section is now boarding. I'm so glad we had a few minutes to talk."

"Me, too. I hope you have an amazing trip. *Ti amo!*"

"*Ti amo*, and you have fun yourself. I'll miss you. *Ciao.*"

"*Ci vediamo.*"

I sat at an empty, unused gate for a few moments and gathered my thoughts. I couldn't help but wonder if her time spent strolling the cobblestone streets of the Eternal City would signal the start of an even longer sojourn as she was still in need of those laps around the universe. I shook off that thought and called my cousin to coordinate a pickup at the airport. These were still pre-Uber days for me.

Barbara worked for the University of Hawaii at an off-campus speech pathology clinic. Her hours were flexible and the office was not far from the Honolulu airport. She pulled up just as I walked out to the designated spot. We hugged and both tried to figure out how long it had been since we'd seen each other. Too long, was the correct answer. Barbara was five years older than me, had curly hair that she kept her natural color of gray, and a petite figure. She looked very much like my sister.

"It's great you finally came to visit your favorite cousin." We shared that secret. "Are you hungry? I know it's only mid-afternoon, but I'm through with work and there is a fun place I want to take you to that's close by."

"Sounds great. It's past my dinner time back in the Mountain Time Zone."

Not far from the airport was *La Mariana* Sailing Club, a fancy name for a truly authentic tiki lounge. It felt like we'd stepped back to the 70s and Steve McGarret and the rest of the *Hawaii Five-0* crew would walk in at any moment for a beer after a hard day of chasing criminals around the island. The decor was made up of a bamboo ceiling, numerous salt-water fish tanks, wicker chairs and tables made from koa. The live music was provided by a husband and wife duo, playing what could be best described as luau music with that distinctive Hawaiian slide guitar sound. I loved the place immediately.

This was a bit of a homecoming for me as I'd lived on Oahu in the late 1970s with Barbara and her parents for the summer right after high school. I felt quite at home, both in the location and the time warp I was experiencing. We settled into our cozy booth and both ordered a Longboard Lager from the Kona Brewing Company, rather than a drink containing an umbrella. The macadamia nut mahi mahi caught my eye, and Barbara picked the Cajun ahi.

"This place is great! Good call."

"I thought you'd like it." She cut right to the chase. "So, you came here instead of Italy? I've got to hear this story."

"Well, it involves a girl."

"I kind of figured that," she smiled.

Barbara was almost like another big sister to me, someone with whom I could talk to about anything. She had been there for me that pivotal summer between high school and college when

I was transitioning from a boy to a man. Girls were very much a part of those conversations on the lanai. She was in graduate school at the time and would marry a Navy pilot a few years later. They were married for fifteen years and tried unsuccessfully to have children during their first several years together. His military career took them to various parts of the world. Her husband, Steven, was tragically killed during a training mission while they were stationed in Pensacola, Florida. Barbara never remarried.

I told her all about Kate and the magical month we had just experienced together and her trip to Rome. I even shared my reservations regarding the staying power of our relationship based on Kate's limited life experiences and her need for them coming so fresh out of her marriage.

"I think you were very wise to give her space to experience Rome on her own. She may have even resented you being there, in hindsight, someday, down the road."

"I'm sure you remember all the details from the Anna experience." She nodded and grimaced a little. "If that taught me anything, it's that you can't skip the necessary steps after a divorce. I'm trying to give Kate all the space she needs but the fact is, we accidentally fell in love in the meantime."

"I don't think I'd ever call falling in love an accident. It should always be a wonderful thing, no matter the outcome." She had a valid point.

"Barb, I honestly don't know how she can juggle all of this. She's still trying to heal from the heartache of a failed marriage. She's essentially only about twenty years old in dating years and now she's in a relationship already. I just think something will eventually have to give, and that thing most likely will be me, specifically my heart."

"Tell me how that heart of yours has felt this past month." I think I knew where she was going with this.

"It's been amazing. I've felt so alive and so in love. In so many ways she's everything I've always wanted. When I simply live in the moment and don't think too much about what I'm doing, it's wonderful. But when I do stop and think about, it feels like I'm living and loving on borrowed time."

"But it sounds to me like it's totally worth it to you, even with the real possibility of it not ending the way you'd like hanging over your head."

"I certainly wouldn't trade last month for anything. Especially for playing it safe and never having experienced everything I did with her. Now that would have been a shame."

"Here's to not thinking too much then and just enjoying the ride." She held her glass out in a toast.

"Cheers to that, Barb!"

Chapter 14

Once in a vision I came on some woods
And stood at a fork in the road.
My choices were clear, yet I froze with the fear
Of not knowing which way to go.

Nether Lands—Dan Fogelberg

IT'S A SAD FACT OF LIFE THAT IT OFTEN TAKES A FUNERAL to bring extended families together. The last time I'd seen Barbara, as well as several other cousins, was about two years ago at my father's funeral. Getting caught up takes a backseat to mourning at such gatherings. This reunion was anything but somber. After experiencing the fun time warp provided by the tiki lounge, we did some catching up while polishing off a bottle of *Pinot Grigio* together at her house located in lovely Hawaii Kai, on the other side of Diamond Head from Honolulu and all its hustle and bustle.

The time difference quickly caught up with me, with a little help from the wine, so I was ready for bed around 9 p.m. or midnight in Utah. It was a work night for Barbara, so she was eager to say goodnight, too.

I was very much aware it was 8 a.m. in Rome. Kate would have already landed at *Fiumicino* by now. I missed her dearly. I fired off a quick email letting her know just that, along with a brief overview of my first night on Oahu. I lay in bed pondering the vast amount of time and distance between us. The full moon that I could see through my window wouldn't even make its way to her until well into my tomorrow. Thankfully, sleep rescued me from my over-thinking self. Barbara had to finish her workweek with a short Friday in the office, so I was on my own that morning.

We'd mapped out my day the night before, picking some sights to visit that were close by. She gave me a ride down the hill from her place and dropped me off at Sandy Beach before heading into work.

The sea air, the sound of the waves crashing, and my toes in the warm sand immediately energized me in a way that is unparalleled. I am most happy and alive when I am at a beach. The irony of feeling alive at this exact spot wasn't lost on me. I had a close call with a rip current here while on vacation as a teenager and, if not for my brother, I very easily could have drowned.

That morning, the waves were not conducive to body surfing since they threatened all comers with a vicious shore break that could snap a spine. I was content to just soak up the sun and watch others who valued life much less than I, doing the surfing for me. Perhaps I possessed some perspective they didn't. I eventually got in the warm water and enjoyed swimming outside the breaker line.

When I left the beach, I walked half a mile up the coast highway to Blowhole Lookout. I watched in wonder as the incoming waves were pushed through a massive lava tube, creating a geyser-like effect.

In the distance, the coastline of Molokai was visible; I even spotted several whales from my vantage point. It was a peaceful and pleasant morning, and I barely gave a thought to Kate and Rome. Mission accomplished. The airfare was paying for itself.

The swimming, walking, and sudden overdose of sunshine left me fatigued, so I took a rare nap when I returned to the house. It was a three-hour doozy. Barbara had come home from work an hour into my snooze but kindly let me sleep.

For the rest of the day we did some grocery shopping, getting items for a Super Bowl party we would attend on Sunday. Then we enjoyed some surprisingly good Thai food from a nondescript-looking restaurant in a nearby strip mall.

Once again, I was ready for bed by 9 p.m., even with the nap. Blame it on the tropical air. I checked my email before bedtime and was ecstatic to see one from Kate in my in-box. She gave me a recap of her first day, which included a tour of the Vatican Museums and a nap of her own. She let me know I was missed, which warmed my heart. I recounted my day for her and sent her my love before falling asleep, hoping she'd find her way into my dreams.

Barbara had a full Saturday planned for me. After breakfast, we went on a glorious hike to the Makapu'u Point lighthouse, which offered a sweeping view of the windward side of Oahu. We made our way up the coast, vintage Hawaiian music playing on the car stereo, and drove past her old house in Kaneohe, where I'd spent that memorable summer. We then had lunch in Kailua before stopping at the stunning Pali Lookout, located a third of the way up the misty green sheer cliffs that divide the island.

The Pali tunnel took us toward Honolulu, and we turned off and stopped for a visit at Punchbowl Crater, also known as the National Memorial Cemetery of the Pacific. An excellent sushi dinner in Kahala capped off a wonderful day.

I was eager to hear from Kate again before bedtime. Hours earlier she had complied.

*I feel so much at home here as I am walking these
streets. It's like I'm connecting with my roots, with
my people.*

She had strolled the *Roman Forum* and toured the *Colosseum* earlier in the day. Later that night, she enjoyed the food and wine. Kate had acclimated to the time change but complained about the cold and rain.

*I plan on going to the Spanish Steps on your
birthday. I love you so much! I want to come back
here with you someday. Ti amo and ciao for now!*

I was thrilled she was having a wonderful time by herself and hadn't yet come to any conclusions about her situation in the broader sense. Maybe I'd dodge that bullet a while longer.

Super Bowl Sunday missed coinciding with my birthday by a day, but Barbara insisted that her work friends include celebrating my big day into the festivities, complete with a cake and candles.

The party was held at the house of a coworker, just ten minutes from Barbara's house. I wore a Patriot's T-shirt and was vastly outnumbered by rabid Seahawks enthusiasts. As a Red Sox fan, I felt compelled to cheer for the other New England teams, even though my devotion to the Red Sox defies logic and geography. My dad spent a few of his formative years in La Jolla, California and went to the same Jr. High as Ted Williams, though a few years behind the Splendid Splinter. So, he followed the hometown hero's career as he became a star in Boston.

I was born into it; infected at birth. It was mostly a painful experience until the Sox finally won the World Series in 2004. I was so happy they won it in my dad's lifetime, and mine, for that matter. I was beginning to wonder if they ever would.

We ate massive amounts of delicious food, and the Patriots won on the last defensive play of the game, an early birthday present for me. After the party, Barbara suggested we burn off some calories by taking a little hike up the side of the crater that forms Hanauma Bay. We were treated to a beautiful view of it to the east with Diamond Head crater to the west. We watched until the sun disappeared into the Pacific.

"Are you sure you want to go back home to the snow and cold?" Barbara asked. "You can stay as long as you'd like."

"If it weren't for Kate, I might take you up on that offer. Assuming she doesn't have her *holy shit* moment while she's over in Rome."

She chuckled at the label I put on her potential epiphany.

"Well, if she does, that's even more of a reason for you to stay," she shrugged. "Let's get back and plan your North Shore birthday excursion. You've got a great last-day-in-paradise ahead of you. You really should have stayed longer."

As I stared toward the silhouette of Diamond Head, wrapped in the orange glow of the fading sunset with the sparkling Honolulu city lights in the distance, I couldn't have agreed with her more.

The next morning, I awoke a year older, at least that's what my driver's license said, although my internal clock didn't agree at all with the new number. I opened *Facebook* and read through all the birthday greetings that various friends had taken the time to write. Kate had a several-hour head start on everyone else and had posted first. We were both private people and decided not to put our relationship on full display on social media, but Kate threw out a *Ti Amo!* for all to see and translate on *Google*, if they wished.

I opened Kate's birthday card to me. She wrote sweet words of love and gratitude, along with a poem from E. E. Cummings: *I Carry Your Heart*. Reading it certainly warmed mine. I unwrapped the small box she'd given me at our birthday dinner. It contained

three small rocks, each with a different word carved in it: *THANKS,
LOVE,* and *TRUST*. The box also contained a note.

> *Birthday Wishes*
> *Each rock represents an offering for the year ahead.*
> *Give THANKS: Think of all you are grateful for and*
> *toss the rock into the sea.*
> *LOVE fully: Ponder the things that fill your heart*
> *and make you happy, and then send the rock into the*
> *crashing waves.*
> *TRUST the Universe: What is it you want from this*
> *life? What do you desire more than anything? Ask for*
> *it, trust that it will be yours, and then offer the rock*
> *to the ocean.*

The gift was perfect and pure Kate. And it just so happened that
my plans for the day included a trip to the beautiful North Shore of
Oahu, giving me a choice stretch of beach ideal for rock-tossing.

As we'd mapped it out the night before, Barbara dropped me off
near the Ala Moana Center in downtown Honolulu on her way into
work. The mall served as the hub for the mass transit system. For the
ridiculously low cost of $2.50, I caught the #52 bus to Hale'iwa, which
was on the other side of Oahu.

The bus route, heading north, cut through the middle of the lush
island, with the popular Dole pineapple plantation offering the most
prominent landmark along the way.

At Hale'iwa, I transferred to #55, which headed east along
the North Shore and would eventually wrap around the island,
returning to Honolulu. I got off at the Banzai Pipeline stop, along
with a young Australian couple I'd met on the ride. Fortuitously,
there was a surfing competition happening with some of the sport's
biggest names competing on the massive waves that were part of

the winter swell. I found a spot among the throng in the shade of a palm tree and enjoyed a good hour of some incredible surfing.

This stretch of beach was far too crowded for me to undertake the rock-throwing ritual, so I walked several hundred yards away and found a solitary stretch to ponder the gift. The huge waves were pounding the steep beach with a ferocious roar. I quickly realized that these rocks had a snowball's chance in hell of being washed far out to sea, no matter how far I threw them. I concluded that the offering was more about intent rather than distance.

The theme of the first rock, *THANKS*, was gratitude. I was thankful for so much: my girls, my mom and other family members, good health, employment, finding love recently, and overall happiness and contentment. I let the rock fly. It made it past the shore break at least, so it wouldn't be washing up at my feet with the next wave.

I thought of the people and things that filled my heart with love and made me happy. Lately, that had predominantly been Kate. It felt amazing to be in love again and to have it all come back to me so generously. I also thought about the other, non-romantic forms of love that I felt in my life and about life's simple pleasures. My heart was full as I threw the *LOVE* rock right into the teeth of the next wave to break on the shore, trying to strictly follow Kate's instructions.

The questions that accompanied the third rock, *TRUST*, had dominated my thoughts during the bus ride through the heart of Oahu. *What did I want out of this life? What did I desire above everything else?* On the surface, it seemed the answers were simple: I wanted to be in love and enjoy a wonderful relationship with someone, grow old with her, sitting happily on a porch together in the twilight of our lives. And currently, I wanted that person to be Kate, a woman with whom I'd connected so well and so deeply.

As I cocked my arm, set to launch the small rock toward the pounding surf, I could have predictably asked for everlasting love, trusting that it would be delivered to me. But instead, as I threw it into the breaking waves, I asked the Universe to bless me with peace.

Chapter 15

In the dead of night, she could shine a light
On some places that you've never been.
In that kind of light, you could lose your sight
And believe there was something to win.

That Girl Could Sing—Jackson Browne

IT HAD BEEN THE PERFECT WAY TO CELEBRATE MY BIRTHDAY, a lap around Oahu coinciding with another one around the sun. The bus pulled into Honolulu late afternoon and within minutes of calling her, Barbara was there to pick me up.

We stopped at the grocery store to get a couple steaks, some asparagus, and *Longboard Island Lager*. We planned to observe my birthday and last night on the island by simply grilling and chilling at home. I'd had a wonderful visit with my cousin, and we treated that last night together as if it would be a while until our next reunion.

I had packed earlier and checked my email from my phone while in bed. Work items were beginning to pile up but oddly nothing from Kate. There had to be a good reason for her silence, especially with it being my birthday, but I did briefly allow my mind to venture to the land of worst-case scenarios. This further validated my choice to ask the Universe for peace back at the North

Shore. *Breathe Deep! She's okay. We're okay! She didn't have her 'holy shit moment' at the top of the Spanish Steps or get mugged! There must be a perfectly good explanation. Relax, boy!*

I did fire off an email to her, thanking her for the sweet card and the box of rocks, giving her a recap of my day and my moments of reflection at Pipeline, but leaving out the specifics. I wrote that I hoped everything was good in Rome and that she was safe and sound. I turned out the light and trusted the Universe that she was, too.

I checked my in-box again after a 2 a.m. trip to the bathroom, courtesy of the Kona Brewing Company, and I was doubly relieved to see Kate's name appear. She'd sent the email right after I'd gone to bed, just after she'd rolled out of hers. Wi-Fi had been out for the entire day and evening before in her apartment, and it killed her to not be able to contact me on my birthday.

> *I hope it was an amazing day, worthy of the amazing man whom I love and adore! I'm glad you loved the rocks! The North Shore was the perfect place to make your offerings. I went to the Spanish Steps yesterday and read your card at the top.*
>
> *Thank you so much for the sweet words of love. I now understand why that is your favorite spot in Rome. It's one of mine now, as well. I walked over to the Pincio Overlook you had mentioned. It was a gorgeous sunset, but then got cloudy and cold and began to rain. I went down into Piazza del Popolo and found a restaurant. I had the waiter take my picture. It's my new Facebook profile photo. I was thinking of you when it was taken, so that smile is a reflection of you and the love I feel for you. Can't wait to see you again. Ti amo!*

All was well in my world again, although I had a difficult time falling asleep with thoughts of Kate swirling inside my head, as well as fresh visions of her. I'd gone to her *Facebook* page and saw the wonderful picture of her smiling, holding a glass of red wine and looking radiant. I couldn't stop staring at her. I lay there in awe of this incredible woman and of the power of love that had a remarkable way of scooping her up from literally half a world away and making it feel that she resided deep inside me.

In the morning, Barbara and I shared a heartfelt goodbye at the airport. I offered her my place in Salt Lake for a reciprocal visit but doubted that anything could pull her away from the island paradise she called home.

After clearing security, I had time to compose an email to Kate and commented on her *Facebook* photo: *Ti amo, bellissima!* The long flight over the Pacific, this time connecting in Los Angeles, was perfect for watching a couple of movies and pondering my life. Kate would have wound up her second to last day in Rome by now, so an email would probably be greeting me, Wi-Fi permitting, when I landed and waited in LAX for my final flight.

There had been no outward signs of her coming to any conclusions or experiencing any epiphanies, but I doubted she'd be sharing anything via email even if she were. Tomorrow she'd turn forty, and it would be her last day in Rome. That could potentially be a very emotional day for her.

I wondered what it was exactly that she was processing. I had no illusions that her thoughts revolved around me or us. I suspected she was mainly contemplating her twenty years of marriage, Jeff and the sting of rejection she felt, Sean and his well-being, and herself. I'm certain she considered her future, being as self-aware as she was, and calculating exactly what she needed to heal and grow and come out of this experience a whole person.

Her incredible depth and that self-awareness were exactly the things that kept me up in the wee hours. My worries would have been relatively minimal had she been a shallow person, oblivious and unconcerned with what she was feeling, simply living blissfully in ignorance. It was ironic; the very character traits that I found so irresistible and attractive were ultimately working against me and us. Yet I inexplicably found considerable beauty in that irony. At this point, all I could really do was just hold my breath and see what would come from all her soul searching. *Focus on the things you can control,* they say. Taking that advice, I would simply continue to love her, as if I had a choice in that matter.

I had a ninety-minute layover at LAX, so I tapped into the airport Wi-Fi and checked my email. The work items were multiplying like rabbits. Going back to the office was going to be a complete joy in the morning. Not. Kate had sent me a lovely overview of her day walking the cobblestone streets of Rome. The only downer had been the weather so far—cold and intermittent rain during her stay. I quickly composed an email to her before boarding.

When you read this, you'll be a year older—happy birthday! Forty has never looked better! I hope you enjoy your last day in the Eternal City. I also hope that this trip has been everything you imagined it would be. You were wishing to connect with your ancestors, and it sounds like you have. I'm thrilled you could make this trip at such an important time in your life. I know these last few months have been quite a whirlwind for you. I'm grateful you've let me into your heart these past several weeks and allowed me to accompany you on part of your journey. I count each day with you a blessing, and I love you beyond words.

As my flight began boarding, I checked the time in Rome and it was just after midnight on February 4th, technically her birthday. I wanted to be the first to post birthday greetings on her *Facebook* page. I did so in Italian: *Buon Compleanno, cara! Ti amo tantissimo e non vedo l'ora di vederti!* (Happy Birthday, dear. I love you very much and can't wait to see you!) *There you have it, Facebook world. Feel free to translate.*

My next day at work was as brutal as I'd expected it to be. It started out with the annoyance of having to wear long pants for the first time in almost a week.

I was swamped with the numerous emails that had piled up, but, of course, the first one I read was from a certain Kate Campania. She had written a brief message before going to bed at the end of her final day in Rome.

> *Thanks for the birthday wishes and the wonderful card. You sure know how to make an old lady feel special! ;-) I had a nice 40th. I decided to go revisit some of my favorite places and went back to my favorite restaurant. I became very emotional on the walk back, not sure why, but I cried the entire way home in the rain. I probably will be too rushed in the morning to write again. I'll call you from NY. (I'll flip off the Yankees for us!) I can't wait to hear your voice and have you hold me in your arms. I'm more grateful for you than you can possibly know. Ti amo, Jamison. Buonanotte from Rome. Good morning when you read this.*

Thankfully, the remainder of day went by quickly. Staying busy has that magical effect on the clock. I was also trying to get back on Mountain Standard Time, too. That may have been part of the reason I had a hard time falling asleep later that night, with the other part being the anticipation of seeing Kate the following day. It felt much like Christmas Eve did when I was a kid. This time, I knew exactly what Santa was bringing me the next day. It was sometime after midnight before I was finally able to turn off my brain.

Most days, I'm the first one to make it into the office. I make the coffee and have the place to myself for about 45 minutes before the others trickle in. I had settled in the next day, sipping my coffee and doing the calculations for when Kate might land in New York, when my cell phone lit up showing her smiling face as part of the caller ID. I'm not going to lie, my heart leapt.

"*Ciao bella!*" I answered, enthusiastically.

"Mmm, *ciao bello*. It's so great to hear your voice."

"I'll say! How are feeling? Tired?"

"Yeah. I didn't sleep much at all. It's going to be so nice sleeping in my own bed tonight."

"I'll bet. I've missed you. A lot." I emphasized the quantity.

"Me, too. I can't wait to see you."

"Is your flight looking like it'll leave on time?"

"Yep. Should be in at 2:30. And I'm not checking my bag."

"All right, I'll be there. Are you doing okay? Sounded like your last night was pretty emotional."

"I'm fine. It just caught me off guard. I'll tell you about it in person."

"Sounds good." I concealed the fact that I was a bit apprehensive as to what this all meant. "I'll see you in a few hours."

"Can't wait. I love you."

"I love you, too, Kate."

The rest of the day limped along at an excruciatingly slow pace. Finally, 2 p.m. arrived. I grabbed my coat and headed for the door.

"Patrice, I'll be back after I drop Kate off at home." Pat, our office manager, was privy to my love life more than the others.

"Really? Just call it a day. It'll almost be four by the time you get back," she said.

"Nah, I'm still playing catch-up from being gone myself, and she sounded like she might fall asleep on the drive home. See you in a bit."

I parked in the short-term lot and headed to the International Terminal. Just as I walked through the automatic sliding doors, I saw Kate coming down the escalator. It took a great deal of self-control to not go bounding up to meet her halfway. When she reached the bottom, we stepped to the side to avoid blocking others who were descending. We were going to be a while. I've never known a hug to convey so much emotion as the one we shared. We silently embraced for a good thirty seconds, maybe more, then finally gazed into each other's eyes and punctuated the hug with a passionate kiss. No words were spoken, nor were any necessary.

We held hands walking to the car and on the drive to her home.

"It's really good to see you. Seems like it's been a month." She took the words right out of my mouth.

"I've got to admit, I really didn't like being on the other side of the planet from you. I prefer you to be in the same city, actually."

"You know, I've got a work trip to Chicago in two weeks, right? I guess I'll either have to quit my job or take you with me."

"Either option is acceptable," I smiled.

Her return smile seemed to have a mischievous life of its own, as if she'd changed subjects in her mind.

"I hope you weren't planning on going back to work."

"I was. I assumed you probably needed a nap right away."

"Sleep is overrated. I'd kind of like to pick up where we left off the night before we flew out. Remember that?"

"Yes. Quite vividly, in fact. But when do you get Sean?"

"Whenever I tell Jeff to bring him home."

"Let me make a quick call."

Without taking much of an eye off the road, I quickly speed-dialed the office.

"Hi, Pat. Hey, I won't be coming back today after all. Yeah, I know, you told me so. Thanks. I'll see you tomorrow."

I hung up and glanced over at Kate who was smiling and appeared to have caught her second wind. *Apparently, there won't be any slowing down at forty for this girl.*

Chapter 16

When you touch me,
The sensation goes so deep.
Your embrace awakens and inspires me,
And I can't seem to get enough.

Kate's Song—Jamison Barrick

EVEN THOUGH WE'D ENJOYED A WONDERFUL HOMECOMING, in the following days, I was a bit guarded, consciously looking for some outward sign that Kate may have had the slightest change of heart regarding us, or more accurately, the timing of us, while in Italy. When I failed to see a noticeable difference, I scolded myself for taking such a negative approach and for setting myself up for a self-fulfilling prophecy to come to fruition. I decided to let my guard down and just enjoy living in the moment.

Kate openly admitted that much of her trip to Rome had involved deep introspection, but she indicated that most of her efforts were focused on the healing that she needed. She never could fully explain the flood of tears on the night of her birthday. She chalked it up to turning forty and realizing so much of her life had changed in the past six months. She was finally releasing it all after holding it in so well since Jeff had moved out.

We both got back into the rhythm of our lives. Kate tried to stick to her formula of Sean time, me time, and alone time. But she allowed the lines to blur and had a genuinely hard time sticking to her self-imposed, rigid guidelines. She had Sean for the weekend after her return, but on Saturday night, I was invited to join them shopping for vinyl records and dinner afterward. The following Tuesday was to be a solo night for her, but she ended up joining me and my mother for our weekly dinner. We upgraded from *Wendy's* to Mexican, considering we had a guest. Mom and Kate hit it off nicely, and Mom was thrilled to finally meet her.

I allowed myself to get pulled a bit by Kate's tides, so to speak. I stopped planning things on the days and nights that she might call on me. I was torn, struggling to maintain a healthy balance, not wanting to be so accommodating as to shun my friends or lose my independence; but I was also drawn to spend as much time as possible with my favorite human. I found it impossible to say no and often regretted it for a couple of reasons. I honestly felt I was impeding her growth by encroaching on her alone time, something to which she was apparently not accustomed. And I didn't like the idea that I might be turning into someone who was always waiting by the phone.

All those internal conflicts were tossed out the window when it was just the two of us on a planned date. The upcoming Valentine's Day was one such instance. I'm not a big fan of this holiday. I don't need to be coerced into suddenly becoming all lovey-dovey one day of the year and doing things that might be out of character during the other 364. Call me a romantic, but I feel every day should be a manifestation of what Valentine's Day embodies. And, in my humble opinion, I think I can say it just as well, if not better than Hallmark.

Nonetheless, I did go above and beyond on this day that celebrates love. I reserved a room overlooking downtown in the *Grand America Hotel*, Salt Lake's finest, while Kate had taken care of dinner arrangements. I kept the hotel choice hidden from her, and I was in the dark as to where we would be dining later. I checked in earlier in the day and placed a dozen red roses in the room to surprise her upon checking in. I also put some *Prosecco* on ice.

The posh accommodations, along with the roses, were a wonderful surprise and set the tone for a perfect, romantic evening. We sipped our *Prosecco* and enjoyed the view of the city lights from our eighth-floor window. Valentine cards were exchanged, minimal wording from Hallmark with the rest of the prose originating from our hearts, in our own handwriting. We both expressed gratitude that we'd found each other and connected so quickly and deeply.

After toasting to love and each other, I shared an observation.

"Do you realize we haven't had a single bad moment since we met? Unless you count the *Twizzler* incident at Sundance."

"You mean the *Red Vine* incident?" she playfully corrected me.

"Yes. It's truly remarkable how well we get along, so effortlessly."

"I must say, it does feel too good to be true at times." I allowed my worst fears to surface and immediately regretted going there on such a perfect night where the 'living in the moment' policy should have been strictly enforced. I tried to recover. "Sorry, tonight isn't the night to get deep."

"No, it's okay. We can talk about anything, anytime." Kate had such an understanding heart as well as a remarkable knack of being able to read my mind. "I know I came fully loaded with warnings and disclaimers, and sometimes I wonder what I'm doing. I'm certain you do your share of wondering for me, too. You've been so amazing to give me plenty of space, and you're so aware of where I'm at on my journey. I couldn't ask for anything more." Her sweet smile melted my heart.

"I just don't want to hinder your progress in any way. You still have a lot to sort out, and I realize there is much you have never experienced. I hope I'm not getting in the way," I said sincerely.

"This isn't exactly how I would have drawn it up, falling in love so quickly after Jeff, but I believe you are a gift. You came into my life for a reason. I truly feel I need to honor that gift. If it's all right with you, I'd like to try and pull this off." Her eyes looked so incredibly hopeful. "I want it all. I want to heal and grow, and I want to try to do it with you by my side."

"I'm all in, Kate. And I'll give you all the space you need. We can go at a pace that works best for you. I, also, want to honor the precious gift that fell from the sky."

"I love you," she said, putting her glass down and kissing me passionately.

"When are our reservations?" I asked.

She glanced at her phone. "We've got an hour, why?"

"I've got an idea how we can kill some time."

It was unseasonably warm, so we decided to walk the three blocks to the restaurant Kate had chosen for us, which happened to be *Takashi*, my favorite. Abbey had suggested it to Kate when she asked her for recommendations. We had to walk rather briskly to get there for our 7:30 reservation, as we'd killed a little too much time back in the room.

We had an amazing dinner of all my favorite rolls and appetizers, but saved room for chocolate fondue at *The Melting Pot*, just two doors down from *Takashi*.

Taking the long way back to the hotel, we enjoyed the balmy night and the energy of downtown Salt Lake City that was filled with like-minded lovers on what would be a Valentine's Day to remember. I could not imagine feeling more in love than I did on this magical night.

The next morning, we shunned the five-star breakfast at the hotel and chose a basic greasy spoon establishment downtown. *What is it that makes chicken-fried steak so irresistible?* We were trying to figure out how to spend the rest of the gorgeous, sunny day when Kate suggested playing a round of golf.

It hadn't snowed since the day I was scraping my windshield in short pants at the airport, and it had been incredibly warm for February in Utah, so a course or two might be open. Sure enough, after a couple of phone calls, we had a tee time. Global warming is apparently not a hoax. After picking up Kate's clubs, we swung by my condo to get mine, and were soon out on an executive course whose holes were mainly par 3's.

We practically had the place to ourselves. It was February, after all, and it was Sunday, which meant a good portion of the fine folks of the Beehive State were in church. Our scores were better than expected, since the last time I'd swung a club was in October, and it had been since August for Kate. I could have triple-bogeyed every hole and still had a blast with my exquisite company.

The 19th hole provided our beer, and Kate took a selfie and sent it to her dad. She assured me that he would really like me, and she was excited for us to meet when he was slated to visit over Sean's spring break from school.

I lived close to the golf course, so we went to my place and sat in the sun-splashed courtyard, me playing the guitar and Kate singing.

Sean was coming home later that afternoon, so I took Kate home, and we said our reluctant goodbye. This farewell was particularly difficult after having enjoyed such an incredible weekend together. We figured out our next rendezvous, planning a lunch together before she had to go to Chicago for work later in the week.

I drove home feeling more optimistic than ever about our chances. I remembered her words at the hotel and found them to be quite soothing. After arriving home, I picked up my guitar and was strumming a few familiar chords when some lyrics floated into my head, or more accurately, my heart. I reached for a notebook that I kept nearby for such moments and began to write.

My musical talent still lagged far behind my ability to put words together in any kind of poetic form. It took me from Sunday night through part of Monday evening until I was happy with the lines. The guitar chords would require much more work until I would consider this a finished song.

I struggled to find the perfect title until I realized it was right there all along, in its beautiful simplicity. I sat back and felt great satisfaction as I read the final verses. It was a hopeful song, full of gratitude and love. I was beginning to feel this fairy tale might just have a happy ending after all.

Kate's Song

When I look into your eyes,
I gaze inside your soul.
I see your beauty,
Through to your core,
And I am lost in your allure.

When you speak to me,
I feel your words of love.
I hear the powerful tenderness
In your voice,
And I know what
You say is true.

How can these weeks
Seem like years?
I feel I've known you
All my life.

When you share
Your words with me,
They go straight to my heart.
They soothe me
From half a world away,
And I grasp
That your love is real.

When you reveal your pain to me,
I see glimpses of your scars.
I fight the want
To take the hurt away,
And I simply hold you tight.

Where did you come from, love?
I've been looking for you
All my life.

When you touch me,
The sensation goes so deep;
Your embrace awakens
And inspires me,
And I can't seem to get enough.

When you love me,
The gratitude overflows.
It's a feeling I've never known,
And nothing can compare.

Do dreams really come true?
I've been waiting for you
All my life.

Chapter 17

She's got a light around her,
And everywhere she goes
A million dreams of love surround her
Everywhere.

She's Got a Way—Billy Joel

"WHERE DID YOU COME FROM?"

Kate's eyes were misty when she asked the rhetorical question. We were at lunch, and I'd just given her my latest song to read, its title bearing her name. I wanted to give her something to make her miss me even more during her business trip to Chicago the next day. If the look on her face were any indication, I would indeed be missed.

I shrugged and answered, "Sometimes when my heart spills over, I feel the need to put it into words. I hope you like it."

"I love it. You spoil me." She exuded appreciation.

"This one actually has some chords I'm trying to match to the words, so I might be able to rightfully call it a song someday."

"You can write me all the love songs you want. They truly touch me." She would, in fact, inspire a few more.

Kate accepted my offer to drop her off and pick her up on both sides of her work trip. It was simply a cheap ploy to spend a few more minutes with her to compensate for her being gone a couple of days.

I used the time Kate was away to catch up with my younger daughter, Bailey. Her boyfriend, Cole, was busy with a study group one night, which allowed us to have some one-on-one time. She came over to my house, and we worked together to make a delicious stir-fry with chicken and vegetables over rice. We sipped some SeaGlass *Sauvignon Blanc* while we chopped veggies and chatted.

Bailey is the more outgoing of my two daughters. She was the one who would emerge out of the wild herd of six-year-old soccer players to run down the field with the ball and score several goals in every game. I would often drag her to Kiara's team practices, and Bailey wouldn't think twice about scrimmaging with girls four years her senior. Her light brown hair was usually pulled back in a ponytail. She had bright, brown eyes and a perpetual smile. And she was smart, just one semester shy of her degree in civil engineering from the University of Utah.

"So, tell me about your girlfriend. Kiara says she sounds normal. You haven't really shared much with us. Are you worried that we'll judge? You know we are just being protective, right?" *Did I mention that in addition to her being outgoing, she was also outspoken?*

"I kind of wanted to wait until I knew she was keeper material before going too public." I was still chuckling from her inquisitive barrage. "I certainly appreciate you being protective. *Rebound girl* taught me to value the approval of my daughters."

"*Rebound girl?* Oh, that one! She was kind of weird. We definitely didn't approve." She cringed.

"I think you'll like Kate. Let's all do dinner sometime soon so you can either accept or reject."

"Would you two like to come to my Ultimate Frisbee fundraising dinner? That way we can meet her, and you can support a good cause." She played on the club team at the U.

"You're always thinking, B. Give me the details, and I'll run it by her. I'll be there no matter what. If she can come, I won't tell her that she'll totally be on trial." Dinner was ready. "Let's eat!"

I retrieved Kate from the airport on Friday afternoon. She had Sean for the weekend, but I still was invited to Sunday dinner. She put Bailey's fundraiser on her schedule, and I had her add another event that was coming up in a couple of weeks. I'd scored tickets to see Stevie Nicks' concert, and Kate was thrilled to be invited. We planned a few more dates and activities for the upcoming weeks, including a scheduled dinner with Abbey, who was feeling a bit neglected and jokingly questioned the wisdom of lining up two of her best friends and finding herself the odd woman out.

As much as Kate and I appeared to be a bona fide couple, she had chosen not to manifest anything publicly on social media. The fact that I even bring it up goes to illustrate how social media has impacted our lives and is part of the dating landscape in the new millennium. I'm a private person and cringe when I see people playing their lives out for all to see on *Facebook*. That also goes for over-sharing a toddler's potty-training stories, gym workouts, or healthy kale recipes. I'm not above sharing facets of my life online and would have been fine posting pictures of me and Kate at various events, but I followed her lead.

I was content living in our own bubble and had no desire to have her click the 'in a relationship' button on *Facebook* and invite all the online fanfare; although it made me wonder a bit.

Jeff knew that Kate was dating me. Sean didn't see any need to hide it from his dad nor did his mom encourage it. I had met Jeff once when I was at Kate's house. Both of us were polite but neither gave the other any kind of indication of being overly impressed. So, Kate's low dating profile had nothing to do with her ex. I just figured she had her reasons and let it go.

However, she did keep up a healthy online presence with the self-awareness articles she posted. Yes, I read most of them. I figured they would offer glimpses into her healing process and the progress she was making on her *journey*. (By the way, the word *journey* made Abbey practically gag, as I assume most of the articles did, too.) I was bracing myself for the day that I opened *Facebook* to find that she'd posted an article entitled: *"How to Recognize Your 'Holy Shit Moment.'"* Thankfully, most of her shared articles appeared to be thinly veiled digs at her ex-husband.

February flew by, and even if there was no trail of pictures on social media to prove it, Kate and I enjoyed many wonderful moments together, which included a few sleepovers when Sean wasn't at home.

I decided to keep more than a toothbrush at her place. I also left one of my guitars, mainly as a convenience since we were playing and singing frequently.

The fundraising dinner was fun, and both Bailey and Kiara flashed me a resounding thumbs-up during the festivities. Stevie Nicks was incredible in concert. Abbey met us for sushi one night, and I was invited to more outings on the nights Kate had Sean with her.

The weather was warming up in Utah, and we were already thinking about hikes, summer concerts, patio dining, and other activities to be enjoyed as the city emerged from winter hibernation.

Kate and I had still yet to experience a bad moment, never even coming close to fighting about anything. We both had personalities that just allowed us to roll with things. The giddiness of a new relationship was past, yet we were still very much in love and constantly trying to demonstrate that to each other. I kept the floral arrangements coming, and the water Kate used in the vases must have sprung from the fountain of youth as the flowers refused to wither at a natural pace. Her Valentine roses we brought home from the hotel still had life in them as we rolled into March. We joked that it was the power of our love that kept them fresh. I know that power, at the very least, made me one happy man.

I was certainly happy enough to have zero desire to look beyond what I was enjoying with Kate. I hadn't even thought of the alternative until I received a call from one of my clients one afternoon. After giving her some pricing for a potential project, Jenny got right to the point.

"Are you seeing anyone these days?"

"I am, why do you ask?"

"Too bad . . . I mean good for you! We hired a new gal recently who is single and totally your type. I hadn't seen any indication that you were dating from *Facebook*, so I mentioned you to her this morning. We even stalked your pictures," she admitted.

I guess clicking on that damned relationship button does have a useful purpose after all.

"That's sweet of you, but I started seeing someone at the beginning of the year. We haven't exactly gone out of our way to post stuff online. What exactly is my type?"

"She's fun and sweet, just like you. Oh well, let me know if things don't work out!"

"You'll be the third person to know. Thanks, Jenny!"

Her proposition did get me thinking. Kate and I had not made any rules nor put labels and expectations on our relationship whatsoever. We never even defined it as that. It had taken me well over a month to even use the word *girlfriend* in a sentence. Everything was simply unspoken. After hanging up the phone, I spent a few minutes wondering how Kate would react if the shoe were on the other foot. And how she *should* react.

Here was a woman who completely missed out on dating. Her gymnastics aspirations left her no time for that in high school. Then she met Jeff at the beginning of her freshman year in Austin. I was certain her friends were trying to line her up upon hearing she was divorced, as well they should, encouraging her to experience that part of life. Kate was quite a catch, after all, and I knew this. I was obviously conflicted on the subject, probably not the ideal friend to advise her.

Had she asked the best friend part of me, and not the lover, I would have encouraged her to date and rack up those experiences. The perspective I gained from my time with Anna would have factored into that advice. But on the other hand, *how often does true love come around in a lifetime and fall into your lap? Would she be foolish to walk away from something so extraordinary just because of less than perfect timing? And what was she willing to gain or lose by searching beyond the horizon?*

This may appear a bit contradictory, but I don't think a little competition is a bad thing. I knew Kate thought the world of me, but I was often being compared to Jeff, not exactly a high bar to clear. Perhaps, she really didn't know what she had in me, because she lacked the experience to compare beyond Jeff. I honestly felt I could hold my own with anyone out there in the dating world— on an emotional level, at least. My Camry and I couldn't compete with a rich lawyer and his BMW, but if that's what a woman was primarily after, then she should probably choose the fine Bavarian craftsmanship and the big bucks.

The fun and games continued through the early part of March. We enjoyed lunches, dinners, movies, either at home, on the couch, or in a theater, and warm and sunny Sunday walks through Sugar House Park. Often, I'd be invited to join Kate and Sean in their various activities. She was beginning to keep her alone time more sacred, and I was totally fine with that. The Sunday before St. Patrick's Day was slated as such a day, and Kate went off the grid. I'd texted her in the morning but didn't receive a response until after 6 p.m.

Sorry for the slow response. I climbed Mt. Olympus today.

Wow! By yourself?

Yeah, not the smartest thing to do, but there were plenty of people on the trail. It was tough. I really had to push myself. I didn't know I had it in me. I was so determined to make the summit. I'm stronger than I thought I was.

Congrats! You're an incredibly tough lady. It was probably very cathartic.

It was. Early bedtime for me tonight. I'm beat. *Buonanotte!*

We met at a downtown bar after work the following Tuesday to sip some Jameson in honor of St. Paddy. Kate seemed a bit subdued. She chalked it up to a busy day at the office and from still being sore from her hike. We made plans for her to sit with me at an awards luncheon on Friday. We had produced the videos honoring some local CEOs, and one of Kate's biggest clients was an honoree. She had Sean, so we called it a night after one drink.

I had tickets for the Collective Soul concert on Thursday, but Kate had to decline as she had Sean that night, and Jeff was out of town. Abbey was more than happy to assume her role as concert buddy. She'd given me some good-natured grief for taking Kate to Stevie Nicks, so it was nice to be back in her good graces. We had a fantastic time, and I honestly never caught myself wishing that Kate had found some way to make it work to join me.

The next morning, while sipping my coffee at work and organizing my day, my phone lit up with a text from Kate. Knowing I was to see her in a few short hours at lunch, I grinned as I began to read her text. My smile quickly faded.

Are you flexible this morning? I really need to talk. I'm an emotional wreck and in no shape to meet you for lunch.

Absolutely. Are you okay?

Not really.

I'm sorry . . . Should I be worried?

Maybe.

She was being kind. The word *definitely* would have been far more accurate.

Chapter 18

It's times like these you learn to live again.
It's times like these you give and give again.
It's times like these you learn to love again.
It's times like these, time and time again.

Times Like These—Foo Fighters

THE MONTH OF MARCH CAN BE A CRUEL ONE. It brings with it the promise of spring after a long, cold winter. It teases with visions of warm, sunny days and is brimming with the optimism of a new season, a fresh start. It was the Vernal Equinox, or as most calendars indicated, the first day of spring. However, it was anything but spring-like as I drove home to meet Kate. The sky was painted a pale shade of gray, and it was cold with light snow flurries falling. *Just perfect*, I thought as I stared blankly at my windshield wipers erasing the droplets of melting flakes.

I had seen this day coming but was to be completely blindsided by the twist. Since I first heard her story back in December, I was justifiably concerned about our timing, about Kate needing more time to heal, and then later needing to perhaps step back and regroup after our love burned so intensely, so quickly. I assumed there would come a time when she would want to experience being truly single for the first time in her adult life. I begrudgingly understood all of this. But I wasn't the least bit prepared for what she was about to tell me.

She knocked meekly on my door, and we embraced as she entered. I could see all I needed to know in her telling brown eyes. Aside from the obvious indication of a tear-filled and sleepless night, they also told me she had some bad news to deliver. We sat down on the edge of my couch, holding hands and facing each other. I took a deep breath before she spoke.

"Ever since I came back from Rome, I should have been the happiest woman on the planet, but I haven't been. And I finally figured out what has been holding me back," she began to slowly explain while I braced myself. "First, I need to say something." Tears began to form and slowly trickle down her face. "You have been so incredible. You came into my life at a point when I needed to feel loved and wanted. You've given me so much, and I will always be grateful."

"That's really sweet of you to say, though I feel a *but* coming." I made a feeble attempt to lighten the moment.

"I'm sorry." Her trickle of tears became a flood, triggering a few tears of my own. "You have no idea how hard this is for me. Hurting you is the last thing I ever wanted to do. I love you more than you'll ever know."

"It's okay." I squeezed her hands tightly. My best friend, my lover's heart was aching. "Just tell me what's going on. It's not like I didn't know this day would come. I understand. I'm so sorry you're hurting." And I truly was. My feelings, for now, were carefully placed on the back burner. I grabbed a box of Kleenex.

"I think it all started that last night in Rome." She began to paint the picture for me. "I cried in the rain the entire walk home from the restaurant. I didn't know why at the time, but I've put the pieces together. I had always envisioned going to Italy with my family. I should have been in Rome with them, not alone. Jeff and I had talked about it for a couple of years, and we planned to go in the summer before he moved out, but things weren't going well enough to justify it. I couldn't go through the motions anymore. That night, I began to realize I wasn't yet ready to give up on us."

I remained silent and simply listened, startled at the direction her words were taking.

"When I told him I wanted a divorce in September, I'm not certain I truly wanted one. I said it all in a desperate attempt to wake him up, for him to realize that he was losing me, to force him to fight for me, for us. He just walked away. We never even talked it through. I realize now that I had absolutely no closure. I have so many more questions than answers. And the lack of answers from him has left me to fill in the blanks myself, to make assumptions about him and what he wants and doesn't want. For all I know I've made wrong assumptions."

She paused to wipe her tears and blow her nose. My tears had stopped. I was trying to process her words and deal with being thrown for a loop. As she often did, Kate seemed to read my mind.

"I know I haven't painted a very flattering picture of Jeff for you. But I've probably shared every single negative thing about him and purposely left out many wonderful moments and a lot of his better attributes. You might think I'm crazy, but I'm still in love with him. I know I still very much love the idea of my family being together. I realize this betrays everything I've said and how I've acted since we met, but I need to give him one last chance. This has been weighing heavily on me for the past week or two. I honestly don't believe that I'll find peace unless I follow my heart and do this." She looked at me, her eyes begging for a response, for some understanding. I finally spoke.

"Does he have any idea how you feel? And has he shown any desire to get back together?" I couldn't quite say what I was thinking. *Did you shake him out of his stupor long enough to get a response? Hell, did you even get a pulse?*

"Yes. We've been talking a lot this week. And we've scheduled some time to talk more next week when my dad comes into town to hang out with Sean while he's on spring break."

Scheduled? That was quite gracious of him to fit you in. My hurt and shock were quickly transforming into misplaced anger. I took a deep breath and a step back in my mind.

"He's actually being very communicative and trying to process my sudden about-face. He's understandably a little skeptical and is probably as surprised as you are."

"I admit I didn't see this coming. Not like this, anyway." That was putting it rather mildly. My gaze shifted to the light snow falling outside my window, and I tried to pull my hands away from her. She gripped me tighter, refusing to let me disengage.

"I'm so sorry." Her tears were flowing again.

"Please, don't say you're sorry. I can't fault you for wanting to keep your family together. Not at all." I was trying to say and feel all the right things. So many emotions were roiling inside me. We sat in silence for a moment. Thirty seconds felt like half an hour. Nothing made sense.

"I have to be true to both of you and to myself." She tried to piece her thoughts together. "I can't make a genuine effort to reconcile with Jeff and still be in a relationship with you. I need to honor that process. And I love you too much to string you along while I go off and try to figure things out with him. I can't have a safety net, I have to be all in," she reasoned.

"And I have no desire to be someone's plan B." My comment was bordering on being snide. My tone softened. "I'm sorry. I really do appreciate you handling things in an honorable way. Most people probably wouldn't. But then again, you aren't exactly most people. That's what makes this so damned hard." It was my turn to soak a Kleenex.

She held me tightly, her tears mixing with mine.

"I'm so sorry," she said, yet again. "I wish there was a way to do this without hurting anyone."

"It'll be all right." I was trying, in vain, to comfort both of us.

All the time that I'd prepared my heart for this day, this moment, and all those logical thoughts I figured would insulate me from the pain of one day losing her were ultimately useless. Seeing it coming doesn't soften the blow of being hit by the train. Not in the least.

Our embrace segued to us lying horizontally on my couch, her head resting on my chest, my hand stroking her hair. Our silence spoke volumes. We were savoring a final, tender moment together, the end of an incredible string of them. Once again, she sensed what I was thinking, though this time she was slightly off the mark.

"I guess we finally had our first bad moment together." Her words were another unnecessary apology.

"I'm going to have to disagree. Even our last goodbye was perfect." But even perfect moments must end.

We eventually gathered ourselves, and she used my bathroom mirror to try to repair the damage her tears left behind. It was unspoken that we would leave all the summations for a later date. We would simply just process things for now.

I did wish her luck with Jeff, which was a stupid thing to say. Luck doesn't have a thing to do with love. They had a massive amount of hard work ahead of them if they were to reconcile. I had serious doubts they could pull it off, but if I truly loved the woman, I had to wish for her to receive what her heart wanted most. I told her I was here for her if she needed to talk, knowing she probably wouldn't take me up on the offer, fearing it would only cause me more pain.

She tried to say she was sorry one last time before walking out my door, but I quickly and gently placed a finger on her lips, stopping her in mid-apology. I then replaced the finger with my lips, giving her a final goodbye kiss. Her eyes welled up again, undoing her futile repair job. I watched until her car backed out and drove away. The snow had stopped. It was the first day of spring, after all.

I went back inside and collapsed on my couch. I could smell a trace of her perfume on my shirt. I inhaled deeply, knowing this and all the other remnants of her would eventually vanish. I lay there wishing the past hour had somehow been a bad dream. I checked the time. It was too late to make it to my luncheon and, as I was planning on being out of the office for that anyway, I decided to take my time getting back to work. After several minutes of solitude, a text came in. It was from Abbey.

I'm here for you if you want. Just got off the phone with Kate. She was bawling. I'm sorry.

Thanks. Maybe I'll call you tonight. I'm still in shock. Jeff? Really?

Yeah. I don't get it either. How about I come over to your place after work and we talk over bourbon?

Even better . . . Thanks

Chapter 19

When you're dreaming with a broken heart,
The giving up is the hardest part.
She takes you in with her crying eyes,
Then all at once you have to say goodbye.

Dreaming with a Broken Heart—John Mayer

I'M NOT SURE I CAN ACCURATELY DESCRIBE what a broken heart feels like. Poets, songwriters, and novelists, with far greater talent than me, have attempted to do this throughout the centuries. I suppose it's ultimately a very personal experience, and no two heartbreaks are alike. In my case, it felt like an elephant had placed one of its massive feet on my chest, inhibiting my ability to capture anything resembling a full breath. And my stomach churned like it used to do at the starting line of a big race during my track days. But in this circumstance, I didn't have the starter's pistol to offer instant relief.

That was my sorry existence for the 72 hours that followed my conversation with Kate on the couch, now my least favorite piece of furniture in my condo. Abbey's visit later that night helped temporarily. My angel of mercy brought with her the only food I could have imagined eating with my stomach so unsettled—take-out from *Morelia*. Chili Verde pairs surprisingly well with Evan Williams' single-barrel bourbon. I sought some insight from

Abbey, but she had none to offer. Kate's desire to reconcile with Jeff caught Abbey completely off guard, as well. And with Kate's father currently in town, they had no plans to get together until lunch late the following week. She insisted I get out of the house over the weekend, so I agreed to join her for a hike on Sunday.

I still had to get through Saturday. I cursed the fact that I lived in a cold, landlocked state. A walk along the beach, or better yet, some body surfing, would have been my prescription for what ailed me. The roar of the ocean, the salt air, and the warm sea breeze had always been my kind of medicine. I settled for a poor substitute—45 minutes on a stationary bike at the gym. I had another thing to curse. The earphones I wore while on my ride seemed to play an inordinately excessive number of breakup songs from my massive *iTunes* library. Shuffle mode was anything but random on that day. It was downright cruel.

The hike with Abbey was pleasant, the sunny weather cooperating nicely. The elephant was kind enough to step off my chest for a while and allow me to climb the moderate incline up the Pipeline Trail, a popular hike in Millcreek Canyon, which rewards hikers with a wonderful view of the Salt Lake Valley. The trail was a little muddy with patches of snow in the shadier portions and was quite popular on such a warm spring day. In a few months rattlesnakes would be a concern. We found ourselves alone when we arrived at the valley overlook. Abbey and I located some large boulders and sat, enjoying the view and sipping from our water bottles.

"You know that you're going to be okay, right? Hardly your first rodeo." She nailed that point.

"Yep. I've miraculously survived every one of these so far. I suspect I'll live through this one, too." *What doesn't kill you makes you stronger, as they say. They sure have a lot to say.*

"What kind of chance do you give Kate and Jeff?" I asked, taking a pull from my CamelBak.

"Not a chance in hell," Abbey responded immediately. "They've got so many issues, and they are such different people. She's only remembering their best of times right now."

"Yeah, a photogenic memory."

"Oh, that's a good one!"

"Song title. I can't claim it as mine." We could hear the faint noise of traffic on I-215 in the distance.

"It really doesn't matter, even if they don't patch things up. She's got such a long way to go to find herself. You really don't want to be part of that journey, do you, Jamison?" Abbey over-emphasized her least favorite word.

"No," I admitted. "And she can't exactly find herself with someone right next to her on that . . . ride. How did you get to be so wise for such a youngin'?"

"Probably from hanging out with old people," she smirked.

"Brat. Let's get going. I've got a hot date tonight. Kidding." My eyes rolled.

"Well, when you're ready to get back on the horse again, I'll help you get set up on *Tinder*."

"Gee, thanks. Maybe eventually. But the body isn't even cold yet."

"Wow, you're full of gems today."

"That one I borrowed from an old western. I promise to have an original thought soon, when I get my mojo back."

That was going to take a while. We began our descent down the trail.

I meandered through the following week, trying to process everything, taking inventory of the damage and missing my best friend. I told only a handful of people. Pat and Dave were two. Dave put a positive spin on things, encouraging me to work on the guitar with my newfound free time. I didn't have the heart to tell my mom about it over dinner on Wednesday night. She mentioned she was looking forward to seeing Kate again and meeting Sean. Maybe I'd tell her the following week. I did tell my daughters, who were very sweet to quickly plan a Sunday brunch at Kiara's house to let their dear old dad know that they had his back.

Abbey called me on Friday afternoon to give me the report from her lunch with Kate. She insisted on being Switzerland as far as taking sides, if it ever came to that. But this was outside the scope of maintaining her neutrality. She was simply sharing information that hadn't been declared confidential. We'd both guessed correctly but hadn't anticipated how quickly talks had collapsed between Kate and Jeff. Within just a little over a week of attempting to reconcile, Kate had thrown in the towel. Again.

"Wow, that was fast. What happened?" I inquired.

"It didn't take her long to realize he was never going to change. Same old Jeff. But she had to try."

"How is she doing? Hurting pretty badly?" I still cared deeply for her.

"Yeah. She's dealing with a lot of emotions. She feels kind of stupid for thinking he might have wanted it as badly as she did. She feels rejected all over again, but has a sense of relief in knowing she gave him absolutely every chance. She said that's a source of strength, at least. No looking back now."

I knew better than to ask if the subject of me had come up at all, as that would have violated the rules. And that kind of information only feeds the ego, not the soul.

"Well, I hope she's going to be okay."

"She will be, and don't even think about trying to fix a single thing for her," Abbey admonished.

"I know. Old habits die hard."

"Just let them die. I know it's not easy, but you have your own journey to worry about." Again, she heavily accented the 'J' word, which gave us both a chuckle.

"Thanks for the download, Switzerland."

I'm horrible at following good, solid advice that makes perfect sense. My heart got the best of my brain early Monday morning at work. I ordered some flowers to be sent to Kate's office. I know, not the smartest thing I've done, and I had regrets just seconds after typing in my three-digit code on the back of my Visa card and placing the order. I didn't include a message and left it completely anonymous as a way of mitigating my actions. Kate was hurting, after all. I got a text from her just as I was winding down my workday.

Did you send me flowers?

Maybe.

That was incredibly sweet of you. Why didn't you indicate they were from you? I thought they might have been from Jeff for a second. They were from the florist he used once.

The jerk continued to ruin things for me.

I'm sorry they were from me and not him.

That's not what I meant! It was a nice surprise and brightened my day. Thank you!

You're welcome. I know you've been hurting. Can I come get my guitar soon? You can toss the toothbrush ;-).

I'm hanging in there. It's been a rough couple of weeks. Do you want to stop by Sunday afternoon for the guitar, or I can meet you someplace? 4-ish?

I'll see you at your place.

Thanks again. You're amazing.

Apparently not amazing enough.

I rang her doorbell, this time with more of a feeling of dread than anticipation. When she opened the door, the magic energy was still present, and there was a sweet tenderness in our embrace. We sat down in the kitchen, and I saw my flowers on her island. She caught my glance.

"They still look as pretty as when they arrived on Monday. Thank you."

"I'm glad you like them."

Our conversation was a bit stilted, which wasn't surprising, but we gradually relaxed. Small talk and work related topics gave way to themes of a more personal nature.

"I hope you had a nice visit with your dad. I was really looking forward to meeting him."

"*He* was looking forward to meeting you, too. I've said nothing but great things about you."

I decided to dive right in.

"I'm sincerely sorry things didn't work out between you and Jeff. Abbey told me. I know that's what you truly wanted."

"Thanks. I should have known better," she shrugged. "But I had to try. I had to know that I did everything in my power."

"I get it. When I left Anna, I knew I'd given it my all. No second-guessing. You can have that same peace now."

"I could use some peace. It's been a hell of a couple weeks. In some ways, it was harder to say goodbye to you than it was to him. Maybe because I already said goodbye to him once before." She smiled slightly, and that familiar and beautiful sight tugged at my heartstrings.

"I have so much to figure out," she continued. "I honestly don't know what I'm going to do going forward. But I do hope that you can somehow be part of my life, eventually, if you want that."

I called upon strength from inside of me I didn't know existed.

"This is what I want." I paused, inspired by words I'd recently written. "Just like the song says, I want you to see and do it all, and leave no stone left unturned."

The Spanish Steps." Her eyes began misting. "I still have that hanging on my wall at work."

"Do what it says. Go out there and live, and have all the experiences you've yet to enjoy. Take a couple of years. That should give you plenty of time to figure things out. By some chance, if your path brings you back, you'll know where to find me. Unless something changes dramatically in my life, I'll be there at the top of the Spanish Steps of Rome at sunset on the Summer Solstice, 2017. Find me."

"You've got a deal." Tears were streaming down her face. My eyes were surprisingly dry.

"I'd better get going."

We hugged at her doorstep for what I assumed would be the final time. I kissed her on her forehead, walked to my car, and placed my guitar on the backseat. I slowly backed down her driveway, and for the first time since we'd met, I didn't look back.

Chapter 20

I wonder what tomorrow has in mind for me;
Or am I even in its mind at all.
Perhaps I'll get a chance to look ahead and see
Soon as I find myself a crystal ball.

Crystal Ball—Styx

THE EXPRESSION *TIME HEALS ALL WOUNDS* implies simplicity, but it's actually a very complex endeavor. Certainly, time does take away the initial sting of a broken heart, but it's a gradual process, not unlike an injury to any other part of the human body. The sting gives way to a manageable, throbbing ache, which, in turn, becomes but a dull twinge, and then it's finally gone. I'm a firm believer that time itself can be manipulated somewhat. What we do with the gift of time can either speed up or delay the healing process. If we can rehab other injuries to get back in the game quicker, why can't we apply the same strategy with our hearts? So, I'll revise the expression to say, *time well spent heals wounds faster.*

Unfortunately, I didn't follow my personal philosophy initially in the days and weeks after Kate and I parted ways. I wallowed in my misery for much longer than I should have before at last snapping out of it and beginning the rehabilitation process in earnest.

Social media enabled my malaise. It was too easy to see what Kate was up to without me on *Facebook* and *Instagram*. She didn't appear to be wallowing at all, but rather thriving. Despite the negative emotions that came with my actions, I kept feeding my morbid curiosity by staying abreast of her social life.

It was nothing more than a silly battle between ego and soul. The loudmouth of the two, ego, nourished my deepest fears and preyed on my vulnerabilities. *Why didn't she choose me? Was it the age difference? Was I not sufficiently successful on a financial level? Did she even miss me?* I covered every possible angle of our demise, far beyond the obvious and logical. I sought answers to pamper a bruised ego, not to gain more enlightenment. That was the role of my soul in this age-old tussle. Had I been able to hear the quiet whispers over the obnoxious roar, I would have been guided to ask questions that mattered, questions that provided answers full of peace, not false gratification. It was a solid month before I finally told my ego to shut the hell up and focus on the gentle and sincere guidance from my soul.

As I emerged from my self-imposed fog, I expected a creative burst to follow. It's been my experience that heartache and angst usually inspire a flood of words to describe the emotions I was processing, even more so than the waves of euphoria felt in the heights of being in love. I'd written two love songs for Kate in our first months together, and I fully expected them to be quickly eclipsed by a flood of lyrics dealing with our goodbye. But the expected deluge was only a mere trickle. I had many stops and starts and created several pages of stand-alone and unconnected lines in my writing notebook. I could not come up with any cohesive themes with which to bind my random lyrics. In frustration, I set aside the words and focused on the music.

I suppose you could describe my next move as retail therapy. I bought a new guitar; a low-end Martin that had me now sitting at the big kid's table in the guitar world; forget the fact that the quality of the instrument far surpassed my ability to play it. I traded up for it. The shiny black Fender I'd kept at Kate's was a fine looking and sounding guitar, but it never felt right. I tried different strings and attempted to adjust the action, or string height, but I failed to truly connect with the instrument. I could draw some simple analogies between women and guitars here, but I'll spare you my conclusions. Suffice it to say that the rather pedestrian-looking Martin sounded and felt like a million bucks. Never again would I be a sucker for a pretty face. Well, in the world of guitars, anyway.

Spring kicked into high gear and with the warmer weather many nights and weekends were spent playing my guitar on the front porch or my back deck. I learned numerous favorite songs from YouTube and improved my playing in leaps and bounds. I bought yet another guitar, this one a 12-string. This was an essential club I needed in my bag, I reasoned. So many of the classic songs I was learning were originally played on the fuller sounding twelve. Besides, it was gently used and didn't break the bank. I was no longer going out on dates, buying dinners, movie tickets, and all the related expenses that come with a girlfriend, so my disposable income had to go somewhere. Right?

I kept myself busy and slowly it mattered less and less what Kate was up to and more what I was doing. One day I sat several tables away from her at an awards luncheon where a partner from her agency was being honored. She arrived late and I had to leave the function early so our only contact was a wave from halfway across the darkened room. It was just as well, as the lack of a face-to-face greeting allowed the knots in my stomach to subside long enough for me to enjoy the chicken.

Bailey graduated from the University of Utah in early May so we celebrated with a big family dinner, Carrie included. Wedding season started up in Utah, where kids marry young. As a soccer coach to literally hundreds of girls over the years, I had many surrogate daughters out there in the Salt Lake Valley. I was honored that I apparently had made a positive impact on many young lives, enough to merit an invite to join in the celebration of their big day.

I purchased a lot of Target gift cards that summer. That's me, Mr. Practical.

The outdoor concert season also began as the weather warmed. I bought several pairs of tickets to various shows and between Kiara, Bailey, Jade, and the ever-trusty Abbey, I didn't concern myself with finding a date. I would spread the wealth and rotate through the ladies in my life. We enjoyed rocking to Collective Soul, Vertical Horizon, Train, America, Michael McDonald, and Toto. The Collective Soul show featured a lot of acoustic guitar, which inspired me to sign up for a songwriting class from the University of Utah Continuing Education department. This would end up having a huge impact on my life.

A week before the summer semester was to start I was notified by email that the course had been canceled due to low enrollment. My disappointment was short-lived. Later the same day I received an email from the instructor indicating that he was willing to still teach the class off-campus if there was enough interest. I indicated that I was in if others still wanted to pursue the class.

Luckily three others were committed as well. He offered his home as our meeting place and the following Tuesday would be the first class. I was excited to see where this adventure would lead me.

In the meantime, Abbey was encouraging me to enter the glorious world of online dating. I hope that you can feel that last line dripping with sarcasm. I wrestled with the idea. The thought of putting myself out there terrified me. I pictured a bunch of women on their lunch break at work chuckling over my profile and pictures and swiping left, accordingly. Anonymous rejection. Who thinks up such schemes?

I remained steadfast in my refusal to submit myself to such ridicule until I heard these magic words from Abbey: "Kate is on *Tinder*." That punch to the gut was the push I needed to finally relent. If she was out there, wading in the sea of online love, then I better dive in myself.

The first step was trying to encapsulate the essence of me into a few sentences and pictures to somehow appeal to the opposite gender. The photograph part was easy. I only had a handful of recent pictures in which I considered myself looking the least bit photogenic. I am what I am, I figured. As to how to portray myself in words, I asked for Abbey's assistance. She was in the office, this time in the role of my client, doing some editing with Dave. We read through a few profiles of men she'd matched with during her sporadic dabbling on *Tinder*. After reading several, I felt the need to apologize for my gender.

I lacked any pictures of me in a gym selfie or firing an automatic weapon, so I selected basic photos of me in real life situations with friends and family. And instead of listing several *musts* like *must love dogs, must like working out*, and demanding that a prospective mate share a similar vegan lifestyle, I went with Abbey's suggestion of describing myself in simple terms and listing some interests and passions. I kept it short and sweet.

Just a nice guy . . . I'm compassionate, respectful, honest and real.
I love laughter, music, the outdoors, travel, sports, friends, family, and
new adventures.

With a simple click, I put myself out there in the cyber world and held my breath. Immediately a bunch of potential matches popped up of women within my pre-selected 35-mile radius and age range. Abbey sat with me on the edit bay couch, and we were doing the very thing that made me cringe when I was picturing the women in their office break room laughing or rolling their eyes at me. Abbey shared her opinions: "She's cute. She's got crazy eyes. She's trying way too hard. She looks like she's high maintenance, she seems normal." We swiped right (the affirmative direction) on several but swiped left on more profiles. We soon finished the first batch of potential matches. I was somewhat overwhelmed by the concept and the process and was glad to shut down the app and get back to work.

Later that evening I went home and grabbed my new Martin guitar, a notebook, and drove to the home of Steve, my songwriting teacher. He didn't live far from my mom's house, near my old elementary school. As usual, I was overly punctual. While I was waiting for the others to arrive with their guitar cases in hand, I opened the *Tinder* app on my phone to see that I had several matches. Yikes! Here we go.

The other aspiring songwriters began to pull up in their cars, saving me from scrolling through the matches, for now. I couldn't imagine at the time that this songwriting venture and online dating adventure would become my prominent themes during the summer of 2015. My life was taking me in directions that were not at all how I'd drawn it up.

Chapter 21

I've gotta find a way to set me free
Cause I have lost way too much of me.
In the mirror, I don't know who I see.
Have it in your heart to set me free.

Vinyl and Bourbon Nights—Jamison Barrick

Tinder
Noun / tin-der
1: A very flammable substance adaptable for use as
kindling
2: Something that serves to incite or inflame

I TYPICALLY LIKE TO KNOW WHAT I'M GETTING INTO before immersing myself. By its very definition, *Tinder* has the potential to provide the spark that could possibly grow into a flame. There is always the possibility that the tiny flicker gets blown out before it ever becomes a blaze. And, of course, with any fire, there is always the risk of getting burned. So, I ventured into the world of online dating with extremely low expectations and my heart insulated with a thick layer of asbestos.

On the surface, the entire concept of swiping one way or another, based on looks and a few descriptive sentences, seems incredibly superficial. But perhaps it mimics real life more than we wish to admit. I liken the experience to a cyber version of being at a party. Out of the dozens of people there, I spot someone from across the room that appears to be, from that limited first glance, attractive, interesting, and nice. If I eventually make my way over to her and say 'hi' and introduce myself, that would essentially be the same thing as swiping in the affirmative direction on an app. Likewise, if someone from across the room doesn't draw enough interest to merit an introduction, that is a swipe in the other direction.

Let me get this out of the way up front. *Tinder* and similar apps (*Bumble* was out there, too) get a bad rap as being nothing but hookup sites. And the term 'hooking up' has changed in recent years to take on a strictly sexual connotation. In my day, it just meant hanging out. (Hell, I better check out the meaning of 'hanging out' in the urban dictionary in case that has changed!) But I digress. What I'm trying to say is that I didn't look at *Tinder* to hook up, and I'd point out that 95% of the women whom I've met on the app didn't use it for that purpose either. I figured there were other, specific sites out there for that very reason. Most of us were looking for love or something like it. Even so, I'll never forget the look on my daughters' faces when they found out I was on *Tinder*. It was a cross between utter disgust and disappointment, despite declaring my best intentions.

Anyway, back to the story. In both worlds, matching with someone either by swipe or introduction, strokes the ego. We all crave the need to be desired. I suppose there is some sort of endorphin rush or a release of dopamine when we connect with another human. I can see how some people would find the whole thing a big game and even become addicted to the high. I admit to being quite thrilled, initially, to be the object of another's interest, but I really didn't know what I was doing or how to proceed and escalate things from texting on the app to a face-to-face meeting.

I will keep the ladies in these stories nameless, so we'll just call my first date *Tinder Girl #1*. She was a savvy online dating veteran who took me under her wing and suggested we meet for a cup of coffee at *Starbucks*. I swear that *Starbucks* is in cahoots with *Tinder/Bumble* as their various locations seem to be the preferred meeting place of *Tinderlings* and *Bumble Bees*. Many a cappuccino has been consumed during an online-generated first date. I arrived first and recognized her from her pics when she walked in. *Oh, dear Lord, do we shake hands or hug?* We'd only shared a dozen lines of texts so far. Thankfully the *Tinder* pro knew what to do and gave me a hug-lite. We ordered our coffee and while sparks didn't seem to fly for either of us, she did point out that I had made a rookie mistake. In one of my photos I had on a name tag. She expertly pointed out that with my name out there I could be more easily stalked. I thanked her for her tutelage. Nothing came from the date other than a deleted picture.

Tinder Girl #2 lived in Utah County, about 30 miles south. We met at a *Starbucks* halfway between us. This info had not been in her profile but it was revealed over hot beverages that she had eight kids, two still at home. She was a Mormon who was struggling a bit with her faith. She did choose hot chocolate rather than coffee so I suspected that she would ultimately toe the line and remain faithful. I shared with her that my idea of church was being up in the mountains on a Sunday, enjoying God's handiwork in nature rather than in a chapel. She was quite lovely, but we were not a good fit.

Tinder Girl #3 liked her Scotch whiskey, as evidenced by one of her profile pictures, and was kind enough to take me on a tour of Scotland one evening at a local watering hole called *Whiskey Street*. I knew my American Bourbon well but was a Scotch neophyte so it was quite informative. We went from the Lowlands to the Highlands to Islay. There wasn't any real chemistry between us, but I learned a lot, including the fact that the tab at *Starbucks* is far less than it is for three rounds of fine Scotch whiskey. Lesson learned.

Meanwhile, back at *Starbucks*, I came to realize that *Tinder Girl* #4 had posted pictures on her profile that were at least ten years old, and I'm guessing fifty pounds ago. I don't consider myself to be a shallow person so my main issue with the discrepancy between her past and present was the lack of honesty rather than her appearance. She had two daughters at home, trashed her ex-husband the entire time, and I got the impression she was looking more for a solid father-figure for her girls than a mate for herself. Eight dollars plus the tip for the *barista* was all it cost me to gain this knowledge. I was now officially a *Tinder* pro.

Lest you think this dating all transpired in a week's time, it was spread out over several weeks. Still it seemed to me like a mad rush, and it left me dazed. After four dates and several other text conversations that didn't go anywhere, I decided to give *Tinder* a rest. Besides, I had assignments to keep up with in my songwriting class.

My first class had been rather intimidating. The instructor, Steve, was a nice man in his sixties who wore his hair in a gray ponytail. I easily envisioned him attending Woodstock and protesting the Vietnam War in his youth. Though I didn't see any, his house smelled like he owned a few cats and smoked a pipe. The other three students, Emily, Jake, and Cal, were all in their thirties by my guess and were much more accomplished on the musical side than I was. Their nice guitars and ability to play them well filled me with envy. We spent a good portion of the class going over equipment needed to record our songs to be able to share them. I realized quickly that I'd picked an expensive hobby and more of my disposable income would be going toward microphones and recording software in the coming weeks.

We talked a little music theory, which was way over my head, and we were given an assignment to have a song completed by the following class. He wanted us to write what he called a groove song—something that was simple, catchy and upbeat. He brought out a bottle of red wine midway through the session, and we all enjoyed a small glass. We were encouraged to bring a bottle of something to share and just like a treat schedule in youth soccer, we each signed up for an upcoming week. I was enjoying this setting much better than having it in a classroom on campus. He'd indicated the cost of the sessions in a previous email and had asked for payment in cash. After our two hours were up we paid him and called it a night.

I wrestled with my song for the entirety of the following week. Lyrically I had nothing and musically I knew I had to keep it simple, given my limitations. I made very little progress as the days flew by, and I probably shouldn't have wasted an evening on one of the aforementioned-*Tinder* dates. I was in full panic mode the night before my next class. I was halfway tempted to pull out one of the songs I'd written for Kate and put some chords to it but neither fell into the groove category.

I was crafting the lyrics first and trying to be quite flowery and complex. Think *Hotel California* by the Eagles. I soon abandoned that idea and decided I better keep it simple. Think *Take It Easy* by the same group. That's when the idea hit me to write a good, old-fashioned breakup song but as an upbeat tune. I flipped back a few pages in my notebook of lyrics and came across the lines I'd written about my breakup with Kate several weeks earlier. They were random but they painted an accurate picture of the process of breaking up with someone, a perfect collection of heartbreak clichés. If I simply filled in some words and added some lines I'd be able to portray all the stereotypical stages of losing someone. I'd have some fun with a typically sad topic.

I had some chords in mind that fit the theme of the song. With my guitar and pen working in unison, I strategically mixed the old words among some new ones, and 45 minutes later I'd written my first complete song, with both music and lyrics. The title came easily as well. I often enjoyed a sip of bourbon while listening to one of the many vinyl records in my collection. Though I'd personally never done so to drown my sorrows, I imagined a jilted lover doing just that.

Without any high-tech gear yet, I recorded the guitar part to my iPhone. It took me a good 12 or 13 takes to get it as spotless as I could. Upon hearing the recorded music as I read the lyrics, I was struck by the fact that I'd written something that sounded like it came from Nashville. And this was coming from someone who rarely, if ever, listened to country music. Interesting. The next day I printed out copies at work to share with the class.

This time we started right away with the wine, a bottle of Kris *Pinot Grigio* that Emily brought. We presented our songs to each other. I chose to go last. Emily composed a song that Taylor Swift would be at home singing. Not bad at all, she had a very sweet voice. Jake and Cal had written great music with decent lyrics. Neither had a particularly great voice but I admired their courage. My heart was beating out of my chest when they all turned their attention to me. I had to start with a confession. I don't sing.

It was way back in the 5th grade during a talent show when one of my classmates tried to sing in front of the entire school. She absolutely crashed and burned on stage. Perhaps I'd already developed the gift of empathy at a young age, but I felt I died with her that day. I was traumatized by the event and it affected me going forward. Other than singing in the shower or in my car, you won't catch me singing. The mere thought of singing in front of others makes me shiver. So, I passed out the lyrics to the group and asked them to read along as I played the guitar. I played the song all the way through with only a few slip ups. I got to the end, looked up, and got approving nods from everyone. Then Emily spoke up.

"Can I give it a shot? I think I could sing it for you."

"Sure! I can use all the help I can get." I was eager to hear my song performed for real.

Steve chimed in.

"Why don't you two take a few minutes and work on it. We'll take a little break, and I'll show the guys my garden out back."

I quickly shared my vision of the singing part with Emily, humming the words as I strummed. She agreed that it had a Nashville flair to it. She caught on unbelievably fast and soon had the verses figured out. The chorus followed, and as we were nailing down the bridge, the others came back in the front room to hear our mini concert.

I started with the intro. Emily came in on cue and absolutely nailed it. I was so mesmerized by her voice giving life to my song that I almost flubbed up my strumming. I played the final chords, and as we finished, the guys gave us a nice applause. Steve looked both stunned and proud of his pupils.

"Wow," he said. "You two might just have a hit on your hands. That has a very commercial sound to it. Well done. All of you!"

As we left Steve's house, Emily and I walked toward our cars.

"Thanks so much for singing for me. You were great. I can't believe how fast you picked that up."

"You are very welcome. That was so fun. Singing and playing are easy for me. I suck at writing words. That was a great song you wrote. Simple, yet there's a lot going on."

"Thanks. I wrote that last night, in a panic," I confessed.

"Seriously? I wish I could do that. I'd actually been working on mine way before I decided to take this class."

"I loved it. You've got an amazing voice."

"Thank you." She paused. "Hey, would you like to get together outside of class and write some music together? We could combine talents."

"I'd love to." I was genuinely flattered.

We already had each other's email addresses, but we also exchanged phone numbers. I knew this was completely a platonic thing with our age differences, but I had more of a rush that night than on any *Tinder* dates so far. I drove home with a huge smile on my face. I didn't turn on any music. In my mind, I was hearing *Vinyl and Bourbon Nights* playing the entire drive home.

Vinyl and Bourbon Nights

I'd feel so much better
Had you not said goodbye.
Can't seem to shake you
As hard as I try.
Life would be easy
If you still loved me.
Instead of in my arms
You chose to be free.

(Chorus)
It's looking like a
Vinyl and bourbon night.
A little bit more
And I'll be feeling all right.
Just one more spin
And I'll give up this fight.
Looks like another
Vinyl and bourbon night.

Wonder what you're doing
And who you're with.
Will you end your night
With just a kiss?
Do you ever
Think of me?
Couldn't you see
We were meant to be?

(Repeat Chorus)

(Bridge)
I've gotta find a way to set me free,
Cause I've lost
Way too much of me.
In the mirror,
I don't know who I see.
Have it in your heart
To set me free.

Hope I find
Someone better than you
To love me forever
And always be true.
She's out there waiting
Just for me.
I'll forget all about you.
Just wait and see.

(Repeat Chorus)

Looks like another
Vinyl and bourbon night.

Chapter 22

Think of me.
You know that I'd be with you if I could.
I'll come around to see you once in a while,
Or if I ever need a reason to smile.

Hello, It's Me—Todd Rundgren

"Oh, shit!" I must have looked like I'd seen a ghost. In a way, I had.

"What?" She was startled by my outburst.

"My ex-girlfriend just walked in with some guy. Don't look now."

"Oh! Is this, by chance, the *Vinyl and Bourbon Nights* girl?"

"I'd be lying if I said that song was purely generic. She's the one."

"Let me know when I can turn around and check her out." Her look went from curious to mischievous. "I hope you don't mind, but if she sees us, I'm going to be uncharacteristically affectionate with you. Your date is quite the young hottie, after all." She winked.

"Oh, yeah?" I couldn't contain my smile. "You are quickly becoming one of my favorite humans."

"Good. But it's going to cost you. You know how it was my turn to buy?" She asked and I nodded. "Not anymore. This one is on you. And I'll probably add dessert, too." Her smirk was adorable.

Emily had been a godsend. Not solely on that humid, late-August night but for most of the summer. Plus, the time spent with her meant that I wasn't dabbling as much on *Tinder*. We enjoyed a wonderful, platonic relationship that had blossomed immediately with our first songwriting/jam session. Our love of music and the shared desire to create it bonded us, making for an unlikely pairing. Emily was pushing for us to complete the trifecta and perform music together, something I wasn't terribly eager to pursue but knew it was inevitable.

A petite, 5 foot 4, curly-haired blonde with kind blue eyes, Emily had recently ended a five-year relationship and sworn off men for the time being. She shared an apartment in the trendy Sugar House neighborhood with a roommate, Karen, whom I didn't meet for several weeks.

Karen was friendly enough, though completely indifferent to our music being played in their home. I suspected that she wondered why Emily has hanging out with some old dude. They also had a cat named Winston who, for some reason, took quite a liking to me and often resented me for giving more attention to my guitar than him.

Emily had an amazing singing voice and a talent to pick up music by ear. If she heard it, she could play it on both guitar and keyboards. She was gifted as a lyricist, but a complete lack of an ego kept her from realizing her immense talent. Her passion for music had been a casualty of her last relationship, and she was anxious to take back that part of her life. Her day job as an accountant completely belied her creative soul. She was sweet, sincere, and devoid of even a trace of pretentiousness. And on more than one occasion, I found myself wishing she were twenty years older.

We typically got together to jam once a week, usually at her place, although when she found out I had a swimming pool at my condo, we logged in a few extra Saturday or Sunday afternoons strumming and swimming. We would both write lyrics and play with chords.

Often, we'd drift from one idea to another and end a session with several incomplete ideas rather than a finished song. We would typically break from our jams to grab a bite at one of the many nearby eateries, taking turns paying, despite my objections and chivalrous intentions. It was fun and challenging for me to keep up musically. She never once made me feel inferior, always praising my ability to weave words together. We also kept up with our lessons with Steve, until he informed us in late July that he had to suspend them temporarily to care after his dying father.

She gladly gobbled up one of my summer concert tickets, joining me to see Todd Rundgren at a nice, intimate venue called The Depot. We also had plans to see Grace Potter and the Nocturnals in early September.

Yes, the time spent with Emily cut into my desire to get on *Tinder*, but I would occasionally fire it up, no pun intended, and see if I had any matches. Nothing materialized enough to even merit a meet up at *Starbucks*. I did have one intriguing match that didn't quite feel right. After a little online investigation, I was certain that I was being scammed. And the culprit was most likely a Nigerian man, based on my research. I let the 'romance' play out a little until, sure enough, I was asked for money to help the supposed 'damsel in distress' who had taken quite a liking to me. It made for a great story around the water cooler at work.

One night Emily and I were in a rare rut. Nothing was coming easily, either lyrically or musically. We decided to take a dinner break. It was her turn to buy and pick the spot. She chose Wasatch Brewery, a lively brewpub, with a fantastic menu, a short walk from her apartment. We would normally gravitate to the patio of any restaurant we chose, but on that night the air was thick and damp with no cooling breeze whatsoever, so we opted for a table inside. Our beers and appetizers had just arrived when I saw Kate and her date walk in the door.

I had not overtly stalked her on *Facebook*, but I also didn't un-follow her to prevent her posts from popping up on my feed. It was apparent from her various posts that she was out there dating. She was still playing it coy and not sharing the identity of her dates for all to see. But it was easy to fill in the blanks from the pics of concerts and dinner and drinks for two that she wasn't lacking for male company. I had brushed all that aside anyway, being too busy and having my own fun that summer to really care. It's amazing how fast those walls can come tumbling down.

Emily could sense everything I was feeling, hence her offer to play the role of my young, hot date. Bless her heart. She knew that my ego was taking a pounding. My soul had already surrendered and gotten up from the table and left. I told her it was okay to discreetly turn around and check out Kate. Personally, I was focused on Kate's date, probably a rich lawyer who drove a BMW. Emily snapped me back to reality.

"I'm going to take a closer look on my way to the girl's room." She got up and, out of nowhere, kissed me on the cheek and winked.

"See you in a minute, honey." I played along and winked back, although I would have preferred to not be left alone.

I was sure that Kate had spotted me across the crowd of diners just as Emily returned and took her seat.

"I think your date tonight is much cuter, and the guy she's with probably drives a great, big truck, you know, to overcompensate." She grinned as she gave her scouting report.

"I'm thinking a BMW and for the same reason." We shared a laugh and our meals came.

I chose to focus on enjoying my exquisite company and completely stopped glancing Kate's direction until we got up to leave, after I'd picked up the tab, of course. The small investment would quickly be worth every penny.

As we made our way to the door, my eyes met Kate's. It would have been extremely awkward to walk up to her table to say hi, so I gave her a smile and a quick wave. As Kate returned the wave, her date looked up to see the recipient of her salutation. With impeccable timing, I felt Emily's hand grab mine, and we walked out the door looking every bit like a happy couple, albeit with a May/December twist, or can we please revise that to June/November?

We were well out of sight of the restaurant before Emily released my hand from her grasp. She was relishing her theatrical role and the chance to play head games with another woman.

When we got back to work, we started writing a song based on the night's events. It showed enough promise for us to want to finish it eventually. Before I left I gave her a hearty hug and thanked her for turning a potentially unpleasant night into a memorable one. She indicated that the pleasure was all hers. *Damn, to be twenty years younger.*

The ride home was quiet and contemplative. I thanked my lucky stars that Emily was on hand to save me as the sight of Kate with someone else could have been deadly. Instead it was just a non-fatal wound from which I would certainly heal. I was determined not to let the Kate sighting set me back more than a one-night funk, but the feeling lingered a few more days.

Hoping to snap out of it, I decided to fire up *Tinder* again before hitting my pool for some Sunday afternoon laps. I scrolled through a few names and faces and had a swipe or two in each direction before eyeing a photo of a beautiful brunette with stunning, blue eyes.

Her name was Vanessa. There was no descriptive profile, but she looked gorgeous in all her five posted pics. The app indicated she was eight miles away and in her early 50s, just a few years younger than me. As I swiped to the right, I sincerely hoped she wasn't a Nigerian scam artist. I felt a bit of a jolt as I was immediately notified of a match, indicating that she had swiped affirmatively for me sometime earlier. Wow. I must say she stood out from all the rest, assuming her photos were reasonably recent.

I grabbed a towel and a water bottle and hit the pool. After several laps, I took a break in the sun and grabbed my phone. I opened the *Tinder* app and was tempted to send Vanessa a quick message. I didn't want to seem overeager, and the glare of the sun on my phone made it almost impossible to see my screen well enough to compose a cute greeting. I shelved the idea until I was back inside my condo.

Once there, I opened the app again and went to message Vanessa, but she was gone. Disappeared entirely from the app! *Dammit!* I had the sinking feeling that I inadvertently deleted her as a match while I was struggling to navigate on my phone in the harsh glare from the sun.

I was going to just let it go, chalk it up to fate, and simply not having the blessing of the Universe on this one. But there was something stirring inside. That persistent feeling eventually pushed me to do something that was completely uncharacteristic for me and far outside my usual comfort zone. I'll be forever grateful that my soul spoke up loudly enough for me to hear it.

Chapter 23

All my instincts, they return,
And the grand facade, so soon will burn
Without a noise, without my pride
I reach out from the inside.

In Your Eyes—Peter Gabriel

YOU USUALLY REGRET THE THINGS YOU DON'T DO rather than the things you've done. Add that one to a growing list of things *They* say. *They*, those enlightened sages whose wise words end up being the answers to an online search for motivational quotes, or become memes posted on social media, or land in the pages of a simple love story. For the record, that expression comes from something Mark Twain once wrote. He earned his place among the mighty *They*. How does the quote pertain to this tale? Let's just say there wouldn't be much of a story had I not thrown caution to the wind.

After stewing over the sudden online disappearance of Vanessa for the remainder of my Sunday, I decided to do something about it. I may have deleted her accidentally, but there was also a good chance that she deleted me, making my next move potentially a rather foolish one. I've often played the fool in the pursuit of love, so I had little to lose but possibly something to gain. The next morning at work, in my quiet hour before the office filled up, I logged on to *Facebook*.

Tinder is tied to *Facebook*. The profile pictures used on the dating site come from the social app, and *Tinder* also shows the various pages one *Likes* and *Follows* on *Facebook*. I suppose the premise is that the more mutual interests between two people, the better the chance they are compatible. After opening *Facebook*, I typed the name Vanessa in the search bar. There she was, the first face in a stack of other women sharing the same name. Her identifying profile picture was one of her five shots that she used on *Tinder*. I checked out her photos. She appeared to have two adult children and a grandson. And she had beautiful eyes. Though it was hard to tell from photos, I believe I detected some sadness in them, belying her smile.

Okay, now that I found her, what could I possibly say in a direct and private message that wouldn't make me seem like a crazed Internet stalker? I had only one chance to get this right, and I figured it was a slim one at best. I went with the supposed best policy: honesty.

> *Hi Vanessa. I apologize for this random message but I didn't know how else to contact you. We matched on Tinder this past weekend and I was on the app in the bright sun, sitting poolside and fear I might have inadvertently clicked the 'un-match' option. You may very well have deleted me as a match, and if that's the case, I apologize for this intrusion. I promise I'm not a creeper and I've never looked up and reached out to anyone before from this app. You just seemed nice from your pictures and I wanted to say hi . . .*

Within seconds of hitting SEND, I felt both foolish and pessimistic that I'd ever hear back from the pretty brunette with the enchanting blue eyes. I logged off *Facebook* and got on with the business of selling and marketing a video production company. No sense in watching a pot that would probably never boil.

Near the conclusion of a rather busy day, I got on *Facebook* as a way of winding down. I immediately saw from the alert that I had a message which could have been from numerous friends or clients who prefer to communicate on the site. I was beyond surprised to see that my message was from none other than Vanessa Grant.

Hi Jamison, that was sweet of you to reach out and I can tell that you aren't a creeper! I deleted my Tinder account Sunday afternoon. I was on it for just 3 days but I realized I have no business doing the online dating thing right now. A friend talked me into it but the timing is horrible. My mom is in hospice care right now and probably doesn't have much time left. I need to focus on her, despite needing to do other things to keep my sanity. Here is my number if you'd like to keep in touch that way. Maybe when life isn't so complicated we can go get a glass of wine?

I didn't worry about appearing overeager or any other silly rules of engagement but felt it in my heart to respond immediately.

I'm so sorry to hear about your mom. My dad passed away recently, so I know how hard it is. Your focus is right where it needs to be currently. Here is my number. If you ever need someone to talk to please feel free to reach out. I'd enjoy staying in touch and when it's a better time, I'd love to get that glass of wine with you. Take care, Vanessa

Later that night I received a response from her and a friend request on *Facebook*, which I immediately accepted.

Thank you so much. I look forward to meeting you soon
and I just might take you up on that offer to talk. I'm sorry
about your dad. I lost mine many years ago and it still feels
like yesterday. Talk to you soon.

Overall the day turned out much better than I'd anticipated. Vanessa seemed sweet enough, and I believed she was being honest about her current time constraints. It would have been a simple matter of never responding to blow me off rather than fabricate such a story. I couldn't imagine someone being terminally nice but then using deceit as a way out. However, I've known people capable of acting in ways that defied all logic and decency. I had a hunch Vanessa was not one of them.

I safely tucked her in my back pocket for the time being. She was a dark horse, a long shot, at best. The idea of eventually meeting her was a pleasant one, but I wasn't going to hold my breath. I would reach out to her in a few weeks and inquire about her mother and see where it would go from there.

Emily was the only person I told about my foray into *Facebook* stalking. Other than that specific detail, it was a non-story. But we were always looking for interesting themes. In fact, we normally started each songwriting session by sharing anything interesting that we'd experienced during the previous week. So that's how the Vanessa-story spilled out. Emily wished me luck and joked that if the two potential lovebirds were to eventually hit it off, she had dibs on me for at least one night a week for our music. I agreed that our time was indeed sacred.

August soon surrendered to September, my favorite of the twelve months in Utah. Warm and dry, never terribly hot or windy, and the nights start to cool off a little, making it perfect patio season. It's also my preferred month to visit my home-away-from-home, which is the La Jolla area of San Diego.

I've taken yearly vacations to La Jolla since I was a pre-teen when my dad brought the family to his old stomping grounds. I fell in love after the very first sighting of the Pacific, and my daughters were eager to be the third generation to feel a deep connection with the beaches of 'the jewel' of the Pacific. I continue to visit one of my favorite spots on earth, often taking solo voyages. I don't mind traveling alone in the least. It's a wonderful dictatorship, not a democracy. I can do what I want and choose when to do it. And, I feel that every moment is precious when I can escape for a beach vacation.

After landing at San Diego International, I began my trip inland, taking a fascinating tour of the Taylor Guitar factory in nearby El Cajon. It was a dangerous visit. I left salivating over the high-end guitars I saw being built from scratch. A mediocre psychic could even guess that a new Taylor was in my future.

I checked into my hotel, quickly changed, and hit the beach. Time was of the essence. Torrey Pines was my best bet to catch some waves and get in a quick bodysurfing fix. The water was the warmest it had been all summer, and the surf was decent, giving me a dozen quality rides before I caught my breath. I sat on the sand, facing west, watching the sun descend toward the Pacific. All was perfect in my world. I didn't even waste a single thought on wishing I were sharing the moment with someone. The dictator was content.

The rest of my long weekend was spent at some of my favorite haunts in the area, like Windansea Beach and the Scripps pier area of La Jolla Shores. I rented a bike to ride along the boardwalk of Pacific Beach and caught a few waves on the north side of the PB pier. I was drawn daily to the water, to breathe in the sea air, and hear the gentle roar of the waves and ride a few. My batteries were being recharged.

One night, I met my cousins for a delicious Mexican dinner at *Alfonso's* in Solana Beach. I took in a San Diego Padres' game another evening, but otherwise kept my nights open to catch the sunset. The La Jolla cove area is renowned for its lovely sunsets, and on my final night it delivered. I posted a picture on *Facebook* of a stunning, brilliant orange sky with the darkened cliffs and ocean below.

I received several Likes on the photo—one was from Vanessa. I felt it was a good time to reach out to her so I composed a quick text.

Hi Vanessa. I hope you are well. How is your mother doing?

She replied within minutes.

Hi! Looks like from FB that you are on vacation—that sunset is gorgeous. I'm jealous. I'm not doing so well. My mother passed away this past Monday. We had her funeral on Saturday. She's in a much better place but I miss her and feel quite lost. Thanks for checking in.

I'm so sorry. I hope you are getting a lot of love and support from your family. Sending you hugs from La Jolla. Please let me know if I can do anything for you when I get back.

Thank you! My brothers and sisters are very close to me so we have each other. We have a lot to do, go through her stuff, sell her house—pretty overwhelming. Maybe we can get that wine together sooner than later. I'll need it.

Sounds like a plan. Take care, Vanessa.

As the crimson sun disappeared into the ocean, I savored the moment with a greater sense of appreciation than I had before texting Vanessa. I also felt the strong urge to call my own mom to say hi and tell her I loved her.

Chapter 24

Drive out the darkness;
Better angels take flight.
Love is the answer.
Step into the light.

Stay in the Light—Jamison Barrick

LIFE WAS WONDERFUL IN THE AUTUMN OF 2015. The Utah weather was spectacular. The mountains that rimmed the Salt Lake Valley were painted in the gorgeous fall colors of yellow, orange, and red. Emily and I continued to make music together, inching closer to performing a set of originals and covers at an open mic event someday soon. I enjoyed a couple of University of Utah football games with the kids. Cole had another year to go at the U, while Bailey, Kiara, Tyler, and I were all proud alums. We sported the team color of crimson and cheered heartily for our Utes, who recently had moved into the Pac-12 conference. The school's athletic nickname honors the indigenous people of the area, with the full blessing of the Ute Nation.

I was content with not actively pursuing a dating life. I'd had an initial taste of *Tinder* and was completely underwhelmed with the experience. I'd had my fill of *Starbucks*, too. I wasn't preoccupied with finally meeting Vanessa. I assumed it would happen when it was supposed to, if it was to occur at all. I would stay in touch and see where it would go from there. Overall, things in my corner of the universe were almost perfect. The rest of the world was about to go mad.

On Friday the 13th of November, in Paris, gunmen and suicide bombers hit a concert hall, sports stadium, and several bars and restaurants in a coordinated attack that killed over 130 people and shocked the world. The Eiffel Tower went dark the next night to honor the victims. The tragedy profoundly affected me. I was horrified at the depravity and utter disregard for life and the brazen assault on all the things that a civilized society holds dear.

I began writing a new song while watching televised images of the most prolific landmark in the City of Light going pitch black. I wrote to sort out my emotions and address the very real pain I felt in my heart. In what would be a huge departure from the usual love songs I've written, this one was shaping up to be somewhat of a political statement, or more accurately, a plea.

The typical posturing had already begun ahead of the 2016 election, and a nationalist fervor grew from the rubble of the terrorist attacks. Hate seemed to be the loudest response to the acts of hatred at the core of the attacks in Paris. Darkness was pitched as the answer to the black hearts that had unleashed such brutal terror. In the meantime, I was touched by the tragic plight of Syrian refugees fleeing their war-torn homeland. Many in our nation saw nothing but a potential threat in the eyes of the displaced, who were mostly women and children.

I had a great start on a song. The words of Martin Luther King, Jr., touching on darkness and light, found their way into the verses, and I also drew on Abraham Lincoln's inauguration speech for inspiration. The guitar chords were simple ones I knew well but the sequence was pleasing and captured the mood of my lyrics splendidly. I was getting close to completion when tragedy struck again on December 2nd, this time closer to home.

In San Bernardino, California, fourteen people were killed in a mass shooting. Social media pages filled with unfettered opinion and toxic debate on both sides of the issue of guns, particularly assault rifles. Politicians offered many thoughts and prayers but very little in the way of concrete answers and solutions.

I included some lines in the song about that incident and the ensuing uncivil dialogue. This composition was taking a while to write. I was finessing it more than usual, wanting the lyrics to be perfect. I was a single line away from completion when I received help from an unlikely and long-distance source.

A few nights before Christmas, I was working on the missing verse when I took a break and had a peek at *Facebook*. Kate had posted a few photos of herself and Sean on a holiday vacation to Cancun. One of her photos was of a heart, etched in the sand, with the caption: Love is always the answer.

Damned if she didn't totally nail it shut for me. Along with Dr. King and Lincoln, the song now had an impactful contribution from my ex-girlfriend, Kate Campania. If it ever became a hit and sold a bunch of records, I'd possibly be compelled to share a tiny bit of the financial windfall with her. I didn't give a single thought as to what the heart in the sand signified or for whom it was intended. I was just thrilled to complete the song and extremely pleased with how it turned out. I recorded the music on my phone, only needing eight takes to get it right this time, and excitedly sent Emily the audio file along with a copy of the lyrics. Her text back warmed my heart.

It's absolutely beautiful! It'll be an honor to lend my voice to it. I can't wait to perform this with you. Send a copy to Professor Steve. He'd love to see your amazing progress.

The lead up to the holidays had been hectic. I marveled at how fast the year had flown by. Another office Solstice party was in the books. This time, no special visitors spiced up the event. I helped my mom single-handedly keep the USPS in business by making several runs to the post office with her numerous cards and packages. I enjoyed visiting several friends and exchanging small gifts. I gave Emily a nice guitar capo before she left town to visit her parents in Northern California. She gave me a subscription to *Songwriter Magazine.* Emily was my biggest fan.

The holiday season peaked with my Christmas Eve flank steak dinner with the gang. I again added to their growing vinyl collections with more must-have albums. We played games, sipped wine, and the guys gave me some fine bourbon, all but assuring that if Cole were to ask for Bailey's hand in marriage in the upcoming year, he'd surely have my blessing. And you may have already guessed that a new guitar was under the tree again this year—a nice Taylor that could well have been in the process of being made during my factory tour. It was a combined Christmas/early-birthday present, and it felt, sounded, and looked wonderful. I suppose it's possible to have all three in one pretty package.

Speaking of pretty, Vanessa and I exchanged several holiday-themed texts. I wished her a *Merry Christmas,* with hope that it wouldn't be a terribly difficult one with the recent passing of her mother. She was grateful for my concern and informed me that she was hanging in there emotionally. I suggested that after the holidays we finally meet for that sip of wine.

I'd really enjoy that. I think I can finally come up for a little air now. It's time to get back to living. Thanks for being so patient with me. You easily could have lost interest. I'm so glad you didn't!

We planned to meet during the first full week of the New Year. I had enough time to do some *Facebook* sleuthing so I'd have a bit of a scouting report going into our first date. She only made the occasional post and added pictures sporadically. I found it appealing that she wasn't consumed by the need to share her life on social media. It appeared from her few posts that she had a son and a daughter. Her daughter was married and had a cute toddler. Vanessa enjoyed her yoga and seemed to have a close group of friends from her studio of choice. Professionally she worked at the Cystic Fibrosis Foundation of Utah, I assumed in marketing. Several of her posts promoted the foundation's fund-raising efforts that captured her in the middle of the activities. The rest was a mystery that would hopefully be revealed slowly, over some red wine.

We selected a downtown wine bar, *By the Glass,* for our long-awaited get-together. As usual, I arrived a few minutes early. It seems that for my entire life, if I weren't a few minutes early, then I was late. Vanessa was late. At 5:35, I received a text and apology that she was running a little behind but was on her way. That scored points. I have always valued when a person showed consideration. My table faced the front window with a view of the sidewalk outside. It was already dark and a typically cold January evening. Five minutes after her text, I saw her approach the establishment. She wore a knee-length coat and was bundled in a wool scarf. My pulse quickened as she entered, spotted me, and approached our table.

It had taken so long to arrive at this point that I'd almost forgotten our meeting came about through *Tinder*. Being a seasoned veteran of the app by now, I knew it was quite permissible to hug upon first contact, which we did rather robustly.

"It's so nice to finally meet you," she said sincerely.

"Likewise," I replied. Then I blurted out the exact words I was thinking. "Wow, your *Facebook* pictures don't do you justice!"

She smiled shyly at my comment, and her grin put the exclamation point on the perfect portrait. Vanessa was quite possibly the most beautiful woman I'd ever seen.

Stay in the Light

As darkness is falling
On the city of light,
It seems that the answers
Are nowhere in sight.

Morning is shattered
Half a world away.
Hold on to your weapons
But remember to pray.

(Chorus)

Drive out the darkness;
Better angels take flight.
Love is the answer,
Step into the light.

Stay in the light,
Stay in the light,
Stay in the light.

They come seeking refuge
Like our fathers before.
Yet we turn our backs
As they flood to our shore.

Those trying to lead us
Don't have a clue.
Inside is your answer.
It's all up to you.

(Repeat Chorus)

(Guitar Solo)

(Bridge)

Defend your positions
And spread words of hate.
Locked in your fear.
Stake claim to your place.
Knowing you're right,
You deserve your own fate.
Oh, stay in the light.

Drive out the darkness.
Better angels take flight.
Love is the answer.
Step into the light.

Drive out the darkness.
Love is the answer.

Stay in the light,
Stay in the light,
Stay in the light.

Chapter 25

I know you're still afraid
To rush into anything,
But there's just so many summers
And just so many springs.

The Last Worthless Evening—Don Henley

I BELIEVE THAT THE EYES ARE THE WINDOWS TO THE SOUL. I found Vanessa's rich, blue ones to be incredibly enchanting as we sat across the table, sipping a flavorful Willamette Valley *Pinot Noir*. But they were also steeped in mystery. I sensed there was a compelling story behind them, though I believed that this single sitting with her would not surrender any clues. I would leave our first date intrigued by the many secrets still unrevealed and completely charmed by layers that she peeled back and shared with me.

Before going back in time and swapping stories, we covered the ground since we connected on *Tinder* in late August. Losing her mom was incredibly difficult, and she felt very much an orphan without a living parent. As if the emotional toll on her wasn't hard enough, she had to deal with the logistics of going through her mom's belongings and getting her house prepared for sale. That was taking much longer than anticipated, even with the help of two siblings who lived in the Salt Lake area.

"I'll be going through her scrapbooks, journals, and other mementos, and instead of getting any work done, I'll start reading. Before I know it, three hours have passed," she explained. "So, the process has been incredibly slow. And it's been quite an emotional ride."

I wondered if simple sadness was what I was detecting in her eyes.

"I can only imagine. I'm sorry it's been so hard. My mom is getting on in years and lives in her home still, so I'm staring down that same scenario someday soon."

"It'll be one of the hardest things you'll ever do in life," she cautioned. "I hope we can get everything done in time to show her house in the spring. It'll be easier to sell then, anyway."

"Where is her house? Where did you grow up?" I asked.

Vanessa took me back to her childhood. She grew up in an affluent neighborhood near the Salt Lake Country Club. She was the youngest of five kids, with two brothers and two sisters. Her father had been a heart surgeon; her mom was a happy homemaker. She grew up in the Mormon faith but 'outgrew' it, in her words, by the time she was in Jr. High. She attended Highland High School, where many of the rich kids went in the valley. She graduated four years after I did and also attended the University of Utah and was in a sorority, a proud Delta Gamma.

She wasn't exactly my type, based on stereotypes and prejudices from my past. I almost asked her if she'd been a cheerleader, which would have completed the trifecta of a spoiled sorority girl with pompoms. But all that was a lifetime ago and, what constituted a certain type so many years ago, was now changed by the sands of time. Once again, that feeling of not being in her league crept into my thoughts. Her father had been a surgeon and mine, a newspaper editor. *If her ex-husband ends up being a lawyer the whole thing is off.*

We ordered another glass of wine each and a small cheese appetizer plate to soak up the alcohol. Vanessa insisted that I catch up with her story so far. I started with my much humbler beginnings and made it through my college days, and let her take the lead again.

She graduated from the U in English, intending to continue to get her Master's in education, and then teach. But she got married her senior year in college and had a honeymoon baby, so she got her BA and became a mom. A second child arrived two years after the first. She admitted to marrying too young and not really knowing herself or her husband. After twelve years they divorced.

"He was a workaholic. His job came first, and the kids and I were a distant second. He was a great provider. We lacked for nothing. We had a nice home in the Avenues, which I kept. He was very gracious in the divorce. I think he felt a lot of guilt that he couldn't really love us the way he wanted to, so he would at least provide for us."

"What did he do for a living?" I had to ask.

"He was and still is in commercial real estate. We're actually great friends to this day."

"I'm glad to hear that. Pretty rare it seems. I'm friends with both my ex-wives."

"I've been married twice myself." She continued with her story.

She was a single mom for six years and then remarried. He moved into her house after their wedding. That one lasted eight years, meaning she'd been divorced now for a little over two. I deemed that plenty of time to eliminate the potential of her still being in that delicate rebound period. I was getting adept at dodging bullets by now.

"That divorce wasn't so amicable. He was cheating on me with his secretary. Just like the stereotypical affair. It was awful. He's a lawyer so he pretty much had all the resources of an entire law firm on his side."

"No shit?" I almost spit out the wine I was sipping along with my exclamation. "That sucks." Both the part about him being a lawyer and her unfair legal battle.

"That first year was very hard on me. My kids were really worried about me. But I survived. But then my mom went downhill so quickly . . . .." She fell silent.

"It sounds like you've had a very rough stretch lately. I'm sorry."

"Thanks." She was quick to take the spotlight off herself for a moment. "So, tell me about your life from college to *Tinder*."

"That sounds like a really bad movie line," I chuckled.

I told her about my first marriage and proudly bragged about my two daughters and the wonderful men in their lives. I took her on a short tour of the Anna years, adding that she wasn't alone—my ex had an affair with a woman, too. That earned a 'no shit?' from her side of the table. I threw in a few *Tinder* tales, including the scam artist who pretended to want my heart but was after my money. I shared the professional side of my life with her and also some recent interests, including the songwriting and guitar playing.

"I'd love to hear you perform some of your songs. Please let me know when you do an open mic. Remember the little people when you make it big time!"

"Some of the lyrics are still without music, but I'm working on that part. I have no illusions of ever being a rock star. I'd be thrilled just have others buy and perform my songs."

I withheld telling her that if she played her cards right, she may someday earn her very own song.

The mood was now light enough for Vanessa to wrap-up her story. She had two kids of whom she was equally proud. Her daughter was married with her husband in law school in Virginia. She had a grandson, Marcus, who had completely stolen her heart. She had made it out to Charlottesville twice this past year, and her daughter had made it back home twice, but it wasn't nearly enough. She couldn't bear having Marcus grow up so far away from Grandma. Her son worked for a tech company located in Lehi, otherwise known as Utah's Silicon Slopes. He was more interested in his job than shedding his eligible bachelor status. We proudly shared photos of our loved ones. Good genes on both sides.

She spoke about the passion she had for her job, sharing the cystic fibrosis story and trying to raise awareness and money to find a cure. CF and similar diseases that affect a small percentage of the population are not funded by government money like the major diseases, so private funding is crucial for research and new drugs. I offered my company as a resource to help with any video production work. We worked a lot with the non-profit organizations in the city. She was appreciative of my offer.

Two-and-a-half hours had flown by, and we had shared quite a lot. I concluded that the ex-husband/lawyer needn't be a deal breaker. We all make questionable choices. I took care of the tab, and we wound down our conversation before walking out into the January cold. I cut to the chase.

"I had a great time. It was nice to finally meet you; very much worth the wait."

"It's been fun. Sorry it took so long to finally get together," she needlessly apologized.

"Don't be. You've been dealing with a lot. I totally understand."

"I'm really glad you tracked me down on *Facebook* after I deleted

Tinder. Thanks for being a good stalker." Her smile was just as beautiful as her mysterious eyes.

"Would you like to get together again soon?" I certainly did.

"I'd like that. It was nice getting out and taking a break from my mom's stuff. I still have a ton to do and need to focus on that, but it would be wise for me to take a break now and then, aside from my yoga. I may need your help to remind me to keep a healthy balance. Once I get going, it's kind of overwhelming."

"I can do that, but I don't want to feel like I'm holding a gun to your head."

"No gun needed, just a gentle nudge is all it will take."

"Deal."

I walked her to her car, a Toyota Forerunner. Her lawyer ex must have been able to keep his BMW in the divorce. She thanked me for the wine, and we shared an affectionate hug. She waved as she pulled away. I had a short walk back to my car. I reached for my phone and dialed Emily. She was aware I had a date and wanted a full report.

"Hi! How did it go?"

"It was great. She's really sweet. I kind of like her."

"Good! I want to hear all about it!"

"You will, next time we jam. I think I have a new song for us to write. So far, I only have the title, no lyrics yet," I teased her.

"Oh yeah? What's it called?"

"I Should Have Kissed the Girl."

Chapter 26

When you see me fly away without you;
Shadows on the things you know;
Feathers fall around you
And show you the way to go.

Birds—Neil Young

THIS WINTER I NOTICED THE COLD AND SNOW MUCH MORE than I had during the previous one. The year before, I was so distracted by falling in love that I was barely aware of the season at all. This one was hard to miss, with frigid temperatures and frequent snowfall that often snarled either the morning or evening commutes. The skiers and the resorts were ecstatic, but I wasn't. This was the time I could have used a Hawaiian vacation to warm my old bones as I aged another year in early February.

I had my music to keep me warm. Emily and I continued our weekly sessions of writing, jamming, and working toward performing live. She had played at open mic events and at coffee shops a few years earlier before allowing her music to fall to the wayside during the time she was in her last relationship. She was raring to go again but patiently waiting for me to catch up. She easily could have taken the stage solo but genuinely liked the idea of a duo this time around. I was warming to the idea of performing, primarily because I didn't want to hold her back. That was my main incentive to keep working to get to a comfortable level when performing in front of others.

I looked beyond a love interest as inspiration for my songwriting and was content to take Emily's lyrical ideas and work on themes that had nothing to do with me. She loved *Stay in the Light* enough to suggest that it would start off our set when we hit the stage. She inquired often about my status with Vanessa, but there was very little to report, and I was content with that even though it meant no love songs were flowing from me. That would change soon enough.

Vanessa and I texted and talked several times a week. We met for coffee a couple of weeks after our wine date. I bought tickets to see Amos Lee in concert in early March and, at the risk of disappointing Abbey and Emily, I invited Vanessa who eagerly accepted. Kiara, Tyler, Bailey, and Cole also had tickets for the concert, so this was to be their first meeting with Vanessa. I anticipated that she'd pass their test for being normal.

She had been busy with work and with her mom's house, and I was doing my own thing in the meantime. There was really no angst in terms of the progression of our relationship, if I could even label it as that. Vanessa was someone I wanted to get to know better and experience had taught me that such things take time. Current logistics served as a buffer that kept both of us from rushing into anything, and that was just fine with me. I was quite content with having the dynamics play out much differently than what I'd experienced with Kate. Fireworks and a speedy cascade into love hadn't exactly panned out last time. Vanessa seemed to agree with our pace, although it's not something we ever discussed.

Before the concert, we all enjoyed dinner together at Bailey's favorite restaurant, *Current Fish and Oyster*. We matched *New Zealand Sauvignon Blanc* with our seafood, and Vanessa seemed to fit in nicely with the kids, appearing to be at ease and engaging seamlessly in the conversation. As we walked the four blocks to the Capitol Theater on a rather balmy night, Vanessa and I held hands. Kiara and Bailey didn't give any outward signs of approval like a thumbs up or an affirmative nod, but judging by their smiles, it was apparent that Vanessa had passed the test. That was fortunate because with each date that we enjoyed, she was passing all of mine as well.

Amos put on a fantastic show, and the acoustics in the former movie-theater-turned-opera house were perfect for his mostly unplugged concert. I finally kissed the girl, so maybe I could put that into song form. In fact, we shared a lengthy goodbye kiss in the doorway of her lovely home in the Avenues neighborhood of Salt Lake. She thanked me for a wonderful night, and I expressed appreciation for her normalcy. I enjoyed the view of the valley from the car with a huge grin on my face as I descended from her lofty perch above the city. *Was that a small bottle rocket that just exploded overhead?*

At the same time that Vanessa was focused on her mother's house, I was concerned about my mom's health. She had been in a slow decline for some time, both mentally and physically. She had met her great-granddaughter a few months earlier when my nephew and his wife visited from California. My brother and sister agreed with me that she seemed to have lost her will to live after that visit. It was as if she really had nothing else to look forward to and live for after checking that box off her bucket-list. She was eighty-eight and missed my dad terribly. It was heartbreaking to see her fade away. I was incredibly torn. Most of me wished for her to live forever, but a small part of me wanted her to be at peace.

Emily and I were wrapping up a productive music session on the night of April 4th. She'd been looking for an open mic opportunity for us and recently signed us up for a Meet-up group that was all about such performances. We were getting close and had worked on our four-song set all night. Before we said our goodbyes, I pulled my phone from my jacket to take it off mute. I had several missed-calls from my brother and decided it must have been important, so I called him back while still in Emily's front room.

"Hi bro," he answered, and my older brother's tone was somber.

"What's going on, Phil?"

"Angie and I stopped by to check on Mom about an hour ago." His voice began to crack. "She's gone." He was now sobbing.

"What?" I didn't fully comprehend his words, nor did I want to. Emily stood closer and touched me on the shoulder, concern etched on her face.

"She was in her bed. We thought she'd just gone to sleep early, but her light was on. She's gone, Jamison."

"Phil, I took her to Walgreen's yesterday!" I protested, my eyes filling with tears. Emily squeezed my arm. "I'll be right there. I'm close by, in Sugar House."

"See you in a few. We're waiting for the police to come. Angie said we needed to call them first. I didn't know what the hell to do. I'll call Jean and tell her."

Good. I was in no condition to drive and break that news to my sister, too.

"My mom died," I turned to Emily after ending my call. I was in complete shock and so grateful I wasn't alone at this moment.

"I'm so sorry!" She wrapped her arms around me and steadied me as my world was spinning. "Are you in any shape to be driving?" I probably wasn't, but I assured her I was. "Call me tomorrow or when you can. I won't bother you, but just know I'm here for you."

"Thank you. That means more than you know."

The seven-minute drive to my mom's house was a complete blur. I pulled up to find a couple of police cars in front. I walked in, and a sobbing Angie greeted me with a hug. My mom had been very fond of her. She had been incredibly kind and took her on more of her errands than I did.

"She seemed fine yesterday," I explained to Angie, trying to comprehend it all myself. "I mean, we've all seen her fading a bit lately, but she was not on death's doorstep by any means. I don't get it."

"I think your amazing mother decided to go out on her own terms," she said, trying to comfort me with words that made perfect sense. "I truly believe she had done and seen everything she wanted to, and it was finally time to be with your dad again." Tears streamed down her cheeks.

"It would be just like Maggie to call her own shot." I smiled at that thought. "But I wish I could have said goodbye." My smile faded quickly.

Phil broke off his conversation with one of the officers and embraced me. He looked shell-shocked.

"They called the mortuary and they're on the way to pick her up. At least all that funeral stuff won't be new to us after Dad . . . ." He tried to compose himself.

"Yeah. I didn't think it would be so soon, though." Our tears flowed freely.

I gathered myself and asked one of the officers if I could see my mom. I appreciated the professionalism and compassion they showed while doing what had to be a very unpleasant part of their duty. He led me into her bedroom, then left so I could have some time alone with her. She looked incredibly peaceful, as if she were simply asleep. It still didn't seem real. *Wake up, Mom. Please wake up.*

Chapter 27

In your arms,
I feel so safe and so secure.
Every day is such a perfect day to spend
Alone with you.

Follow You, Follow Me—Genesis

I ONCE READ AN INTERNET MEME THAT SAID: *The greatest love is love that shows up when you need it the most.* I found this to be true in the days and weeks after my mother passed away. I felt such an incredible outpouring of love from many dear friends. I'll be forever grateful for each person who reached out to me during that trying time. The event certainly brought me closer to one person, who came through when I truly needed her.

Before leaving my mom's house, Phil and I divided up the list of the many people we needed to call and notify of Mom's death. I left before the mortuary came to pick her up. It was strange, but I no longer felt her presence in the home. I didn't want to linger and make the calls there, so I headed home with my brother's blessing. Earlier, Phil had to cut his call to our sister short when the police arrived, so she was my first call. I called Jean on my drive home and spent most of the call trying to convince her not to feel guilty.

She had often expressed her frustration that she couldn't do more to help with Mom and genuinely felt bad that she lived two states away. I tried my best to express that guilt had no place among the myriad of emotions we were experiencing. We would talk much more over the next few days but she was already making plans to fly out for a probable Saturday funeral.

I called family first, starting with my aunt who also lived in Salt Lake and a few close cousins, including Barbara in Hawaii. It was well after 10 p.m. when I decided to leave the rest of the calls for the next day. It was eerily quiet in my condo. I usually have music playing all the time but not on that night. I felt a rare emotion for me as I sat there in the dark—loneliness. My mind drifted to thoughts of Vanessa. I didn't want to bother her with a call at that late hour, so I sent a short text, not knowing if she'd get it before bedtime or in the morning. I was not really expecting or seeking a response. I just felt the need to reach out to the one person whom I knew could relate the best.

My mom passed away tonight.

My phone rang within seconds.

"Hi, I didn't know if you'd be up," she abruptly cut me off.

"Oh, my God! I'm sorry, Jamison. Are you doing okay?"

"I'm still in shock. Hasn't really sunk in yet."

"It may not for a while. Would you like some company? Can I come over, or do you want to be alone?"

"I wouldn't want to put you out this late."

"It's not putting me out at all," she gently scolded me. "Unless you absolutely want to be alone, I'm coming over."

"That would actually be very nice. Alone is sucking right now."

"You told me roughly where you live but text me your address, and I'll be right there."

"Thank you. I really appreciate it."

I had just enough time to tidy up a little before I heard a knock on my door. My text had caught her in full-on 'ready for bed' mode with no makeup, hair pulled back, wearing yoga pants and a red University of Utah sweatshirt.

"Sorry, you didn't exactly get me at my glamorous best," she shrugged before wrapping her arms around me.

"That's funny, because I was just thinking that you were a beautiful sight for sore eyes. Thanks for coming."

"Of course. And those tears in your eyes are fogging up your vision, but thanks."

We sat on my couch, and I gave her all the details from the night, still in complete denial that what I was telling her was true.

"I know it doesn't feel like it right now but in many ways, you are lucky she passed this way. To see someone you love suffer over a long period of time is excruciating. She sounds like an amazing woman."

"I suppose you are right. If she were writing her own script, she'd probably choose to die in her *own* home, in *her* bed, on *her* terms. I just wish I could have said goodbye."

We held each other in the dim light and talked softly about life and death and everything in between. The clock struck midnight, and I started to feel bad for keeping her up so late.

"I should let you go. It's a work night for you. I'm obviously not going in tomorrow. Not looking forward to planning a funeral."

"Would you mind if I slept here, at least for a few hours? I don't want you to be alone tonight. I know too well what you are feeling inside. You don't have to face this alone," she said lovingly.

"I'd like that a lot."

"Can I borrow a T-shirt, and do you have an extra toothbrush?"

"Yeah, I have a complete sleepover kit always at the ready, just in case a lady comes calling," I joked.

"I'll definitely get more dolled up in the future for an official booty call," she winked.

I led her upstairs, picked out a Boston Red Sox T-shirt for her to wear, and dug out a fresh toothbrush. She changed in the bathroom while, for some illogical reason, I hastily made my unmade bed. I then turned down the freshly made bed for her and she climbed in while I brushed and changed. I joined her under the covers and she kissed me goodnight before laying her head on my chest and gently caressing my hand. Her warm touch turned a terrible night into a tender one. Within minutes, a wave of exhaustion washed over me, and I was fast asleep.

I was awakened to a soft kiss on my forehead and Vanessa's gentile whisper.

"I didn't want to slip away without saying goodbye."

"What time is it?"

"About 5:30. You go back to sleep. I'll let myself out."

"No, I'll . . .," I began to protest, but she put a finger to my lips."

"Sleep. You've got a long day ahead of you. Call me if you need anything. Food later. You name it, okay? I'm here for you."

"Thank you. You've been incredible."

"I'm keeping your Red Sox T-shirt. I kind of like it." She kissed me goodbye, leaving me smiling for a moment, before I remembered the reason for her visit in the first place.

The following week felt like a month. I spent more time at the mortuary than a living being should. I got my mom's obituary placed, which she had written herself, and logged several hours on the phone with government agencies, insurance companies, banks, and various friends and family. The logistics of planning a funeral and the many details that accompany death often push the grieving to the back burner to be dealt with at a later, more tranquil time. I had to be there for my daughters, who had lost another dear grandparent and also consoled my brother and sister. I knew I was heading for a crash after the funeral when things would be quiet again.

It was a gorgeous spring morning the Saturday after her passing and a beautiful service. Somehow, I made it through my remarks without becoming overly emotional. My two ex-wives, children, stepchildren, nieces, nephews, and many friends and co-workers all came to honor my mother. Emily and Abbey met each other for the first time, and my sushi buddy, Courtney, also attended. I even received a nice text from Kate, offering her condolences. Barbara was off to China for a conference but had sent a beautiful bouquet of tropical flowers typical of those from Hawaii.

Vanessa felt horrible that she was unable to attend as it fell on the same day as one of the biggest CF fundraisers of the year: a 5K and 10K road race with which she was heavily involved and simply couldn't miss. I assured her that it was quite all right, and I had sincerely appreciated her incredible support all week. But no words could allay her guilt.

Sunday saw the departure of my sister and her family back to California. Two nieces had crashed at my place, and I was sad to see them leave and take their youthful energy with them. As I had expected and dreaded, my world became suddenly very quiet. I was overwhelmingly melancholy Sunday night. I knew this was just a short breather before moving onto phase two: dealing with my mom's affairs. We had a house to sell along with all of her possessions and accounts. My appreciation for what Vanessa had been dealing with for several months was uppermost in my mind, and I would soon understand why such matters take much longer than you'd assume.

I strummed a guitar for the first time in almost a week. That offered such sweet solace and made me excited to begin making music again. The seed for a new song was planted that night, beginning with a guitar lick that came to me along with a few words that swirled in my head. I decided to write a song describing the emotions that accompany the loss of a loved one. It would take me until September to finish it.

Even though my mother's passing brought Vanessa and I closer, I anticipated some sort of exponential growth to occur between us, but it didn't happen that way. We both had a great deal of work ahead of us with our mothers' respective estates, which prevented us from seeing each other often. But even when we did get together, we lacked the intensity I was expecting. Some of the reasons for this were obvious, while another one was carefully and purposely obscured.

I fell into a little funk in the weeks and months after the funeral. Not prepared for the emotions I felt, I painfully came to grips with the fact that I was an orphan, of sorts, and now part of generation-next—taking a step forward in the mortality line with no one left in front of me. For several weeks after mom's passing, I would instinctively reach for the phone around 10 a.m. to have my routine check-in call to her. With my daughters now out on their own and fully independent, looking after Mom had become my primary purpose during the years since Dad had passed. Without that constant in my life, I was a bit lost.

I imagined that Vanessa had been going through the same emotions, with a half-year head-start on me. Initially, I chalked up our inability to take it to the next level to our collective despondency and all the logistics that consumed us; but, slowly I became aware that there was much more to it than that. She would only allow me in so much. Just when it appeared that some unexplained walls were coming down, she would quickly rebuild new ones. Despite all the caring and tenderness that I saw in her eyes, they were still shrouded in mystery. They painted a picture of a woman who was cautious, not a stranger to pain, and perhaps concealing a secret.

In time the mystery would unravel, and her secret would be revealed. It would dwarf the one that Anna carried with her for so long. I had become adept at hitting the curve balls that life threw at me, but I would soon be faced with a reality that would test me in ways I couldn't possibly imagine.

Chapter 28

From a distant stare,
Your gaze returns my way.
What's to keep me
From drowning in those azure pools?

Untamed—Jamison Barrick

WINSTON CHURCHILL ONCE DESCRIBED RUSSIA THIS WAY: "It is a riddle wrapped in a mystery inside an enigma." In my mind, this could also accurately describe a few women I've known and loved. It fit Vanessa. She was inviting yet elusive, loving but aloof, trusting and also wary. I was drawn to her complexity. I feasted during the times she was generous with her heart and was left to wonder why when she felt the need to be guarded. Even two steps forward and one back still added up to progress, I concluded. Besides, I was content with the pace and felt no sense of urgency. We both enjoyed each other's company and neither of us were going anywhere, so it worked.

In the meantime, I was moving forward with my music. In early June, Emily and I performed at our first open mic event together. The night before our performance, we were taking a break from working on our set when we came to the realization that our band lacked a named. We hadn't even thought about it, so we kicked around a few names but nothing stuck. I dug deep into my collection of Italian words and presented her with *Ecco*. It's a tough word to directly translate. The Latin roots translate as *behold*, and in modern Italian it means *here*, or *look here*. Emily took an immediate liking to it. We would be introduced as *Ecco*. It flowed much better than Emily and Jamison.

The open mic evening was held at the home of one of the members of an online *Meet-up* group of like-minded people. I was glad we were starting at a home rather than a coffee house with paying customers. It seemed like an enjoyable bunch with a common goal of having fun, sharing music, and supporting one another. The sound system was set up in the patio area of a massive backyard, complete with a swimming pool. The homeowner, Brad, didn't play or sing but was gracious enough to invite a bunch of aspiring musicians and songwriters over. He even had an assortment of adult beverages to offer the group. Vanessa came to support me and met Emily for the first time. They clicked nicely, as I had expected and hoped.

We were fourth in the lineup. I was nervous as hell. It was one thing to play on my couch or patio and another to perform in front of people. Emily had much more pressure than I did. She was singing as well as playing, yet she seemed incredibly calm.

We began our set with one of her songs, and then followed it with *Stay in the Light*, receiving generous applause. The few times I looked up, I was greeted by encouraging gazes. We then played the song Emily first sang at our songwriting class and ended with the sassy and snappy *Vinyl and Bourbon Nights* as our encore.

The enthusiastic applause we received instantly made my lifelong fantasy of being a rock star come to fruition, even on this small scale. It was a rush. Emily was back to doing what she loved, Vanessa seemed quite thrilled for me, and I had at least one groupie. I'd call that a perfect night.

Later that month, Vanessa and I enjoyed seeing a real rock star, Matt Nathanson, in concert at an outdoor venue nearby called the Sandy Amphitheater. It was a typically warm evening, and we had a great view of the sun setting in the west with a full moon rising in the east above the imposing Wasatch Mountains.

During one song, I noticed Vanessa looking off into the distance, a slight breeze gently tossing her hair. I briefly pictured her in a convertible, riding along a desolate highway without a care in the world. She snapped out of her trance and looked at me, smiling. I wondered where she'd gone in her mind for that instant. I filed the moment away. A new song had been conceived.

Blame it on the full moon, the buzz generated by the live music, or her simple beauty, but I felt the need to articulate what I was feeling in the moment. I tilted my head toward her and whispered in her ear.

"I love you."

I saw so many things in the look she gave me upon hearing those words. I could see so much love, hope, and appreciation. I also detected a glimmer of doubt and hesitation. Her reciprocal words, however, were instant.

"I love you, too." She wrapped my arm in both of hers and rested her head on my shoulder. "Please stay the night," she added, without looking up. I gently kissed the top of her head to indicate I thought it was a dandy idea. I was turning cartwheels inside.

As the sun finally slipped beneath the horizon, and the stars came out to play, it suddenly struck me that this evening fell on the Summer Solstice, the longest day of the year. Until that moment, I hadn't given much thought to the Spanish Steps, Rome, Kate, and the summer of 2017. I wondered for an instant where I'd be a year into the future on this night. I assumed I'd be with Vanessa. Things between us were slow but steady.

As Matt was belting out his new hit single, *Run*, I couldn't imagine myself in Italy a year later or having anything to do with Kate. That song I'd written was about a fanciful notion and would likely remain just that, never coming to pass. Or so I thought. The Spanish Steps would beckon.

The concert was a nice respite for what had been a busy summer so far. Vanessa had finally listed her mom's house. I spent a few weekends helping her get it and the yard ready to show. She appreciated my efforts, and I scored valuable points with her local siblings. So far, there had been several showings but no offers.

Vanessa was fighting off discouragement and the realization that they may have to drop the price. As for my mom's house, I was incredibly lucky. My brother and his wife decided they wanted to move into it. It was an upgrade for them in terms of location and size. Jean and I made it easier for Phil to buy us out of our shares of the house by deducting what we would have paid in real estate fees and the money it would have cost to make some needed upgrades and get it looking good enough to place on the market. Despite the vast amount of paperwork involved, it ended up being a win/win for all of us.

That arrangement also allowed us to go through all my parent's valuables at a much less frantic pace than was the case for Vanessa. I had been spending a few hours every weekend slowly going through the mementos and albums. My sister flew in for a week in early July, and we concentrated on the task during her entire stay. Just as Vanessa had described from her experience, the process was slow and emotionally difficult. So many items had sentimental value and decisions had to be made as to which child or grandchild was more closely tied to a particular object. Much of my childhood was being relived, which was accompanied by mostly sweet memories. Mine had been a happy one, but tears were often present as I took my nostalgic stroll down memory lane.

I wondered on more than one occasion if the parallel experience that Vanessa had gone through was behind that look in her eyes I couldn't quite comprehend. Was it simply reflective of a state of prolonged melancholy? It had been a difficult summer for me to sort through my parent's possessions. Perhaps the strain also showed on me. Would I see joy in her eyes eventually with the sale of her mother's home? Was that holding her back, leaving her in a state that could best be described as emotionally stationary? One night while sipping wine on her patio, we talked about our collective experience.

"Have I told you how much I appreciate you being there for me since my mom died? You already blazed that trail for me with the insight you've shared. You've been a lifesaver."

"I don't know if I've been much help. It hasn't really been a case of me telling you what to expect as much as you just observing me slogging through all of my stuff."

"You're not giving yourself enough credit. You've been there for me while still dealing with your own issues. I appreciate it more than I've shown. Thank you, V." I used the nickname often.

She reached out and squeezed my hand gently.

"I should be the one thanking you. I honestly don't know how I would have made it through all of this without you. You're the lifesaver."

"I guess we are both lucky." I leaned in and kissed her softly. "I'm now fully appreciating what you've been through since even before your mom passed away. This is the hard shit in life no one warned us about. Our own mortality becomes real. And going through old items and reliving memories is bittersweet."

"That's been the hardest part. Some pieces of my childhood weren't very happy. Reliving the past has reopened some old wounds." She fell silent.

I wasn't going to press her on something that was obviously a sensitive subject. I sat quietly, waiting for her to continue, but she changed the subject. That would be as much as she'd reveal on that warm midsummer's evening. She had offered me the first glimpse of what might be behind that often sorrowful look in her otherwise beautiful blue eyes. I would eventually come to find out that, while my childhood had been happy and carefree, a huge part of hers had been hell.

I set aside the dark possibilities when I sat down one evening to write the song that had its genesis the night of the concert, when I caught Vanessa wistfully looking off in the distance, her mind a million miles away for an instant. I expounded on that theme and focused entirely on the lyrics. I figured Emily could help me with the music portion of the song. I tried to capture the essence of how I saw Vanessa and that I'd barely scratched the surface of truly knowing the woman. Because I didn't have the musical side to slow me down, I had the verses completed in half an hour. Despite the potential ramifications my words might have on Vanessa, I was eager to share them. I called to tell her goodnight and causally added that I'd written a song for her.

"You did? Wow! Send me the lyrics. Girls love this kind of thing. Send it now," she demanded.

"All right, but first a little disclaimer. It's not overly sappy and romantic. It's kind of deep. I'll put you on speaker and send it."

I texted the lyrics from my iPad and heard her put me on speaker. I waited patiently for her response. Guys who write songs for girls love that kind of thing. About five minutes passed before she said anything, which had been enough time to read the lyrics several times.

"Wow. I love it. It appears you find me both irresistible and mysterious. I'm glad I can keep you guessing. How boring would it be if you had me all figured out? *Untamed*? Yes, that's me." I could hear her smile through her voice.

"Well, some days I have you figured out. Other days, not so much. But if you read the words carefully, I don't seem to be complaining. I'm glad you like it."

"I really do. It'll be cool to hear you perform it. I'm really flattered." Her tone turned serious. "And I know you aren't complaining, but I wouldn't blame you if you did. I admit, I hold a lot in and keep so many things to myself. I promise to open up more. It's not that I don't trust you. I do completely."

"Hey, I'm not asking you to change a thing. The song was not meant to coax you to do anything."

"Oh, I know," she responded. "I'm saying this because I know I need to do better at giving you more of me. You deserve that. You've been so patient and wonderful. I know I'm not easy. But to answer your question in the song, I will share with you my secrets. Soon. I promise."

"When you're ready, V. Only when you are ready."

Part of me wasn't completely certain I wanted to know what she was hiding. It was my soul delicately whispering to me, *be very careful what you wish for.*

Untamed

Cruising to nowhere,
Feet up, top down.
You pick the tunes.
Will I someday
 Be your favorite song?

From a distant stare,
Your gaze returns my way.
What's to keep me
From drowning in
Those azure pools?

A Cheshire grin,
Wind whipping your hair,
Having its way with you.
Is the breeze the only
One that does?

(Chorus)
Will I ever truly know you?
The wild horse within?
I know I'll never tame you;
Oh, but what a ride.

Sun on your face,
You match its glow;
Needing nothing and no one.
Do you see me
As your brightest star?

Soft candlelight
Illuminates every move
Of your mesmerizing dance.
Won't you let me
Deep inside?

(Repeat Chorus)

(Bridge)
Would you care
To share your secrets?
Will you finally
Shed your skin?
Can you tell me
What you're hiding?
Will you completely
Let me in?

Will I ever truly know you?
The wild horse within;
I know I'll never tame you.
Oh, but what a ride.

Chapter 29

There's an emptiness inside her
And she'd do anything to fill it in,
But all the colors mix together—to grey;
And it breaks her heart.

Grey Street—Dave Matthews Band

HER CURSIVE HANDWRITING REMINDED ME OF THE PENMANSHIP of my daughters when they were that age. The deliberate yet soft lines and curves exuded youthful exuberance and restlessness. In the case of my girls, I remembered that I could also discern abounding innocence in their text. That singular element felt absent from the carefully chosen words that Vanessa had meticulously inscribed in her journal, and for good reason. She was painfully documenting the chilling details of how her innocence had been utterly and brutally stolen from her.

July gave way to August, and the harsh 100-degree days were finally in the rearview mirror for the parched citizens of the Salt Lake Valley. The canyon winds began to have a pleasant, cooling effect at night, offering a tiny hint of the next season. Near the end of the month, Vanessa and her siblings sold their mother's home, at last. Her emotional ride didn't end with the signing of the closing documents, as her temporary relief over the sale gave way to the sad realization that her childhood home was now gone. The new owners were already talking about renovations that would change the character of the home. Our celebratory dinner a few days later was a rather subdued event.

Vanessa was trying hard to be more engaging, but she simply didn't have it in her that night. From across the table she looked emotionally exhausted.

"I'm sorry I'm not very good company tonight. I usually snap out of it once we get out the door."

"I understand. You've got a lot on your mind. It must be hard to lose a piece of your life like that. I'm sorry, and I get it. I'm so relieved that Phil was able to keep my mom's house.

"Thanks," she smiled appreciatively. "It feels like one of the biggest chapters of my life is now over. The one constant in my life has been that home—and the people inside it, of course. I've lost my anchor." A single tear rolled down her cheek.

"Maybe this celebration was a bad idea." I felt bad for pushing it.

"No, it was a great idea. Thank you for being so thoughtful. I thought I'd be fine. Sorry I can't seem to rise to the occasion."

We skipped desert, paid our tab, and I took her home. She was silent the entire ride, staring out the window; her thoughts were far away. I reached out for her hand, and she turned and offered a slight smile. We pulled into the driveway, and I turned off the car.

"What are you thinking?" I asked, not expecting much substance in her answer.

"I'm thinking it's time," she replied, staring straight ahead. "I've got something to show you."

We walked into her house. She disappeared into her den for a moment and returned holding a small stack of brown, leather books. Little Post-it notes marked a few sections. We sat in her living room as she struggled to find the right words to continue. I swallowed hard, wondering where this was leading. She finally spoke.

"These are a few of my journals, from Jr. High and High School. I've marked the parts I'd like you to read. Don't read them all; you don't need to know all about my 8th grade crush or the times I wanted to kill my brothers." She forced a smile. "These have been buried in my bedroom closet at Mom's house all these years. I found them a few months back when I was going through things."

She took a deep breath to compose herself. "These contain the secrets I promised to share. I feel they are safe with you. I feel safe with you. I love you." She was sobbing at this point. "My first husband knows but not my second. You'll be the only other man I've loved to know my story. These old words do a better job of painting the picture than I can now. Take them. Please read them." She paused as I nodded affirmatively that I would. "You may not want to be with me after you know everything."

"Don't be ridiculous," I interrupted. She cut me off quickly and forcefully.

"No, please listen. You'll soon learn how truly damaged I am." Her tears flowed freely. "I'm broken, Jamison; probably beyond repair. I know I need help. I . . . I owe it to you; you deserve to know everything, so you can make the choice of whether you want this or not."

"V, I love you! Nothing in these journals could possibly change that."

"You don't know that. Take them home, and read what I've written. Take a good day to let it all sink in, and then we'll talk about it. I promise I'm not trying to scare you away. But I love you too much to keep this from you anymore."

I held my lover tightly for several minutes until her crying subsided. I reluctantly left. It was apparent she needed to be alone, and I had been given a strict assignment. I looked back at her standing on the front porch as I backed out of the driveway. Her face showed such contrasting emotions. I saw mostly sadness and fear but also a trace of hope, and even relief. I drove home, the journals stacked on my passenger seat, wondering what they would reveal.

I opened the first one within minutes of arriving at my condo. I had a hunch as to the nature of the secrets hidden within but nothing could truly prepare me for what I was about to read.

The first entry that Vanessa marked was dated November 13, 1977. I quickly did the math and placed her in Jr. High at age thirteen.

My friends are so boy crazy it makes me sick! It's all they ever talk about. Last week Carol liked Jim and Lori liked Todd. Now Carol has a crush on Todd and Lori isn't talking to either one of them. Way too much stupid drama for me! Everybody is always talking about kissing and sex, too. I wish I could tell them that it's not that great. It's actually awful. They'll find out someday soon. I feel so different from all my friends. I can't relate to the things they do and how they act. They seem so immature to me. But maybe they are normal and I'm the one who isn't. I know they haven't been through what I have. They wouldn't understand and they wouldn't even believe me. God, if anyone ever found out . . . I thought about him today. I think about him most days and I hate it. I hate him. I can still smell his after-shave, feel his rough hands, see his hairy arms, and smell his bad breath. I wish he'd have a heart attack and just die. Some days I want to die. Today is one of those days. I hate life today. I hate boys. I hate girls, too. I hate a lot of things lately. Mostly I hate Uncle Asshole in Oklahoma. I hope a tornado hits that state and kills him, but not Aunt Vickie, Carli, and Scott. I'll probably still hate him even after he dies.

Oh, my God, I thought as I thumbed through the pages to her next bookmark. I felt sick inside. She revealed more in her next entry, dated almost a year later, on Aug 6, 1978.

Mom and I had another ugly fight today and this one was pretty bad. I wish I could tell her the source of all my anger towards her. I'm sure she thinks the church stuff is teenage rebellion. I can't tell her the real reason I won't go into that building ever again. I won't go there and take the sacrament and pretend to be all pure and innocent when I'm not. I can't sit there and hear all about a loving and protective God. Where was he when I needed him the most? I won't do it, as much as she tries to force me to go. I almost blurted it out when we were screaming at each other. I was so close to telling her that it's her brother's fault that I'm so angry, so moody, so withdrawn. And she's partly to blame, too. She had to know. She left me alone with him. She let me have sleepovers with my cousins. She didn't do her best to protect me from a monster. She had to know about his dark side—he probably did those things to her, too. Maybe she suspects that he did those things to me. Maybe her guilt makes her angry, like mine does to me.

My heartbeat was racing as I read these deeply disturbing words, which were written on paper with such sweet handwriting. My eyes could not stay dry. My heart ached for Vanessa, both the younger and older version. In the second journal, the next marker opened to a folded notebook page. It looked like a class assignment that had never been turned in. It lacked a grade or any teacher comments. No, this never made it to her teacher's desk.

Vanessa Grant   Mrs. White — 5th period   3/27/79

Stolen Innocence

It was never in the darkness
But always in the light
He'd do his filthy deeds
And then hide in plain sight
He'd tell me I was pretty
Had the audacity to call it love
I'd close my eyes and tremble
While I prayed to God above
His strength was overpowering
And I knew it wasn't right
I'll hate myself forever
That I put up too little fight
I have other names I go by
Call me slut and call me whore
But I hated every moment
Never once did I want more
I'm left to pick up the pieces
Each day I see the cost
When I look into the mirror
My innocence is forever lost

Her third journal had several Post-it notes. I only made it part way through the first one. I couldn't go any further. It was too personal, too painful. I felt I was intruding in her private hell, even though she'd invited me.

June 6, 1981

> *Brandon tried again to get me to go 'there' tonight. It would have been so easy. His parents and his brothers and sisters were all up in Bear Lake for the weekend. We had his house to ourselves for once. I really want to do it. We love each other and it feels right. All our friends are doing it. It's time. But I just can't. I'm so screwed up about sex. And I know why. It's amazing that something that happened over 8 years ago still affects me. But it does. I don't know what to do about it. I don't have a single person in the world to talk to about it. I want it to be a beautiful thing when it happens. It's still so very ugly to me . . .*

I had read enough. It was 10:30 p.m., but I didn't hesitate to call Vanessa.

"Hi." Her voice sounded tentative. I suspected her tears had resumed after I left.

"Oh, my God, V. I have no words that could possibly convey my sorrow. I can't even imagine . . . ." I literally had no words.

"It sometimes seems like a bad dream to me. I just never wake up from it."

"Can I come over? I know it's late, but I want to just hold you, love you. Something. I feel so helpless right now."

"I appreciate it, but I honestly don't have it in me tonight. Can we get together after work tomorrow? I'll fill in all the blanks. The journals only give a little glimpse."

"Yeah, let's meet tomorrow. I just want to say one thing tonight. You wondered if I'd still want to be with you after knowing your secrets. You need to know that I love you more than ever, and I'm not going anywhere."

"Thank you," she mustered through her tears. "I love you."

I wasn't going anywhere. Regrettably, I would soon find out that *she* was.

Chapter 30

But we carry on our back the burdens time always reveals
In the lonely light of morning, in the wound that would not heal.
It's the bitter taste of losing everything I've held so dear.

Fallen—Sarah McLachlan

VANESSA CHOSE TO MEET ME THE FOLLOWING EVENING at Sugar House Park. The large expanse of green space sits adjacent to Highland High School, her alma mater, and not far from her childhood home. Perhaps she found comfort in returning to her old stomping grounds. I spotted her near our rendezvous point, at the edge of Parley's Creek, sitting on a large rock, with her toes dipped into the gentle stream. She wore a floral-patterned sun dress and was illuminated by the tiny bit of sunlight that penetrated the shade, provided by the canopy of tall trees that lined the water's edge. I stood and watched her for a moment. She was deep in thought and unaware of me standing a short distance away. Despite the hell that was churning on the inside, she looked more beautiful than at any time since we met. My heart both swelled and ached for her.

We embraced in silence as I took my place beside her on the boulder. Words were futile in this tender moment. Our hug ended, and we sat there for several minutes, mesmerized by the sound of the rushing water and the sight of the filtered sunshine glistening off its surface. She spoke the first words, abruptly going back in time, over forty years ago.

"I've blocked so much of it over time, but I was eight years-old when the abuse started. I'm not even going to mention his name. As you read in the journals, he was my uncle on my mom's side. He lived here in Salt Lake at the time, married with two kids. My cousins were close in age, so we hung out a lot together. I was over at their house all the time. My aunt Vickie was a nurse, so she always worked different shifts and wasn't home a lot. It started during that summer when my mom and dad went to Africa for almost a month on some sort of humanitarian mission, like Doctors Without Borders, but with a different name that I can't remember. My cousin, Carli, was at a dance camp for a week and my other cousin, Scott, was always off with friends. Vickie was working long hours, so I was alone a lot with him."

She said the word *him* with complete disdain.

"I do remember that it was gradual. We played these stupid games where he got to see some of my body, and he showed me his. I remember his tone was very sweet and gentle. I was too young to recognize how creepy it must have been. Things progressed; he always told me it was all right and normal. And then it escalated to full on child rape. All the other words that sugarcoat it really piss me off. *Molestation* isn't even a harsh enough term for it."

She paused to collect herself. I was in dire need of composure myself. The tears forming in my eyes went hand-in-hand with the sick feeling in the pit of my stomach. I honestly couldn't even begin to comprehend such darkness and depravity.

"Over the next three years, he continued raping me every chance he got. The bastard was such a master manipulator and opportunist.

He created so many occasions for being alone with me, and no one was the wiser. Like I wrote in that English assignment you read, he hid in plain sight, playing the role of such a nice guy and this sweet, doting uncle. It was our little secret, this special thing between us. I hated it and deep down knew it wasn't normal, but I was so young and was easily manipulated. I started to try and get out of ever being with him, but my parents insisted and he was pretty much my main babysitter. I don't think they realized how little Vickie was around, with her crazy schedule. He made me afraid to tell my parents, spinning it somehow that I'd be the one in trouble if I ever shared our secret. The son of a bitch knew what he was doing.

"I suspect he was probably abusing Carli, too, but it's something that we have never talked about. And we won't ever. I'll tell you why in a minute. The rape continued until I was eleven. I was growing up, getting bratty, and more independent. I think he was afraid I was nearing the age where I wouldn't play along anymore. So, it finally stopped. Then he moved. I was the happiest person in the world when I found out that they were moving to Tulsa. He worked at the Chevron refinery in North Salt Lake and got a promotion to relocate to Oklahoma. A hospital there hired Vickie, so they started packing. We hosted this big farewell dinner for them, and my mom grounded me for a week for being rude by running off with my friends and missing the final goodbye. There was no way in hell I was going to hug that monster goodbye."

Vanessa hadn't made much eye contact with me while she recounted the horrors of her childhood. She stared blankly at the stream, speaking matter-of-factly, only allowing emotion to flavor her speech on occasion. She continued.

"I kind of tucked it all away in this little box and tried to forget about it. That worked for a couple of years. But then I hit Jr. High, hormones started kicking in, my girlfriends got into boys, and I was suddenly being bombarded by these awful memories. I felt so different from my friends. Religious guilt kicked in, like I had done something wrong, like I was unclean and unworthy in the eyes of God. I stopped going to church. It was a huge point of contention with Mom for a long time. My dad never attended, so he supported me. She eventually gave up and even stopped going herself. We had some rough years. I felt a lot of resentment toward her. I thought that she somehow knew. As I read about the subject later, I learned that my uncle was probably abused himself, and I assumed he might have molested my mom when they were younger. He was five years older, so that made sense. She later claimed that he never touched her and had no idea that he was capable of doing such vile things, or she'd have never left me alone with him. I eventually let go of any bitterness or hostility toward my mom, recognizing that our relationship was just another victim in this horrible story.

"During high school and into college, I recognized a pattern of not being able to sustain normal relationships with guys. I was a mess. There was a lot of self-sabotage, anxiety, guilt, low self-esteem, unhealthy views of intimacy, all the textbook stuff. I've failed at almost every relationship I've ever had with a man. I want to break the pattern." She paused. "I desperately don't want to fail with you."

Her tear-filled eyes found mine. I finally understood the indescribable message that they had been sending since I first gazed into them. They had exuded sadness, fear, and doubt, accompanied by much love, tenderness, and hope. But in that moment, I saw incredible determination. I finally spoke.

"You won't fail, because you aren't alone. I'm here with you."

She quickly looked away and was silent for a moment. Her response was not at all what I expected. She again picked up her story where she'd left off.

"It was near the end of my sophomore year in college when it all finally boiled over. I'd just broken up with a guy I dated for a few months, and then I simply went off the deep end. I had several one-night stands and was basically using men to self-medicate, or something like that. Again, these were all textbook actions for someone in my shoes. A sorority sister pulled me aside one night and told me she was really worried about my behavior. She flat out asked if I'd been sexually abused when I was younger. I denied it. She didn't believe me and then revealed that she had been abused herself and had gone through a very promiscuous period in her life. She'd recognized the similar warning signs in my wild conduct. She was a lifesaver. I finally got some help and went to a counselor she recommended. I was still on my parent's insurance, there was no privacy back then, so they knew something was up.

"After a few sessions, I found some inner strength and wanted to relieve myself of the burden of carrying this secret for so long. I finally sat down and told my parents what had happened to me. And shit totally hit the fan. My dad believed me immediately, but it took the initial shock to wear off for my mom to believe me, too.

"Dad went completely ballistic, called my uncle, and threatened, at the minimum, to send him to prison and, at worst, to kill him. Things got so ugly. Of course, he denied it. My dad had his lawyer look into it. Back then the statute of limitations in Utah was four years after a victim's 18th birthday. I was still within that window. I wasn't sure if I wanted to do anything legally or what was even best for my healing. My dad kind of hijacked the whole thing from me and started talking about different actions to take without really asking me. He went nuts. We were in the midst of trying to figure out whether to press charges when we were informed that my uncle had put a bullet in his head." She delivered that line with cold detachment. I found her tone chilling, yet I understood.

"Oh, God," was all I could say.

"Yeah, just what I needed. Another thing to screw me up even more. Sorry if that sounds incredibly selfish, but when you're just barely surviving, everything is about you. Part of me was relieved. His death gave me a little closure in knowing he'd never touch anyone else ever again, but the eventual guilt that came with it was almost more than I could take. It totally blew up our extended family. My mom and her siblings never quite recovered. I've hardly spoken to my cousins since, so I'll never know if Carli was abused, too. Vickie sent me the most heartfelt letter about five years after his suicide. His name was Ted, by the way. In her letter she pleaded with me to not carry any more guilt regarding his death, and that she truly believed me. It was an incredible gesture, and I'll always love and adore that woman for her amazing kindness and strength."

Vanessa suggested we get out of the shade so we walked a short distance and found a spot to sit on the grass in the warm sun that was going down in the west.

"I never told you how my dad died. It was about three months after Ted's suicide when he suffered a massive stroke that left him almost completely debilitated," her voice began to tremble. I held her hand while she continued. "We had to put him in this rehabilitation center. My healthy, proud, strong, indestructible father; my hero, my protector, couldn't even feed himself." She began to sob, reliving the scene as if it were yesterday. "He slowly withered away.

"I visited him every day for nine months until the day he died. I can still see his eyes. His body was failing him, but his soul was still so very strong, and the only way he could demonstrate that strength was through his eyes. There was so much love in his eyes but sorrow, too—not for his own state of being, but for me. He was telling me with his eyes how sorry he was that he hadn't been able to protect me. I would talk to him and tell him repeatedly that I was going to be all right, not to worry about me, and not blame himself. I think he held on until he finally believed that his little girl would be okay. I miss him dearly. I carry around so much guilt about his death. I'm convinced that he wouldn't have suffered that stroke had I not told them about what my uncle did to me. I've had to live with that every day since."

No words were spoken as we caught the tail end of a stunning September sunset. She tried to lighten the moment.

"So, I'll bet you're so glad you decided to stalk me on *Facebook* after I disappeared from *Tinder*. Such a simple, uncomplicated woman, with no baggage," she joked, smiling for the first time.

"Yeah, it sucks how you can't chose who you fall in love with," I played along for a moment. "You've been through so much but you've also shown remarkable resilience." She smiled appreciatively, then dove back into her tragic tale.

"Anyway, I continued going to therapy for a few months after my dad died. Then I met my first husband at the U, got married, had a kid and got busy. I stopped getting help and just tried to push that dark stuff out of my life. I talked myself into pretending that it never happened. But that little box full of secrets was never very far away, and I'm certain the fact that I never truly dealt with it affected both my marriages. And I admit to still being messed up. It was quite apparent from going through all those family photo albums and my journals that I still need a lot of help. And do you know what the final straw was for me to push me to finally get help?"

"What?" I asked, clueless as to where she was going with this.

"It was the song you wrote for me. You were being way too kind. I'm not *Untamed*; I'm unwell. I'm quite broken, Jamison. And I realized that I've been subconsciously keeping you at arms-length. I'm afraid to fail again, and I honestly doubt my ability to succeed because giving all of me is essential in making a relationship work. I don't have one hundred percent of me to give. Those lyrics made me realize how incomplete I am, how inadequate I am as a partner."

I was shaking my head No, but she was correcting me by nodding Yes. She finished her thought.

"Your song showed me how much you really love me. I recognize that I have something here; someone who is worth fighting for."

The grass felt cool on her bare legs, so Vanessa suggested we finish our talk in her car.

"I've decided to get some help. I didn't go into work today. I was online looking at therapists and reading reviews. I've got my first appointment with a good one on Thursday. I'm going to give this every bit of my focus and energy. I'm going to put in the work and become whole again." She sounded so determined.

"I hope you know I'll be here for you, every step of the way, as much as you want me to be." I was just as determined to help her through this grueling process.

"I need to talk to you about that." Her tone was cautionary. "I've been thinking about this all day. I need to do this alone. I know you. You'll want to be my wonderful knight in shining armor, and

I love you for that; I really do. But I can't have a crutch. I can't have a safety net. And among my many lovely issues, a huge one is that I don't do well in relationships. I don't believe I can be in a relationship while I figure out how to be able to be in a successful one, if that makes any sense." She started to tear up.

I was momentarily deflated, the ego portion of me, that is. But my wise, old soul quickly seized control and, in a voice much louder than the usual whisper, told me in no uncertain terms that her strategy was absolutely the correct one. The fear of the unknown was hard to set aside, however. Vanessa read my mind.

"I am not breaking up with you—far from it. I'm doing what I need to do to make it work with you. I want this. I want you. I'm just not ready for you, not how I am right now." She spoke with such sincerity and conviction. "My family will be my support group. Things with them are uncomplicated, and there are no romantic entanglements involved. I feel deep in my soul that this path gives me the best chance of getting where I need to be. Time and space will help me focus on healing. I hope and pray you understand."

There was still much to say and ground rules yet to be figured out. But I spoke the only words that mattered in the moment.

"I do, love. I do."

Chapter 31

As daylight fades, the nights grow cold.
The sun slips away and I let go.
This is one summer, I can't wait to end.
On this moonless night, you call to me.

Everywhere—Jamison Barrick/Emily Paich

THE GROUND RULES VANESSA LAID OUT WERE SIMPLE ENOUGH, yet incredibly difficult to live by. We wouldn't see each other, but we would talk weekly on the phone to stay connected and so she could share updates on her progress if that didn't impede her treatment. She admitted to not really knowing what she was doing and assured me that this arrangement was just as hard on her as it was on me. I believed her. After a couple of sessions, she received confirmation from her therapist that some separation wasn't a bad strategy. She felt great relief in knowing that her decision had been a sound one, though it didn't make it easier on either of us.

One of the first people I called after our 'breakup that wasn't really a breakup', was my sister in California. Jean had a Masters in social work and was experienced in the ugly arena of child sex abuse. I was seeking her professional opinion in strict confidence. I explained the situation and gave her some background, hoping to receive an informed opinion regarding how long this process might take. She was candid with me and cautioned me not to get my hopes up for quick results from the therapy. There was a massive amount of damage for Vanessa to deal with, and it was going to take time and a lot of work. She wished the best for Vanessa and for me, as well, but felt confident in the ability of someone to heal from even the worst scars that life can inflict. I hoped she was right.

I, predictably, moped around for a few weeks with no idea if this was just a temporary break and better days with Vanessa were over the horizon, or if it was the beginning of the end. One night while working on a new song with Emily, she tried to snap me out of it.

"You need a road trip!" she proclaimed. "And I know just the place."

She had been planning a trip to Nashville to see an old college girlfriend and suggested I tag along for part of the vacation set for late November.

"Fly out with me and meet Amber. We'll probably ditch you for most of the time, but there will be plenty for you to do. The Predators might be in town." She knew I was a huge hockey fan. "Amber knows a friend of a friend who is in the music business. Maybe we could meet with her to learn a little about the business and how to get discovered or sell our songs. Apparently, this lady finds musicians and gets songs wrangled for that TV show, Nashville."

"I thought it was canceled." I was aware that they showcased several new songs each episode, and the show had created a bit of a cottage-industry for aspiring songwriters trying to get their music out there.

"ABC did, but it got picked up on cable; the CMT network, I think."

"That would be cool to at least learn the ropes," I admitted. "Let me think about it. You are right. I could use a little change of scenery."

We were working on a new song that I'd originally started in April. I struggled all summer with the void that my mom had left in my life, and one night I sat down to finish the song, about the loss of a loved one. After penning the initial verses and coming up with the guitar chords for the entire song, I decided to take it to Emily to round out the lyrics. It would be our first Lennon/McCartney-style song—a true collaboration. We decided to take the advice of our one-time songwriting instructor and expand on the theme of the song to make it more universal, more appealing, and relatable. It would be a song about loss in terms of a lover, in the sense of a doomed relationship.

I obviously had some fresh material for inspiration with the sudden departure of Vanessa from most of my life, and Emily used her most recent breakup as her muse. Together we created a beautiful song that had deep meaning for both of us. The song was completed that evening. We decided it would be inserted into our set list for any upcoming open mic nights.

The next day, I Googled the various attractions that Nashville offered. It looked like an amazing town with a vibrant music scene, even though country wasn't my thing. It appeared to be the exact kind of place to pitch a song like *Vinyl and Bourbon Nights*. And the local NHL team was in town during the dates that Emily had chosen. I was all in. I needed to get the hell out of Dodge. It was all part of my master plan to stay busy, not wait by the phone and continue with living my own life while Vanessa was figuring out hers. That was my recipe to maintain my sanity.

Of course, I kept a concerned eye on Vanessa through our weekly phone call. She indicated she was making decent progress, seeing her therapist two times a week. We kept our conversations from getting sentimental and emotional, figuring there was little sense in complicating things with that. Our relationship was truly in a holding pattern. We were not feeding the fire. It was bound to become just a flicker. The subject of me dating never came up. Knowing Vanessa, she would have never put any restrictions on me, but I had no desire to see anyone else. I wanted to see it through, as long as that was her desire, too.

I went ahead and bought my airfare to Nashville, which wasn't cheap as the trip was scheduled over the long Thanksgiving weekend. The NHL's Predators were hosting the St. Louis Blues on Friday night, so I bought a nice seat on StubHub. Emily would be staying with her friend, Amber, so I booked a hotel downtown, within walking distance from everything. The room wasn't cheap, either. The trip was about to get much more expensive. Emily called me a few weeks before we were scheduled to leave.

"We should probably take a guitar with us in case we can meet with that agent I told you about. Do you want to pack one or shall I?"

"I'm glad you brought that up. I'm actually considering buying one while I'm there, so I'd only have to check it on the return flight."

"Do you realize you might have a little guitar problem?" She asked, half joking.

"Yes, I do. And admitting it is the first step. There is this amazing guitar shop on Broadway, and I thought it would be cool to buy one in Nashville. I've had my eye on a nice Martin, anyway. And besides, without an actual current girlfriend, I've got to spend my disposable income on something."

"Oh, you boys and your toys. I'm actually happy for you. That'll be fun, and you'll have a great story attached to that guitar. Okay, I won't worry about packing one, but I'll work on getting a meeting set up with that agent. I can't wait!"

She didn't have to wait long. Time flew by the fall of 2016. Work was busy, the gym beckoned me on days when it was too cold to ride my bike, and Emily and I performed at another open mic event before we left for Nashville; this time at a coffee shop. We dropped *Stay in the Light* from the set list and added the new song, *Everywhere*. I was much more nervous with an actual coffee-purchasing audience than our casual Meet up friends. Kiara, Tyler, Bailey, and Cole all came to support us. I think the girls were proud of their dad for pursuing a passion. We received generous applause from the crowd as we wrapped up the set with *Vinyl and Bourbon Nights*. I was becoming addicted to this new passion and having a blast. Bring on Nashville.

I had my gang over for Thanksgiving dinner the night before the official turkey day. The kids were all heading to Palisade, Colorado the next day for mountain biking and wine-tasting, and I was hitting the road myself. It was difficult not having Mom around for the holiday, providing me another good reason to leave town. I could already foresee a rough first Christmas without a living parent there for me. I had a wonderful evening with my family, and it was made even more special when Bailey and Cole revealed that they were engaged and planning a May wedding. I broke out some of my very best bourbon to toast them, a nice bottle of Four Roses single barrel. I'd been saving it for a worthy occasion, and this moment definitely qualified.

Vanessa had flown to Virginia a few days earlier to spend Thanksgiving with her daughter and her husband and, of course, her little Marcus. She was glad to get a little break from her therapy sessions and recharge her batteries among family. She seemed excited for my Nashville trip and never said as much, but must have been relieved to see that I was keeping busy and not waiting on her. That factored into my strategy. I figured the last thing she needed was to worry about me. Her plate was full.

Emily took an early flight out but I elected to take a later one. I had something to attend to before leaving town. I'd been playing in a football game with my college track buddies since we attended the University of Utah over thirty years ago, and I wasn't going to miss this year. Nashville could wait a few hours. The game represents one of the longest traditions I celebrate in my life, and I'd only missed a few over the decades when Thanksgiving weekend youth soccer tournaments took me out of town. We used to play tackle, but now we wisely play touch, in sunshine or a snowstorm. This year it was dry but cold.

It was great to see my friends, and for a couple of hours it seemed like we were back in time, in the prime of our youth, forever young. Among the many things I'm thankful for, I must include my long-time friends, this yearly gathering, and my good health to still be able to play a kid's game.

~ ♡ ~

After a quick shower, change of clothes, and an Uber to the airport, I was sitting on a plane bound for Tennessee and excited to see what kind of fun awaited me in Music City. There would definitely be many sights, sounds, and delights to experience, but there would also be an unexpected temptation awaiting me, another one of life's curve balls thrown my way. As any good batter knows, the pitch that strikes you out is the one you didn't see coming.

Everywhere

As daylight fades,
The nights grow cold.
The sun slips away and I let go.
This is one summer
I can't wait to end.
On this moonless night,
You call to me.

(Chorus)

Everywhere I go, I'll see you.
Everywhere you go, I'll be there.
Everywhere I go, I'll feel you.
Do you feel me?

Everywhere.
I'll be there.
Oh, baby,
Do you feel me?

I always knew you'd walk away.
We lived inside this fairy tale;
Our hearts frozen,
Longing for a way.
How can I lose
What was never mine?

(Repeat Chorus)

(Bridge)

I can't tell you
All I want to say.
You will never know
All that I feel.
What we had
Is so far away from real
When you lose your fear,
And you're free;
Find me.

I hear voices inside my head
Saying things better left unsaid.
There's nothing left to say
To change your mind,
So, for now . . . I'll just fly.

(Repeat Chorus)

Everywhere . . .
I'll be there.

Chapter 32

Save me from the dark of night.
I'm drifting like a satellite,
Miles from understanding
Where this love will lead.
Heaven let your light fall down on me.

Worlds Apart—Jude Cole

THERE WAS A LIGHT RAIN FALLING WHEN I LANDED IN NASHVILLE, but it was still a good twenty degrees warmer than when I left Utah. I was now able to cross Tennessee off my list of the few states I hadn't yet visited. I hoped to visit Alaska, Minnesota, and Vermont soon but, because of Uncle Ted, I was not in any rush to step foot in Oklahoma. My Uber driver was friendly and gave me several sightseeing recommendations upon hearing it was my first time in Music City.

I checked into the downtown Sheraton and immediately set out on foot to meet Emily and her friend Amber. We had chosen to gather at *Roberts Western World* on Broadway to catch some live music, eat some barbecue, and drink some whiskey. Emily spotted me before I could see her in the large crowd, and I was quickly introduced to her old college roommate. Amber was an outgoing redhead who swore like a sailor and had a strong southern drawl.

We hit it off immediately. The band was playing authentic, old-school country music.

"None of that crossover pop shit," Amber shouted out her musical preference.

"We are buying drinks all night for Amber," Emily announced. "We have a meeting set up on Saturday afternoon with that agent, thanks to her."

"Sweet!" I chimed in. "I guess I better buy that guitar tomorrow."

"Are you getting it at *Gruhn's*?" Amber asked, and I nodded. "If you're a guitar junkie, you're going to love that place and won't want to leave."

"Yeah, he's got a little addiction problem. How many will this one make?" Emily already knew the answer, but I held up five fingers for Amber's benefit, with a shrug. I changed the subject.

"So, tell us about the agent—and thanks for setting this up."

"You bet! She's a friend of one of my good friends and is kind of doing this as a favor to her. Works for the TV show Nashville, among other things. I've met her a couple of times. You'll like her. Name's Regan Waters. She's a pretty southern belle. If nothing else, she can educate you two about the business."

"I'm not leaving town until we have a record contract," Emily joked.

"What are you two drinking?" I asked the ladies, who needed a refill.

"Jack and Coke," Amber answered for them both. "I'm kinda partial to the local brand."

I liked Amber. She kept us thoroughly amused the rest of the night.

———♡———

I was on my own the next day, free to roam Nashville at will. I decided to take in the sights before purchasing the guitar. Broadway seemed to have as many coffee shops as bars. I got my caffeine fix at *Casablanca Coffee* while I mapped out my day with help from some brochures I got at the hotel. I was initially reluctant to visit the Country Music Hall of Fame but I was glad I did. Even though country isn't my cup of tea musically, I was fascinated by the history and the imprint that the genre made on the American music scene; especially its influence on the evolution of the guitar. It was well worth the visit. I strolled down Broadway with the sound of music and the smell of southern cuisine wafting onto the city's main boulevard. I then walked along the Cumberland River before taking a tour of the historic Ryman Theater. I had to pop into *Third Man Records*, being the vinyl junkie that I am. For lunch, I enjoyed some incredible ribs at *Jack's BBQ*. When in Rome, right? I was painfully aware of the fact that I was likely to gain several pounds on this trip.

It was finally time to check out *Gruhn's Guitars*. I was like a kid in a candy store, feasting my eyes on the largest inventory of guitars I'd ever seen. The second floor contained the rare treasures. Some of the vintage Martin collectibles were in the five and even six-figure range.

I came back down to earth and the first floor and focused on my purchase. I sampled several models and couldn't help but be intimidated by the ability of the others strumming to the left and right of me. One kid, no older than ten, was blowing me out of the water with his picking prowess. I sheepishly narrowed down my choices by softly strumming a few Barrick originals on two guitars I really liked. I settled on a sweet-sounding Martin dreadnaught made from mahogany. She was an absolute beauty.

I must admit, walking back to my hotel room, carrying a guitar case, made me feel like I was a country music star for a moment. The passersby had no clue that I was merely a hack. I played with my new toy for a good hour before hopping into the shower and changing for the hockey game.

The Bridgestone Arena was a short walk from the hotel. I decided to eat there, guessing correctly that some outstanding items would be on the menu at the concession stands. The hockey game was exceptional, with the local Preds defeating the Blues in OT. I only get the equivalent of double-A hockey in Salt Lake, so anytime I can catch an NHL game, I'm in heaven.

I spent a good part of the next day catching some live music at several bars that line Broadway. I was seeking some inspiration ahead of our meeting at 4 p.m. with a bona fide Nashville agent. We planned to meet in my hotel room where it would be quiet, and we could play for her. Emily and Amber got there an hour early so we could rehearse and go over everything we were hoping to accomplish from the meeting. There was a knock at four o'clock sharp. I opened the door and was treated to my first look at the stunning Regan Waters.

She stood just barely less than six feet tall, most of it legs that were quite visible under her short skirt and unbuttoned knee-length coat. She wore very little makeup, letting her natural beauty shine through. Her shoulder-length, auburn hair framed a pretty face and unusually green eyes stood out among her many attractive features. I guessed her to be in her forties, confident and comfortable in her own skin. But the most enchanting part of her was revealed when she spoke.

"You must be Mr. Barrick." Her southern accent damn near did me in, sounding like how I remembered Vivien Leigh's voice from *Gone with the Wind*.

"And you must be Regan Waters. Thanks so much for meeting with us." I tried to sound like Clark Gable. I took her coat for her like a proper southern gentleman.

Amber hugged Regan, introduced her to Emily before opening a bottle of, fittingly, Gentleman Jack, and preparing some glasses for us. Regan proposed a toast.

"To your first time in Nashville and to your music!"

We got comfortable in the chairs and on the edge of the bed while Regan told us about her background, including her work procuring new music for *Nashville*. Shooting for season five was nearing completion, and the first episode was set to premier in two weeks. The success of the new season would determine whether the network would pick up another.

She took us through the process of becoming discovered, which was what Emily wanted, and the ins and outs of selling songs, which was more my dream. She tutored us on the publishing process, copyright laws, and the necessity to record a quality demo, indicating that there were several studios in town that specialized in demo recoding.

"Enough of that, let's hear some of your tunes," Regan suggested.

She could have been ordering a colonoscopy, and with that sweet voice and accent of hers, I would have eagerly complied. Instead, I took my Martin out of her case (guitars are feminine, I've concluded) and checked the tuning while the ladies all admired my pretty, new baby.

Emily and I went through our most current set while Regan recorded the audio on her phone. Amber tapped her toes enthusiastically, providing us with a rhythm section. We ended, as usual, with *Vinyl and Bourbon Nights*.

"I like them all! You two have potential." Regan was being kind. "That last one was snappy. I could imagine a few male country stars singing it. I just hear a man singing that song for some reason. Many of them don't write their own lyrics, so you just never know." Inwardly, I was beaming.

We showed Regan several more songs we'd printed up. She

seemed impressed by our lyrics or was simply being nice to a couple of novices from Utah.

"I won't take these copies with me because you sweet things haven't copyrighted them yet. My first piece of advice, don't go trusting anyone in this business. Get these copyrighted, record yourselves some quality demos with a full band backing you, and I'll see what I can do for you. Y'all are sweet, and I'd love to help."

Regan suggested we all catch a little live music together on our last night in town. Emily and Amber were heading to nearby Franklin to meet friends, but I was definitely free. After saying goodbye to the girls, she led us to a bar close to the hotel. She'd chosen it since it was more a locals' hangout and not as crazy or loud like the bars on Broadway. We settled into a booth back from the stage and ordered some appetizers and bourbon. The band was more rock than country, which was fine by me.

We talked about music at first, and she shared her honest assessment of our songs. She felt Emily had some work to do to cut through the thousands of similar female voices. She described a world full of Taylor Swift sound-alikes and wannabes. A successful female vocalist needed to be unique to stand out from all the others. She used Adele as an example. In her words, I "have a good way with a line," and she thought my songs had potential. The trick was to match the lyrics with the perfect recording artist. And that's what she did for a living and wanted to help. I was very encouraged.

I was also quite enchanted by her personality and mannerisms. We clicked rather nicely. Had it been a real first date, it would have been one of the more comfortable and enjoyable ones I'd ever had. The conversation came easily and the laughter flowed. And that accent. And those green eyes. And those legs . . . *Is that the bourbon talking?*

We swapped tales and life stories. She was forty-nine with a daughter who was a freshman at Louisville. She was happily divorced. We shared photos of our kids on our phones and complimented each other's excellent genetic makeup. She'd been to Utah a couple of times, once to visit southern Utah's red rock country and another time for a ski vacation in Park City. She eventually asked if I was in a relationship. Tough question under normal circumstances, even more so with a nice buzz going and a beautiful woman sitting across from me.

"Kind of. Not really. It's complicated," was my honest reply.

"Well, from where I'm sitting, she's a bit of a fool for allowing you to describe your relationship in such uncertain terms. If she were me, I'd be getting nothing but a 'hell yes' out of you."

I wasn't about to go into the details regarding Vanessa. Other than my sister, no one else knew the specifics of our taking a break—not even Emily. I kept my response simple.

"Thanks. And your ex is a bit of a fool himself."

"That, he most definitely is," she said with a modest smile.

Damn, there was strong chemistry brewing in our booth. We ordered another round and continued getting to know each other better. I was extremely happy I'd decided to visit Nashville.

Regan excused herself at one point to visit the ladies' room, and I pulled out my phone to check the time. It was almost midnight. Time flies when you're having fun. I had a text from Emily.

I hope you two are having fun. Enjoy and remember that you are technically a single man! :-)

I wasn't sure about that, but I did know that I was a slightly tipsy man and my lovely companion was feeling pretty good herself. She sat back down and just looked at me from across the table, smiling and saying nothing for a long moment.

"How about we go back to your room, and you strum a little for me on that new, gorgeous Martin of yours." The implication was very clear.

I thought of Emily's text, which led me to think about Vanessa. I had not seen her in almost three months. In that moment she seemed light years away.

"Why not?" I replied.

Regan took my hand as we left the bar. The cool humid night hit my skin, and I shivered slightly.

We walked into the hotel lobby and got on the elevator alone. As soon as the doors closed, she leaned into me and our lips met. We kissed passionately until the doors opened on the 11th floor. We were about half way down the hallway to my room when I suddenly stopped. I turned and faced Regan.

"I'm sorry. I'd really love to but I just can't. I'm sorry I let it get this far along. Kind of shitty of me."

"Don't be sorry, darlin'. I got a little caught up in things myself. I don't normally do this kind of thing, jumping in like this. And I never mix business and pleasure. I guess I kind of like you."

"The feeling is very mutual, believe me. I guess my situation back home isn't that complicated after all, at least my feelings for her, if that makes any sense."

"It does. Damn," she sighed. "And then you had to go and be a decent man, too. Timing is everything."

"Don't I know that, Regan. Do you think it's possible to maintain our professional relationship after this, umm, near miss? I'd still love to work with you."

"Of course, Mr. Barrick. I'd love to stay in touch. And if that gal back home doesn't lock you up soon, well, you just never know." She smiled and kissed me on the cheek. "I better get me an Uber."

"I'll go with you until it shows up." We walked toward the elevator.

"Such a gentleman, too." She wrapped her arm around mine on the way down.

We exchanged phone numbers before her driver pulled up. Before she got in the car, we hugged, and she looked back and spoke in that irresistible southern accent.

"Write a song about tonight and that beautiful near miss, okay? You've already got your title."

"You can count on it." I watched until the car had turned the corner and was out of sight.

Chapter 33

Well, some say life will beat you down,
Break your heart, steal your crown.
So, I've started out for God knows where;
I guess I'll know when I get there.

Learning to Fly—Tom Petty and The Heartbreakers

"HI! HOW WAS NASHVILLE?" It was comforting to hear Vanessa's voice at the other end of my call.

"It was fun." *Almost too fun.* "I'm at the airport now. How was Thanksgiving with your daughter and her hubby? Or did you even notice them?" I was only half joking, knowing that being Marcus' grandma was her greatest joy in life.

"Oh, I noticed them a little. Dan was busy studying, so I got a lot of time with just Britt and Marcus. I don't want to leave for home tomorrow. He grows up too much in between the times I see him."

"Christmas will be here soon, so I doubt he'll be driving a car or growing facial hair by then." I could always make her laugh, and that sound was one of the many things I missed about her. We were still connected enough to sense what the other was feeling in the moment.

"I miss you," she said. I could hear raw emotion in her voice. "Would you like to grab a cup of coffee before the holidays get too crazy for me? I'd love to see you."

"I'd like that very much." I could have said so much more, but my tone in those few words packed a punch.

"I'm sorry for all this time apart. I know how hard this has been on you. I wouldn't blame you at all if you gave up on me and moved on with your life." There was sadness and uncertainty in her voice.

"Don't be sorry. I'm pretty certain it's been much harder on you than me. I admire your bravery in dealing with your issues from the past. I know things like this take time. I'm not going anywhere. If you haven't scared me off by now, I doubt you will." We both laughed at that.

"Good point." Her serious voice returned. "I just need you to know that I'd understand if you did. I love you too much to ever hold you back."

If only I could have told her about last night, and that my love for her was quite sufficient in doing just that by itself.

"Well, thanks for your concern, but unless you are trying to get rid of me, I'm fine right where I am for now. And I love you more than you know. I can't wait to see you." That *for now* part kind of slipped out.

"Me, too. I love you. And no, I'm not trying to get rid of you. For now," she added with a cute laugh. *Damn, the girl didn't miss a thing!*

Vanessa chose to meet me at a *Starbucks* the Saturday morning after our company *Winter Solstice Luau.* I assumed she picked a neutral and safe spot to avert any fireworks that could have potentially exploded had we met at either of our houses. Even so, our embrace was long and emotional, and we were probably being judged for an excessive public display of affection. We didn't give a damn. She looked even more beautiful than the last time I saw her, taking my breath away when she walked in.

"Wow. You look amazing; even better than those pics on my phone and my distant memories."

"Thank you, sir. And you are looking great yourself. You've lost some hair, though." Her smile lit up the room and warmed my heart. Her eyes had a fresh sparkle to them.

"Well, I've kind of got this girlfriend who makes me pull my hair out."

"Ouch. I guess I deserved that," she chuckled.

We ordered our coffee and found an empty booth. I quickly scanned my surroundings, trying to spot any first-time *Tinder* daters. I didn't miss those days at all.

"I have an early Christmas present for you." She handed me a wrapped package. Its shape gave it away.

"You shouldn't have," I feigned. But I was well prepared and pulled a small, wrapped box from my coat pocket. I also handed her a larger gift that I carried in with me. "This wasn't covered in our rule book, apparently." I smiled.

She insisted I open mine first. I was delighted to receive a special edition of Led Zeppelin's *Physical Graffiti* album on vinyl. It appeared to contain a bonus record. The neighbors on both sides of my condo would soon be hearing from the mighty Zepp.

"You shouldn't have, but I'm glad you did. This is awesome. Thanks! You know me well! Your turn. Open the small one first."

The small box contained some cute earrings I'd bought in Nashville. I had chosen well. Vanessa loved them. Slowly peeling back the wrapping on the second package revealed a white, leather-bound journal. She looked up, understanding its meaning even before I explained.

"I hope that you fill this one with nothing but wonderful memories."

Her eyes began to mist, and she got up and came around to my side of the booth to give me a kiss and a grateful hug.

"Thank you. You're amazing."

We were teetering on the brink of getting overly emotional, which would have created a scene but also possibly set us back in our attempt to give Vanessa her needed space. We reeled in our feelings and kept things rather generic for the rest of our time together, coming out unscathed with just a kiss by her car as we said goodbye and exchanged Christmas wishes. I didn't ask when we might see each other again. The last thing she needed was me hovering.

On the drive back home to put my new vinyl on my turntable, I concluded that this months-long separation had been one of the hardest experiences I'd ever faced in my life. And there were no guarantees of a happy ending. My self-pity was short-lived when I considered how difficult the entire process was for Vanessa. I gave myself a disgusted look in my rearview mirror.

The holidays were difficult. I missed my mom and my dad. I finally got around to grieving his passing, something I'd set aside while trying to comfort and care for Mom. I was still coming to grips with the fact that I no longer had either of them to call when I needed an answer to something I didn't know. As a new member of *generation next*, I certainly didn't have all the answers for my daughters.

Aside from the joyous time I spent with the girls and their guys, this Christmas was quite somber and even a little lonely. A pretty, mahogany Martin guitar under my tree offered some solace. I imagined a day in the future when I would bequeath it to a grandchild starting out on his or her own musical adventure.

On Christmas night, I was contemplating the circle of life when a text chimed on my phone. A long, lost name appeared on the screen. Kate Campania.

Hi! I know it's been forever, but I wanted to wish you a Merry
Christmas. I know it's the first one without your mom. Just wanted
you to know that I am thinking about you and hope this finds you
well. *Buon Natale!*

Merry Christmas! I have been missing my mom. Thanks for your kind
words. I hope things are great in your world. Tell Sean hi for me.

He says hi back. Maybe we can grab a cup of coffee sometime and
catch up. It's been way too long.

What is it with coffee? No wonder there is a *Starbucks* on every
corner. My response was short and reflected my ambivalence.

That would be nice. It has been a while. *Buon Natale*, Kate.

Emily and I had been energized and excited about our
songwriting since our trip to Nashville. After the New Year, she got
into a nice groove writing new material. A new man in her life was
behind her inspiration. She warned him in advance that once a
week she got together with her songwriting partner to work on our
music. I met him one evening, and he seemed comfortable with
our arrangement. He must have deemed me harmless. I wasn't yet
sure if I approved of him for Emily. Time would tell.

I got a look of amusement and surprise when I pitched some
lyrics for a new song called *Near Miss*. It took a little while to
convince Emily that nothing had happened that one night between
me and Regan Waters. She seemed a little disappointed, but I was
glad I escaped mostly unscathed. I had texted Regan a few times
since the trip, keeping it cordial and professional. But I won't lie,
I've thought about that night more than once.

Instead of working on other new material, I wanted to focus on
getting some music paired with my songs that only consisted of
lyrics and needed my partner's more advanced musical talent to
pull it off. I shared several of my poems/wannabe songs with her.

Emily was especially intrigued when she read *The Spanish Steps*, so I gave her some background into the song's origin and how my parting words to Kate revolved around its lyrics.

"When was the last time you were in Italy?" she asked.

"I took the girls there before I met Anna; a quick week in Rome, Florence, and Venice. It was at least twelve, thirteen years ago."

"You need to go back! You should be in Rome for the Summer Solstice like in your song but without the girl." I hadn't told her that Kate had recently texted me out of the blue.

"It's been a while and my Italian is getting too rusty. Hmm. I just might." On a cold January night, summer in Rome sounded rather enticing.

"Are you and Vanessa ever getting back together? You could take her." Emily didn't know the details of our separation. I'd only revealed that Vanessa needed time 'to figure out some things.'

"Who knows? I'd be fine traveling alone. I don't mind that at all. Or maybe I can pick up Regan on the way." I winked.

"There is this great Instagram account that lists airfare deals. You should follow it, and see if anything for Rome pops up." I took note of the name and started following the account.

A few weeks later, I was scrolling through Instagram and noticed a post that indicated a very reasonable price for airfare to Rome and a few other European cities on American Airlines throughout the spring and early summer months. I searched flights to Rome and some offered a single, brief layover in each direction—Dallas outbound and Chicago inbound, under two hours in each city. Why not? It was anyone's guess as to where I'd be in my relationship with Vanessa by June. I needed to keep filling my life with fun experiences and adventures.

The low-fare calendar showed some great prices around the third week of June. *Why not be there for the Solstice?* It would have nothing to do with my song or with Kate. She was out of the picture. I liked the idea of being there on that date. It was also a good week to take a little time off work, as things generally slowed down in the summer. I took my Visa card from my wallet, and within minutes, I had booked my trip to Rome.

We often don't realize the ramifications of our decisions in the moment we make them. Time eventually reveals the outcome of all that we set in motion with our choices. Unbeknown to me, my several days in Rome would rank among the most pivotal times of my life.

Chapter 34

Drive me to where the sun dips in the sea,
The crash of the waves sets us free.
Beauty surrounds us, just you and me;
But your smile rivals all that I see

Highway 1—Jamison Barrick

MOMENTS AFTER SAYING GOODNIGHT TO JIMMY FALLON and turning off the lights, my phone lit up, playing Vanessa's ring tone. My first thought was that something was wrong.

"Hi," I answered.

"Sorry for calling so late. I hope I didn't wake you."

"You didn't. Is everything okay?"

"Yes, and no." She paused. "Things have been going very well with my therapy. I'm making so much progress. I think I've come a long way, but I know I still have miles to go."

When we'd talk weekly, usually on Sunday nights, she didn't go into much detail regarding her therapy. Our conversations were about work and our families, and, generally, were just a vehicle to stay in touch and somewhat connected.

"That all sounds very positive. What's the bad part?" I asked.

"I'm in dire need of a break. A reward if you will. I also really need to reconnect with you in a more meaningful way. I want to share with you all the growth I've experienced. Our weekly phone calls aren't enough. There's so much to say."

"What do you have in mind?"

"Well, I know this is completely out of character and breaks all my rules, but I'd like you to take me away for a long weekend." I hadn't seen this coming at all. "President's Day weekend is coming up next month. Do you have plans to go anywhere?"

"No, I haven't made any yet. But are you sure about this?"

"Yes, I think it would do me some good. I'd pay my share, of course, but I'd love it if you'd plan the entire trip and just pick me up and totally surprise me with the destination. Tell me the kind of clothes to pack, flip-flops or boots, shorts or a parka. I honestly don't have the energy to plan a trip. I trust you completely. Wherever you choose will be perfect. What do you think?"

"I think it's a great idea as long as you do. And I think I know just the place. Can you get off early on that Friday so we can get a jump on things?"

"Yep, no problem. Thank you so much. I literally can't wait. I really need this! Sorry to throw you a curve."

"Are you kidding? I need this, too, almost as much as you do. Just don't change your mind."

Another birthday came and went. I didn't let anyone make a big deal out of it. I insisted that our getaway would be my gift from Vanessa. I was treated to a fun sushi-making night with the kids at Kiara's house. Emily and I ate out after one of our jam sessions, and Abbey took me to *Morelia*. I told her that I bought my airfare to Rome and when I'd be flying out.

"Why did you pick those dates? Is there something you're not telling me? You haven't been talking to Kate, have you?" She knew all about the Spanish Steps, both the song and the tourist attraction.

"No reason in particular, and no, I'm not talking to Kate. I did get a Christmas text from her and one yesterday for my birthday. She has nothing to do with my trip or the dates I'll be there. Besides, things are looking up with Vanessa. We are going on a little weekend getaway in a couple of weeks."

"Really? That was out of the blue. I must admit, I don't understand that relationship at all." I didn't expect her to, without knowing all the facts. That was Vanessa's story to tell, not mine.

"I know you don't. Can we change the subject, please?" My love life, real or imagined, was off limits for the rest of the night.

"Sure." *See what I mean about that annoying word?*

"Where are we going?" Vanessa asked excitedly on the way to the airport. I decided to drive and park in the long-term lot instead of taking an Uber. I wanted both the privacy and the intimacy.

"You'll find out when I hand you the boarding pass." I gave her a sly grin.

"You had me pack for quite a range in weather, so I don't have a clue."

"Here, I can't keep the secret any longer." I removed her boarding pass from my coat pocket.

"San Jose?"

"Just a starting point. You'll see." I changed the subject slightly. "I've been thinking. We've never traveled together. What if we find out we really don't like each other?" I joked.

"You're right. We could totally hate each other by Monday. We're off to a rough start already. I secretly wanted to go the Cabo. San Jose? Really?" She couldn't keep a straight face.

"Cute," I responded. And she was in every possible way.

We had a delightful time on the flight. It felt as if we had never been apart. I was ecstatic to spend time with the woman I loved, a simple pleasure I could never take for granted. We picked up our rental car and drove west on Highway 17, crossing the Santa Cruz Mountains, part of the Pacific Coast Range. We had beaten the heaviest rush hour traffic by about an hour and were hoping to catch the sun setting in the Pacific when we dropped down to the other side.

"Santa Cruz! Good call, Mr. Barrick. It's been years since I've been here. It was beautiful."

"It's the first stop. I hope you like where we are staying. It's an Airbnb near the beach and boardwalk area." I paused for a moment. "I didn't want to make any assumptions, so this place has two beds. I have no idea where you are in your therapy with things." *Things? Really?*

"Thank you. We'll play that by ear. I am in the process of working through those exact things."

"I'd prefer to err on the side of caution. I'd hate for you to go home with regrets," I stated. I quickly glanced her way and saw a look of love and appreciation in her eyes. She reached over to squeeze my free hand.

"I am going to want to fall asleep in your arms, at the very least," she said softly. That sounded wonderful.

We pulled into town just in time to watch the sun sink into the ocean, setting the sky ablaze. A cool breeze hit us, and I wrapped my arms tightly around Vanessa as we breathed in the sea air. I lacked for nothing in that moment.

We checked into our apartment on Beach Street. It was a third floor, two-bedroom unit with a spacious kitchen and living room and a balcony that looked out over the Santa Cruz Beach volleyball courts. Vanessa heartily approved. After settling in and unpacking, we walked across the street and had dinner at the *Ideal Bar and Grill*, sitting on the deck, under a heat lamp, overlooking the water. Vanessa displayed a content smile the rest of the evening. I wore one myself as she fell asleep, her head on my chest. The only thing preventing this from being a perfect moment was the gnawing feeling that my euphoria was temporary. Or was this simply another typical case of me over-thinking and fearing the worst?

We spent Saturday morning exploring Santa Cruz, never straying too far from the water's edge. In the afternoon, we drove north on Highway 1 for a few miles and stopped at the picturesque Shark Fin Cove. We walked a short distance to the secluded Davenport Beach. My attention was split between the beautiful locations and my gorgeous sidekick. She sat there, gazing out toward the thunderous surf, lost in her thoughts. Inspired by the sight, I reached for my phone, opened my Notes app, and began to tap out several verses of a new song. I was waiting for Vanessa to open up about her therapy, but so far she had been mum. I wouldn't press the issue. She didn't reveal anything later as we enjoyed dinner and a lovely view of the harbor at the *Crow's Nest*. She did thank me again for planning such a nice weekend getaway. The pleasure was mine.

The next morning, Vanessa made me breakfast in bed before we left our Airbnb and made our way north once again on Highway 1. We took our time and made several stops along the way. Each mile gave me more inspiration for the song I was writing mostly in my head. I needed to find some time and put it on paper. I got my chance in the afternoon.

We checked into the Half Moon Bay Lodge and unpacked before driving the short distance to the State Beach, a four-mile long strand of paradise. We walked barefoot in the sand, hand in hand before I excused myself and sat down on a weathered bench. Vanessa continued her stroll farther down the beach. I could see the massive breakers of *Maverick's* in the distance, one of the premier big wave surf locations in the world.

I pulled a small notebook from my pocket and began composing the song, rewriting the few verses I'd entered on my phone. Vanessa joined me on the bench just as I finished.

"Here, I wrote another song for you. I promise, this one won't trigger any epiphanies." I winked.

She took the notebook and slowly read her song. As she finished, her smile was even more beautiful than the view in front of us.

"I love it. You're right. It's light, just perfect. I love the way you see me. Sometimes I wish I could see me as you do. That's what I'm working on." She turned away and looked out to sea before continuing. "I was planning on telling you all about my therapy and my progress so far, but I almost don't want to spoil this trip by bringing it up. I'm enjoying this so much. I love being with you."

"You don't have to get into it on this trip. Just relax and have fun. And I'm loving every minute with you."

"I will just say that I've been putting in the work I should have done so many years ago. I usually go twice a week. I've also attended a few group sessions. That was something I was dreading at first, but it's been helpful knowing that I'm not alone. My therapist has been holding up a mirror, and I'm facing what I see in it for the first time. Together, we are revisiting old wounds and dealing with the pain and the scars. I'm learning to love myself. I'm growing so much. It's been incredibly hard, the most difficult thing I've ever done, but it will all be worth it." She looked at me with a confident smile. My love for her swelled inside me.

"I don't want this to sound patronizing in any way, but I'm so proud of you."

"It doesn't at all. Thank you for your support. I feel it every day, and it means more to me than you'll ever know. I love you." Her glowing eyes told me so.

"I love you, V."

Our last day in the Bay Area went by much too quickly. We drove the short distance to San Francisco but didn't stop in the city. We crossed the Golden Gate Bridge, visited Stinson Beach to bid farewell to the Pacific, and then had a relaxing lunch in Sausalito. We reluctantly began our drive south and beat the worst of the traffic, arriving back at the airport by late afternoon.

Vanessa was subdued during the flight home, content to rest her head on my shoulder. Perhaps she was feeling the same thing I was. It was going to be extremely difficult to say goodbye. I wondered what impact this trip would have on our immediate future. *Would this open the door to spending more time together? What, if anything, would change between us?* I would quickly learn the answers to my questions.

Vanessa didn't say a single word during the ride back to her house. She appeared more troubled than deep in thought. I helped her with her small suitcase. I had to ask.

"Are you going to be okay?"

"I don't know," she replied honestly. "I may have jumped the gun by suggesting this trip. I don't want you to leave tonight, and it's probably too soon to feel that way." She peered deep into my eyes. Hers were sad and confused. Mine reflected only sadness.

I had seen this coming. "I don't know if I'm just scared, or if I'm truly not ready. I don't dare resume things with you until I am. I can't fail again. I'm sorry I'm such a mess." She began to cry and I held her tightly, her tears soaking my shirt. "I'm going to lose you while trying to find me."

"No, you're not." I tried to comfort her with logic, amid a purely emotional moment. "Let's just savor the time we spent together and take a few days to process everything; let the emotions subside a bit. We're going be all right. We won't let this derail your progress." I may have been trying to ease my own fears as much as hers. She collected herself.

"Thank you for understanding. I seem to keep saying that a lot. I wouldn't blame you if you ran and never looked back."

"I'm not going anywhere, Vanessa." I attempted to project the same conviction I had when I last spoke those exact words.

I had barely pulled away from her neighborhood when I steered my car to the side of the road and turned off the ignition. I sat and stared out at the twinkling lights of the valley. The warm serenity of the ocean felt a million miles away. For the first time, I wondered how long I could continue to ride this emotional roller coaster.

Highway 1

Take me away,
Far from these city lights.
Let's find ourselves lost
In the full moon tonight.
The galaxies sparkle
As you hold me tight.
Your blue eyes
Are my favorite sight.

(First Chorus)

Come run away with me;
Darlin' it's our turn.
Let's live that second life
After all we've learned.
Run away . . .

Drive me to where
The sun dips in the sea;
The crash of the waves
Sets us free;
Beauty surrounds us,
Just you and me.
But your smile rivals
All that I see.

(Second Chorus)

Won't you take
A chance on us?
Don't let me be wrong.
Please pack your bags tonight,
I've waited for so long.
Take a chance . . .

(Bridge)

Please tell me
That this will never end;
We may never pass this way again.

Come with me,
Where mountain meets sky,
Above the clouds, we will fly.
Just take my hand
And don't ask why.
Baby, you're still my sweetest high.

(Repeat First Chorus)

Chapter 35

And tell me, did Venus blow your mind?
Was it everything you wanted to find?
And did you miss me while you were
Looking for yourself out there?

Drops of Jupiter—Train

I WAS FORTUNATE THAT MY CAR KNEW THE WAY HOME from Vanessa's, as I was in a bit of a daze. The euphoria I felt during the long weekend had been quickly replaced by a feeling of discouragement. There was no way of knowing the ramifications of Vanessa's slight panic attack. Time would tell. I understood her concern, and it was hard to argue with the logic. She needed to be as whole as possible before inviting me back into her heart completely. Logic and reason did little to soothe my troubled soul now, or more accurately my ego. That voice was speaking the loudest; it was all I heard.

My phone chirped, indicating an incoming text. I assumed it might be Vanessa. Much had been left unsaid before I left her house. I was trying to be a safe, upstanding citizen, so I waited until I had exited the freeway and pulled into my carport before looking at the screen. Surprisingly, the text wasn't from Vanessa. Even more startling, the name on my phone was Kate Campania.

Hey you! I hope you are well. Would you like to grab a coffee or a drink sometime soon and catch up?

Timing is indeed everything. Had her text come in at any time during the past four days, it would have elicited a smile and, most likely, a polite, non-committal response. The fact that it came when it did made me wonder if the Universe was sending me a not-so-subtle message. I'd had my fill of coffee lately; something a little stronger sounded more inviting. I returned her text while still sitting in my car.

A drink sounds great. What does your schedule look like next week?

I decided to let Vanessa process the emotional fallout from our getaway weekend and allow her to come to me when she was up to it. I received my usual phone call on Sunday night.

"Hi. I was hoping I'd hear from you again. You left me thinking that I'm a horrible travel companion." I tried to keep our conversation light from the start. She chuckled.

"I'm just glad you took my call, and that you understand that a girl can freak out every now and then," she played along. "I'm really sorry. I wasn't expecting the flood of emotions to hit me like that. But I hope you came away with the most important message from my little meltdown: That I still want you more than ever, and I'm determined to do this right. That is, if you still think I'm worth the wait."

Her words warmed my heart but also pierced my conscience. I would be seeing Kate in a few days.

"I did take away that message, and yes, you are definitely worth the wait. I believe in you, V."

"That means the world to me. I know this hasn't been easy. You deserve the very best of me. And I'm getting there."

"Hey, I'm a work in progress myself. I'm trying to be the best version of me I can be. You don't have the market cornered on this self-improvement thing. I'm hoping to have my own shit together, so you don't leave me in the dust." I had clearly panicked more than she had the week before.

"Get your ass in gear then, boy, because I'm coming on strong," she laughed. I adored this woman.

Her tone turned serious. "My therapy session this week was all about how to move forward. She guided me a bit but let me come to my own conclusions. I think that when the time comes where I feel like I am finally there, we should practically start over. I know that sounds confusing but hear me out. I'd like to start dating all over again. A first date, a second one, and if I still like you, maybe a third," she said with a giggle.

"You're assuming I'll be impressed enough to ask you out a second time," I countered.

"Oh, you will be. I'm going to be a much better catch the second time around. But seriously, I want to take baby steps and get to know each other all over again, because I'm not the same person you fell in love with once. I've changed. I've grown so much. I want us to see each other through fresh, new eyes." She waited for my feedback.

"That makes a lot of sense, not picking up where we left off, but rather experiencing a brand-new start. I'm good with that strategy. It seems your sessions are paying off, oh wise one."

"Thanks. I've got to get my money's worth from all this therapy, after all. It's not cheap, yet it's absolutely priceless." Her confident tone told me that I better get my ass in gear.

I started right away. I texted Kate the moment I hung up with Vanessa. She deserved the very best of me.

I won't be able to meet for drinks this week. It's a long story, too much to text. Can you chat over the phone soon?

Call me now if it's a good time for you.

"Hi! Long time, stranger." Her voice instantly took me back in time. My heart felt like it skipped a beat or two.

"Ciao, bella." She could still somehow draw that beautiful language from my lips.

"I'm bummed that you can't meet me this week. What's this long story? Does it involve a woman?" I was certain she already knew the answer, as she spoke often with Abbey.

"I'd say good guess, but I'm sure our friend has told you I'm in a relationship that's kind of complicated. I'm sorry, but for the moment it just doesn't feel right."

"She did tell me. We would only be having a drink together. I'm sure your girlfriend would be all right with that," she reasoned.

"She probably would be. It's me, not her."

"She's either got quite a spell on you, or you're afraid you won't be able to control yourself when you see me," she laughed.

"Yeah, probably a little of both," I had to chuckle, too. "So, tell me what you've been up to these past two years. I saw you once at the restaurant, and I see glimpses on social media, but your pics don't reveal much."

"You know me, I've never been one to put my life out there for everyone to see. I can't believe it's been almost two years. But when I look back, I realize I've packed a lot into that time. I fell in love a couple of times. I let two men into my heart and had what you'd call a relationship with each of them, both lasting a few months. I broke one heart and then had mine broken, too. I got a pretty good taste of the dating scene. I met some nice guys and more than a few jerks, too."

"Yeah, there are a lot of banged up people out there," I added my own assessment.

"So true. It's been good, though, to have those experiences I never had when I was younger. I didn't exactly go crazy or anything, but I tried to do and see it all." She let the lyrical reference to *The Spanish Steps* hang in the air for a moment. I didn't bite. She continued. "I learned a lot about love and life and how to live alone and be content. I've grown a lot since we were together."

"Sounds like you could write a hell of a fine article for Elephant Journal," I joked.

"Funny," she replied with feigned amusement. "How about you? What have you been up to? I have seen the photos from your open mic events and your pretty guitars on *Facebook* and *Instagram*. It looks like your music is a big part of your life. Were you dating your singer? You two looked pretty tight at the restaurant."

"Nah, she was just playing that part for your benefit. She is a sweetheart, but too young for me. The music has been fun. I've been writing a lot of new songs. Performing is still scary for me."

"I'd love to come see you in action sometime, if you wouldn't mind that."

"Sure," I said. I wasn't sure of that at all.

"What's up with your girlfriend? Abbey says it's been a bit of a roller coaster ride for you."

"She's just working through some things, and I'm giving her some space. I don't share all the details with Abbey."

"What is it with you and complicated women?" She laughed, including herself in that elite group.

"It's just a gift I have," I surmised. "What can I say?"

"Abbey tells me that you're going to Italy. Good for you. You're way overdue. Are you taking your girlfriend?"

"No, just a solo trip. I honestly don't know where she and I will be in June. But I've got to keep living, doing my thing."

"Yes, you do. You'll be there during the Summer Solstice?"

"Yeah. It seemed like a good time to go."

"I'm glad to hear you haven't lost your romantic side. I must say, I've met a few guys these past two years, and you're one of a kind. I mean that in the best way. You are so self-aware and sensitive, but not overly so. You aren't afraid to show your emotions, and you know how to treat a woman. You're the kind of man I'd like Sean to become." I was deeply moved by her words.

"Thank you, Kate. That is the greatest compliment I could ever hope to receive."

"I mean it. Most of the guys I dated never got to meet Sean. Even the ones who did, well, I always wondered if deep down he approved of them. He sure loved you."

"He's a great kid. Please give him my best."

"Maybe if you change your mind, or if things don't work with your girlfriend, we can all grab a bite to eat some night. Not that I'm wishing that for you at all. I hope it works out, if that's what you want. I just want you to be happy. You deserve that. I hope she knows what she's got in you and doesn't make you wait forever."

I hope she doesn't either, I thought. I wasn't about to share any frustrations with Vanessa with my ex-girlfriend. "I happen to think I'm the lucky one. She puts up with a lot from me."

"I highly doubt that." She changed the subject. "Are you only visiting Rome? Anywhere else in Italy?"

"Just Rome for now. Maybe a quick side trip to *Sardegna*, but mainly the Eternal City."

"Will you be visiting the Spanish Steps on the night of the Solstice?"

I paused before answering. "Probably. You know me," I admitted.

"Yes, I do; the hopeless romantic that you are. Who knows, you just might meet a pretty Italian girl up at the top. Or maybe even an American tourist. The sunset is gorgeous from that vantage point."

I chuckled at her obvious reference to the song and my parting words to her.

"It certainly is," I said calmly.

I delivered an Oscar-worthy performance to play it cool and conceal the fact that all the emotions I felt when I first wrote that song had come flooding back to me. I did well hiding it from Kate, but I couldn't deny the feelings that were stirring from within. I would run from those feelings for as long as I could, but I would eventually have to face them head on. That showdown was destined to occur among historic sites and on cobblestone streets. All roads were leading to Rome.

Chapter 36

Lover arrive, lover arrive;
Take me on wings into your heart;
Find a new start.

Lover Arrive—Ambrosia

VANESSA HAD GIVEN NO INDICATION IT WOULD HAPPEN SOONER than later, but for some reason, I thought our renewed courtship was to begin soon after she presented her plan to me. By thinking that way, I'd violated a personal philosophy of mine: *It's better to be pleasantly surprised than bitterly disappointed.* As far as I know, that's a Barrick original, not borrowed from *them*.

March had thawed into April, and it appeared that its showers would surely produce May flowers. But the month had yet to bring forth that highly anticipated first date—round two—with Vanessa. During one of our Sunday night chats, I let my frustration show. And I did so rather clumsily.

"So, tell me, V, when you feel you are ready to start dating again, do you ask me out on that first date? Or do I take a chance and ask you?" The words had barely left my lips, and I felt horrible. I heard only silence for several agonizing seconds. I was just about to apologize when she spoke.

"You're getting frustrated with me, aren't you?"

"No, I . . .," I began to answer but caught myself in my own lie. I righted the ship. "You have been incredibly honest with me throughout this entire process. I owe it to you to give you a truthful response. I'll admit, I expected us to progress a little quicker after our Bay Area trip. That's on me. You didn't do or say anything to give me any indication of that. I'm projecting my own expectations, and I'm sorry."

"Don't be. I appreciate your honesty, and I understand. You've told me to focus on me and not worry about you, but I'll be honest, I worry about your side of things all the time. I often feel selfish and guilty, and I worry you'll resent me for all of this or just give up. But I am getting closer, I really am."

"I'm not giving up, and I don't want you to worry about me at all. You have enough on your plate. But I'm going to ask you a tough question while we are speaking so honestly. Are you waiting to feel one hundred percent ready before moving forward? Because I don't think anyone is ever totally ready to commit to another. There's no such thing as a perfect situation; there's always a risk of failure. I completely understand that your healing process can't and shouldn't be rushed. I'd simply ask if your expectations are realistic with regards to being ready to go deeper with this relationship."

She didn't rush her answer. While I awaited her reply, I was relieved to get some things off my chest, to share my concerns, and not in the passive-aggressive manner that started our conversation.

"Those are very fair questions. I don't have answers for you right now, but it's something I need to figure out. You're right. Fear shouldn't hold me back. Thanks again for your honesty."

"There is a selfish motive at play," I confessed. "I'm about to book my lodging in Rome, and I was asking for a progress report to know whether you might possibly join me."

"That is so tempting, and I may very well be ready by then; but I honestly think it might be overly ambitious to commit to that right now. I wish I could say yes, but you should probably plan on going alone."

"Don't be surprised if Kate shows up in Rome while you're there," Abbey suddenly blurted out between sips of her miso soup.

"What?" I almost choked on my edamame. "Are you serious? Why?"

"Well, you pretty much invited her, didn't you? You should be more careful with what you write in your songs." She made a good point. "I'm just sharing with you the vibe I got from her when we had dinner the other night."

"What did she say?" My lunch date had my full attention.

"Nothing concrete. But I have a pretty good idea of where she's at in her life right now and what she's capable of doing."

"Do tell." I tried to seem indifferent, but I was dying to know.

"I get the feeling she's ready to settle down. She's had her fill of dating and got a lot out of her system. She even had her heart roughed up a bit out there, which I think was probably good for her, an important part of her, you know, the journey thing. She still has feelings for you. You had something special, if not for lousy timing."

"Our timing isn't any better this time around," I alluded to my relationship with Vanessa.

"Look, I don't know all the details about you and Vanessa. You've kept things closely guarded for some reason, but I know that Kate is many things that Vanessa isn't. For one, she's available. And she's ready, she's vibrant, she's whole. And I believe you still have feelings for her. She's also a romantic, like you. She's just crazy enough to fly to Rome and surprise you on the Summer Solstice. I would never try to steer you in one direction or another. I just want you to be happy and fulfilled, but I truly wonder just how happy you are in your current relationship. Remember, I'm Switzerland here and don't have an agenda, but I would point out that Kate went and did everything you mentioned in your song. She took her laps, and now she's back. She figures if things were really that great between you and Vanessa, you wouldn't be going to Rome alone."

I didn't have a witty comeback for that valid point.

"So, having said that, is it okay if I invite Kate to your open mic next week?"

"Sure. Why not? Vanessa won't be there."

Vanessa and I were still in our total honesty phase, so in the spirit of that, I told her Abbey had invited Kate to my next performance with Emily. When we first started dating, we had both shared our recent love stories, complete with names and pertinent details. And I eventually showed my song lyrics to Vanessa, which also included the back-stories and personal connections to each song.

"I just wanted to be completely up front with you. It wasn't my idea, and I hope you are okay with it. Obviously, nothing is going on, I haven't seen her in almost two years."

"I'm fine with it, but thanks for the heads up. That will be fun for her to hear a song that was written for her." *Was that a feline-like hiss in her voice?*

"*Vinyl and Bourbon Nights* isn't really about her. It's more of a generic breakup song. We are getting very close to performing *Highway 1.*" I reminded her that I'd written love songs for her, too. "You better come when we debut that one."

"I definitely will. You wrote *The Spanish Steps* for Kate, right? Are you and Emily playing that song?" *Wow, the female mind can be a steel trap when it wants to be.*

"You have a good memory. Yes, that was for her. But we haven't written the music for it yet."

"Well, break a leg, or whatever you musicians say before a concert." Her tone made me wonder if she were wishing an actual bone fracture on me. I'd never seen this side of her. *Meow!*

Our open mic was a smashing success. Emily stole the show. I was getting more comfortable in front of a crowd, and our music was well-received by the audience that packed the small coffee shop. One of the other performers recorded the entire night and later emailed me the audio files, which I forwarded on to Regan in Nashville. I could hear her accent when I read her responding email.

"You two are getting better and better! Now get that demo recorded, darlin'!"

Kate couldn't attend our performance—an emergency at work kept her in the office late. I got a sweet text before we took the stage, wishing me well and expressing her regrets for not being able to attend. I was actually relieved by her absence, as I was now able to fully focus on the music without the distraction of a long-awaited reunion with my old girlfriend.

Shortly after I got home, still high from the performance, I received a rare, midweek call from Vanessa.

"Hi, this is a nice surprise."

"I wanted to hear all about your performance."

"It was awesome. Emily was in great form, and I hardly screwed up at all." I quickly addressed the elephant in the room. "Kate was a no show, FYI. Got stuck at work."

"Oh, I wasn't even concerned about her; I just wanted to know how it went." *Did I detect relief in her voice?* "Hey, what are you doing next Wednesday?"

"Let's see . . . May 10th? Nothing."

"Good. I would like to ask you out on the official first date of Vanessa and Jamison, the sequel. How about *Takashi*? I'd say we are overdue for some quality sushi."

"That sounds wonderful." I had waited for this moment for such a long time. I was ecstatic but also realistic, wondering if the emergence of Kate had anything to do with Vanessa's invitation. I quickly pushed aside such thoughts. This was a time to celebrate, not overthink. "I can't wait for next week."

It's not easy being a rock star. The groupies can be a little overwhelming. Kate called me the next day at work, asking about our open mic performance.

"I'm sorry I missed you! Things blew up at work. Abbey said you two are really getting good."

"It was fun. Emily killed it. And I've come a long way since those days when I played that black Fender on your couch. I'll let you know when the next one is. We might sneak in one more before I go to Rome."

"Are you getting excited?"

"I am. I've been cramming the Italian, and I just booked my Airbnb."

"Which part of Rome, near the Spanish Steps?"

"Not too far, closer to *Piazza Navona* and the *Pantheon*. But not a long walk to the Steps."

"June should be perfect over there, not too hot yet. How romantic. I'm so jealous."

Did I detect a devilish tone in her voice? I was beginning to believe that Abbey's hunch was correct. Kate was planning her own trip. Kate and Jamison, the sequel. Things were about to get complicated.

Chapter 37

My heart is old, it holds my memories.
My body burns a gem-like flame.
Somewhere between the soul and soft machine
Is where I find myself again.

Kyrie—Mr. Mister

"Wow! Your pictures don't do you justice. I'm Jamison Barrick. It's nice to finally meet you, Ms. Grant." I extended my hand. She shook it and played along.

"It's a pleasure to meet you, Mr. Barrick. Won't you come in a moment? Let's enjoy a sip of wine before we leave for sushi."

She did look stunning. Even more so than the first time I saw her photos on *Tinder*. I'd done the math on the drive over to her house. It had been a few months shy of two years since we first connected on the dating app. And it had been about sixteen months since our very first date. We had taken the tortoise's approach in this race.

Kate and I had come and gone in the time it took me and Vanessa to finally meet after our first online contact. The hare lost that race, if I recall correctly. It had also been an agonizing eleven weeks since I'd seen Vanessa in this very room, after returning from our trip to Northern California.

Enough with the numbers and back to Vanessa's beauty. She looked as gorgeous as I'd ever seen her. It was her eyes. They now had an unmistakable sparkle, replacing the look that had both intrigued and baffled me initially. She appeared to be very much at peace. Nothing obscured my view into her soul. She was whole. I let her dictate the flow of our date. Obviously, we couldn't pretend to completely start over again, but we had plenty of catching up to do.

After dinner, we walked around downtown and enjoyed the fresh, spring weather. Vanessa was craving ice cream, so it became our mission to find some; which we did.

As we strolled the busy sidewalks of the capital city, I reached out and took her hand. The smile she flashed me made it feel like the first time all over again. When we returned to her home, I walked her to the doorstep and treated it like the new beginning it was.

"I had a great time. It was nice getting to know you, Vanessa."

"I did, too, Jamison. I'd love to see you again soon."

"I'd love that, too." I hugged her tightly for a moment, gave her a quick kiss on the cheek, and started walking to my car.

As I got in, I looked back and saw pure love painted delicately on her smiling face—and a tiny, sarcastic sneer. The girl had wanted a goodnight kiss. That's why we have *second* dates.

Our second date was the wedding of Bailey and Cole. I had always envisioned Vanessa by my side for this huge life event but wondered during these past few months if she would be far enough along in her progress to attend. I was thrilled that she shared in my immense joy on that special day. She looked absolutely gorgeous. We danced into the night and I *definitely* kissed the girl.

I was on my back deck playing the guitar when my phone rang. It was Emily.

"Do you want to hear what I've done with your lyrics to *The Spanish Steps?*"

"Of course. I didn't know you were working on that."

"Yeah, I've had a bit of a creative surge with it. All my words were sucking lately so I pulled out this one of yours yesterday and have been having fun with it. Let me put you on speaker. Okay, here is what I have for the verses."

She started strumming her guitar and singing the song I'd written over two years ago. It had just been poetry until Emily's sweet voice brought it to life in an instant. *You shared with me your journey in a noisy, crowded bar. . . .* The music that she had composed far exceeded anything I could have imagined. It was beautiful.

"What do you think so far?"

"It's incredible!"

"Here's what I have for the chorus," she said excitedly and resumed strumming and singing.

I hope you see and do it all, and leave no stone left unturned . . . . She finished the first chorus and again asked my opinion.

"I'm stunned. You've knocked it out of the park." And she had, indeed, with the bases loaded.

"I'm glad you like it. Here's the bridge." *. . . Where you are is where I wish to be . . . .* "I think I'll use the chords from the bridge as the intro. I don't have that nailed down yet, but I'm close. I was so excited, I wanted to call and play it for you. I hope I've done your amazing lyrics justice."

"Are you kidding? You've done a remarkable job."

"I want to play it at the next open mic before you go to Rome, a farewell present of sorts. I'd like to do it as a solo, if you don't mind. I know you'd want a month or two to learn it and practice. Would you be cool with that? I think it would be incredibly romantic to play it right before you leave."

"I'd be truly honored. When is the next gig?"

It was to be on June 1st, and that would be the third date for me and Vanessa. We were pacing ourselves, seeing each other once a week, letting things between us grow organically, as if it were our first dance together. I had hoped to have *Highway 1* ready to perform but the band, *Ecco,* wasn't quite there yet. In hindsight, that song would have been a much better choice than *The Spanish Steps* for a certain audience member.

We started our set with *Stay in the Light*, as a tribute to those killed and injured in yet another terrorist attack, this time at a concert hall in London the previous week. Unfortunately, my song would sadly continue to be timely and relevant. Emily announced our second song, a solo.

"This next song is one that Jamison wrote the words to over two years ago, and he gave me the green light to write the music. It's about bad timing, a romantic notion, and a cool place in Rome. It's called *The Spanish Steps*." She began to play.

I had the rare opportunity to be a spectator from my position on the stage. Normally, I have my eyes glued to the strings and frets of my guitar, but I was now able to look up and watch Emily enchant the crowd and enjoy its reaction. My eyes met Vanessa's. I could feel what she was thinking, and it wasn't good. We wrapped up the set with one of Emily's songs and received a nice round of applause from the audience, many of them fellow musicians. We stayed for a few more numbers before slipping out to go enjoy some wine at Vanessa's. She was rather subdued on the drive to her house.

"I think I know what's bugging you," I started the conversation after she poured us each a glass of white wine. "It's the song, right? *The Spanish Steps?*"

"It's not so much the song. It's more about the girl. The song is beautiful; Emily was amazing. You must have loved Kate very much when you wrote it."

"I did; well over two years ago," I pointed out. Then I added, "And I loved you very much when I wrote your songs. I still do, in fact." She forced a smile.

"I just wonder if you still have some unfinished business with her. I hadn't heard her name in so long, and now she seems to have resurfaced. Is anything going on?"

"No there isn't. I'll be honest, we've shared a few texts and talked on the phone a couple of times, just catching up, but I haven't seen her. I don't feel I have any unfinished business. She might, but that has nothing to do with us and isn't relevant."

"She *might*? What does that mean?" Vanessa's tone was calm, not catty.

"Abbey speculated that she has it in her to surprise me in Rome. But she also knows I'm in a relationship with you, so I highly doubt she will. There is a little more to the song than just the lyrics."

I shared with Vanessa how they played into my parting words with Kate, down to the last detail. She listened intently, her breathing becoming deeper, her eyes avoiding mine.

"But that was so long ago. Like Emily described it tonight, it was just a romantic notion. I'm being completely honest with you. Nothing is going on. My trip to Rome has nothing whatsoever to do with Kate. I wish you were joining me."

"Maybe it's best that I didn't commit to going," she said coldly. "Sounds like you might still have some things to figure out while you're there."

"I already *have* things figured out *here*." I overemphasized the words *have* and *here*. "I don't quite understand why you are doing this. I'm telling you the truth. Why are you pushing me away?"

"I'm not. Maybe I just need a little time to process this," she said thoughtfully.

Perhaps it was hearing the word *time* after so much of it and after all the waiting. I snapped.

"Take all the time you need. Thanks for coming to hear us play tonight. I need to go."

I walked straight to the door and let myself out. As I pulled away from her home, I wondered if I were doing so for the last time; and for the first time, I let myself entertain the idea of Kate surprising me in Rome. Life felt very short as I drove toward the freeway. I was halfway home when it sunk in that I was not being completely honest with myself.

~~~♡~~~

I didn't hear from Vanessa for the remainder of the week and well into the next. And I didn't feel a strong urge to break the deadlock. I started my packing process, buying some travel-sized toiletries, and changing a few dollars into euros. Then I received a text from Kate.

Come va l'Italiano?

My Italian is coming back to me slowly. I hope it comes flooding back once I get to Rome.

Hopefully I'll chat with you before you leave but if not, *buon viaggio!*

I had some business during the week with Abbey over the phone. I flat-out asked her.

"So, how serious is Kate about going to Rome?"

"I honestly don't know, and even if I did, I wouldn't tell you. That's a surprise I wouldn't dare ruin. She's gone kind of silent on the matter, which may or may not mean anything. Why do you ask?"

"Just wondering. Between us, things are a little rocky with Vanessa right now. I'd actually be open to Kate showing up. Not necessarily in *The Spanish Steps* kind of way. The company would be nice, that's all. Don't say anything to Kate."

"Sure. I'm Switzerland, remember?"

Vanessa called me on Sunday, a week before I was to leave for Italy. I was about to break down and call her myself. It was comforting to know we were still in sync.

"Hi. I was just about to call you. I've missed you."

"I've missed you, too. I'd really like to see you before you go. Can I cook you dinner on Saturday night? I won't attempt anything Italian," she chuckled.

"I'd love that. I didn't like where we left things. I'd like to leave on good terms."

"I agree. I've been doing a lot of thinking and have so much to say. But I'd like to talk face to face."

"Should I be worried about what you have to say?"

"No. Not at all. Unless you were hoping to be done with me."

I was completely packed and ready to fly out the next morning before I left for Vanessa's. She fired up her grill, and we sat out on the patio. Pacifico beer paired nicely with the grilled chicken, asparagus, and the warm, summer evening. We didn't talk in earnest until we began eating.

"I'm really sorry about the other night. I let my insecurities get the best of me," she eased into our much-needed conversation.

"I'm sorry I got up and left and didn't talk it out. I let my frustrations get the best of me."

With the apologies out of the way, we dove deeper into the reasons for that earlier disconnect.

"If I'm being completely honest with myself, I was pushing you away again," she confessed. "I'm quite adept at that, as you know. But it's way past time I face my fears about the future with the same effort I'm putting into my healing, which will be an ongoing process for me. This may seem very sudden, but I've thought a lot about this the past week. I would like us to take this to the next level. I'm finally ready. I love you, Jamison, and I want to be with you."

She looked intently in my eyes for a reply. It was my turn to be honest.

"Wow. You know I've wanted to hear those words for a long time. But I didn't exactly envision hearing them on the heels of a fight. As much as I've wanted to hear you say that, I need to know it's coming from the right place and not a reaction to Kate or anything else. There can't be a gun to your head. It feels a little like push has come to shove. Vanessa, my heart is doing cartwheels right now, believe me. I just need you to be certain and for all the right reasons."

"I thought you might feel that way, and I'm not at all upset by your response. Sometimes events can put things in the proper perspective. I was not threatened by Kate as much as I was simply doubting *me*. It's time I believe in myself. I hope she shows up in Rome. I really do. I hope you both get the closure you need on the Spanish Steps on the Summer Solstice. I'm confident you'll come home to me, because for the first time since you've known me, I'm worth coming home to."

I had never heard such conviction in her voice or seen it in her eyes. She continued, "You have been incredibly patient with me during my healing process. I owe it to you to let you have some time to be certain I'm who you want. Your trip to Rome might not give you enough time to figure that out, but it's a start. So, please go, enjoy, and if Kate shows up, all the better. I need you to be certain, too, with no gun to your head, either."

I didn't know how to reply, and she didn't appear to be seeking a response. There was very little to say. I could have admitted I actually needed some additional closure with Kate, that perhaps I had unfinished business myself. But Vanessa already knew this to be true. Time had made her my soul mate. In that moment, I realized such an intimate connection isn't born out of fireworks.

She looked incredibly beautiful across the table in the shade of her patio, her gorgeous backyard as the backdrop. She radiated love and confidence. I felt compelled to capture the moment.

"Would you mind if I took your picture right now? It'll make the miles feel much closer while I'm in Rome. I want to take with me the beautiful image of the woman who owns my heart."

We made love that night for the first time in ten months, not that anyone was counting. Fine, maybe I had been. It was passionate and tender. And it was completely different from the first time. There was a depth, a more intimate connection, that I had never felt with Vanessa. It was perfect. I didn't leave her side until 5 a.m. I still had to shower, change, and get to the airport. I insisted she stay in bed and not walk me to the door. I kissed her gently on the forehead.

"I love you, Vanessa. I'll see you when I get back."

"*Ti amo,* Jamison." She'd done her homework. "I'll be right here. I'm not going anywhere."

Chapter 38

Strada facendo vedrai
Che non sei più da solo.
(Along the way, you will see
That you are no longer alone.)

Strada Facendo (Along the Way)—Claudio Baglioni

June 18, 2017

I DIDN'T WANT TO PUT ANYONE OUT AT SUCH AN EARLY HOUR on a Sunday morning, so I caught an Uber to the airport. The magic of the night before had not worn off and was still fresh and dancing in my mind as I half-heartedly made small-talk with my driver. I stared out at the downtown skyline, still a silhouette with the sun rising slowly over the Wasatch Mountains. I wondered what the hell I was doing, heading off to Rome alone. A trip back to Italy was long overdue. That part I understood. But this inexplicable need to fulfill prophesy from the words to a song I'd written so long ago made very little sense, especially considering the events of the night before. And the temptation to invite Kate back into my life in such grand fashion was a bad idea all around. The risk was huge. I stood to lose Vanessa just when I had finally, truly found her.

"Terminal one or two?" The Uber driver snapped me out of my contemplative trance.

"One, American. Thanks."

I was a bit sleep-deprived from the night before and tried to nap. But, as usual, it was futile for me to try to catch a few zzz's on an airplane, as much as I needed them. The flight to Dallas, and the short layover went quickly. I swapped dollars for euros in my wallet, and dug my passport out before boarding my flight to Rome. I did a quick scan of the boarding line for a possible Kate-sighting. It was a remote possibility that if she were coming to Rome, we might end up on the same flight. But then I remembered she was a Delta girl. I literally had an eye-roll moment walking down the gate ramp.

My destination felt one step closer upon hearing announcements being duplicated in Italian, and I could hear the sweet language being spoken in small clusters on the plane. For a moment, I felt the joy of returning to one of my favorite places on the planet, regardless of the complicated reasons for my traveling there. I tried to squeeze my 6 foot 2 frame as comfortably as possible into my aisle seat of this glorified cattle car. The couple to my right was completely lost in their own world, so thankfully no small talk would be required. I killed the hours with several movies, brushing up on my Italian, listening to music and eating. The food and beverage carts seemed to roll every three hours or so. The one thing I didn't do was sleep, aside from a few tiny, fitful naps.

I decided to postpone any deep thinking about my love life, this trip, and that damned song until I was firmly entrenched on Roman *terra firma*. I did indulge in one of the few things my Internet-disabled phone would allow—scanning through my photos. I scrolled way back to the 'Kate days' to pictures that I never quite had the heart to delete. The intensity of those exhilarating three months with her was evident; the sparkle in her eyes, her smile, her glow, and mine, too. Our brief timeline was well chronicled from early January through a good portion of March. *Beware those damned Ides of March!* There were shots of us in Kate's kitchen, of her on her own trip to Rome, of Valentine's Day, at Sundance, celebrating St. Patrick's Day, and then nothing. My photos afterward reflected the lonely remnants of life after love.

I scrolled ahead to the photos of Vanessa. Very different from the story that Kate's pictures told, these conveyed a much slower pace over a longer period. I could see the uncertainty and even glimpses of pain in Vanessa's eyes in the earlier shots, and then little by little, I could see her glow brighten, her smile widen, and her burden lighten. I always felt she was the most beautiful woman I'd ever met, and she had grown even more so in my eyes during our time together. She looked radiant in the last photo on my phone, sitting across from me on her patio the night before. I stared at that one for several minutes, mesmerized by her beauty while wondering, again, what the hell I was doing.

I decided to turn off my brain. I connected my phone to the USB charger, watched another movie, ate the American Airlines version of a breakfast entrée, and, as the credits rolled, we began our descent into Rome. Dawn was barely breaking over *Fiumicino*.

June 19, 2017

I'm getting too old to be pulling all-nighters, which essentially is what I'd just done. I was showing my age as I waded through the line to flash my passport and continue my way. I caught the Leonardo Express train to *Stazione Termini*. I texted my Airbnb host, Emiliano, through an app we'd prearranged to use for our communication during my stay. I also texted Vanessa that I'd arrived safely. It was her bedtime, but she responded within minutes, wishing me a fun trip and sending hugs and kisses, emoji-style.

I caught a taxi at *Termini* and ventured toward my apartment through Monday morning rush hour traffic. The streets of Rome were loud and chaotic. I had forgotten what it was like in the Italian capital. My taxi driver didn't help instill any confidence that we'd arrive alive, as he fumbled putting the address into his GPS device, all the while dodging scooters and cars weaving their way through the crowded streets and busy roundabouts. I had always wondered why they even bothered painting lanes on the streets of Rome as they were regarded as mere suggestions, at best.

We drove west, toward the Tiber and Vatican City. My driver finally punched in the address just before turning off *Vittorio Emanuele* onto a side street, then pulling into a narrow alley and stopping at my location, situated between *Campo Di Fiori* and the banks of the Tiber. I'd chosen this apartment both for its great reviews, quiet location, and because it was within walking distance to the main sights on my agenda. All the buildings on the cobblestone-paved lane were either three or four stories tall, and a few had businesses on the ground level. Potted trees and climbing vines provided some greenery. The location was tranquil and pleasing, and I'd call it home for a few days.

I texted Emiliano, and he soon arrived on his bicycle. He knew I spoke some Italian, so we started in that language before he assessed my limitations and gradually, and quite politely, switched to English. He was energetic and friendly with an athletic build, and he shaved his head bald, just like me. I liked him immediately and guessed him to be in his mid to late 30s.

He showed me around my apartment; a tidy, single bedroom unit on the second floor, adorned with a generous book collection and several photos and paintings of the more popular sights of Rome. It was as homey as it had looked in the online photo gallery. He had graciously allowed me to drop off my luggage several hours before the official check-in time to accommodate my early arrival. The cleaning lady arrived as he was showing me the location of the main sights and some of his favorite restaurants and *gelaterias* nearby. He was incredibly helpful and validated my decision to get more of a local flavor by going with an Airbnb host over a hotel experience. At the time, I had no way of knowing that Emiliano would play a pivotal role during my visit.

"Is your stay in Rome solely for pleasure and not for work?"

I chuckled internally at his question.

"Yes, just pleasure." Yet I knew full well that there would be a fair amount of emotional labor involved, as well.

"It sounds like you know the sights you wish to visit. Let me know if you need help purchasing any tickets. The Vatican Museums are very popular this time of year."

I thanked him for his helpful suggestions and decided to kill the time it took for my apartment to be cleaned by walking toward Vatican City and St. Peter's Square. I filled my water bottle, said my goodbyes to him and the cleaning lady, and made my way toward the Tiber. I caught my second wind.

It was a perfect early summer morning in Rome, sunny but not terribly warm and not a cloud in the sky. Traffic hadn't noticeably eased since rush hour. I walked along the river, crossing it at the famed *Ponte Sant'Angelo,* which leads to the imposing *Castel Sant'Angelo.* The distinct, round structure, once a mausoleum, then a fortress, now a museum, has always stood out for me from all the other structures in Rome in style and color. Its rather drab brown contrasted greatly from the bright blue sky on this June morning.

I took a few pictures on the bridge and of the castle before turning onto *Via della Conciliazione,* the pedestrian boulevard leading to St. Peter's Square. The street vendors were out in full force, and so were the tourists. The Square was packed with a long line snaking its way into the famous *Basilica* and filled with rows of chairs I assumed were for an upcoming mass or appearance by the popular Pope Francis.

I had visited the inside of St. Peter's on several occasions, so a look inside wasn't on my list for this trip. Instead, I took some artsy shots of the massive columns and statues that framed the Square, already scheming how I would splash the images on social media. I sat for several minutes and watched the massive sea of humanity in the Square, hoping against hope, that the other sights in the city wouldn't be as crowded.

I suddenly felt quite fatigued. Aside from some tiny catnaps on the flight, I'd been awake for a long time. I was too exhausted to even attempt to do the math to count exactly how many hours. I certainly didn't have the energy to think about my love life, either. *Domani*, I thought to myself. I took a different route back, crossing the Tiber on another bridge and in fifteen minutes, I neared my apartment. To ensure the cleaning lady had enough time for her duties, I walked into an adjacent bar.

The day was getting warmer, and I was thirsty, so I ordered a *Peroni* beer and sipped street-side in the shade. I looked at the time on my phone and realized how confused my body clock was. It was only 11 a.m., and I was already drinking a beer, but a tasty and refreshing one, at that. After returning to my apartment, the beverage helped me fall asleep easily, as I immediately crashed for a much-needed nap.

As I've aged, I seem to have lost the ability to sleep in and take decent naps (or sleep on planes). I suppose my body didn't know which way was up or down, because I was able to sleep deeply for four and a half hours. I slowly came out of my near-coma and settled into my apartment, which included a small balcony that offered some fresh air and a limited view of the inner courtyard. I unpacked, hung up clothes, and ate a little from a provided fruit bowl. A hot shower never felt better than the lengthy one I took, almost draining the small, Euro style hot water heater. I dressed and stepped out for the evening, looking for a spot to enjoy an early dinner.

I kept it close to home my first night, choosing a rather touristy restaurant in nearby *Campo di Fiori*. My criteria were simple: Pick a place with outdoor dining, one with the least obnoxious greeter charged with corralling patrons into his establishment. I enjoyed a glass of delicious *Chianti*, a basic salad, and a pizza *margherita*. I was reminded that the *Napolitani* have the market cornered on these things more so than the Romans. Not an ambitious dinner, but it did the trick. I had a few days ahead of me to do it right. And perhaps I'd have a dinner date on my third night in Rome for the Summer Solstice.

I resisted the urge to wander the city after dinner, figuring a fully recharged version of me would better tackle the chores that awaited me on the eve of the Solstice. I did overshoot my apartment on the walk back, so I could take a few photos along the banks of the Tiber. The dome of St. Peter's Cathedral was prominent from my bench, as well as the *Trastevere* neighborhood across the river. I watched the sun slowly dip in the west, but left for my apartment before it fully set. On that short stroll, I selected the site I would visit in the early morning, just after sunrise.

June 20, 2017

I left the apartment just after dawn, feeling rested and caught up on my sleep. The city was relatively still at this early hour, which made for a peaceful stroll. I was more focused on my destination than the many charming sights I passed along the way. The night before, I decided to go directly to the Spanish Steps to start the new day, the eve of the Solstice. Though it wouldn't at all resemble the experience I'd have at sunset the following night, I was anxious to get there, to make some sort of preemptive strike and get ahead of the emotions that I would certainly feel there.

As I turned off *Via del Corso,* I saw *Piazza di Spagna* through the narrow lane that dead ends there, *Via Condotti.* The Spanish Steps rose from the square and were topped off by the *Chiesa della Trinita dei Monti.* I barely noticed the *Fontana della Barcaccia* as I started to ascend the marble stairs. It was a splendid morning, and the setting was as romantic as I had imagined when I wrote the song.

Sure enough, the emotions I'd expected to feel did wash over me as I climbed. I wondered if I should have just left the song in the past, where it belonged. Kate and I had our time, and now I'd allowed this old, romantic notion to threaten the reality of what I currently had with Vanessa. Why was there such a longing inside of me for absolute closure? The situation I found myself in was self-induced. I used the song as a vehicle to leave the door slightly ajar for Kate's improbable return. I was the one who encouraged Emily to bring the song to life, which had triggered a strong reaction from Vanessa. I was in this predicament by my own doing. My life was imitating the art I'd created.

Reaching the top terrace, I envisioned how it would look the next evening from Kate's perspective; seeing me there waiting for her. I was flooded with questions. Were all the hints mere coincidence, or did they truly indicate she would show up? What would she feel in her heart after being apart for so long? How would I react seeing her take those final steps to the top? Had my feelings changed? And the most nagging question of all—why was I not experiencing this vacation in Rome with the woman I loved who was half a world away?

I came to the painful conclusion that I had many more questions than answers. There was a knot in my stomach that came with the realization that I had just a little over 36 hours to figure it all out. I needed a quiet, peaceful spot to sort out the emotions that were troubling my heart and making my head spin. Luckily, I was very close to one of Rome's most serene settings, the *Pincio* gardens on the edge of *Il Parco di Villa Borghese.* I set out in that direction with a great sense of urgency.

Chapter 39

When you found me, I was a broken man.
The winter tides had stolen all the sand.

The Long Goodbye—Jamison Barrick

THE PATH BETWEEN THE SPANISH STEPS AND *IL PINCIO* offers a panoramic view of Rome to the south and west. The church domes visible from that vantage point numbered in the dozens, with the massive *duomo* of St. Peter dwarfing them all. I soon arrived at my destination, which is essentially a gateway to the lovely *Parco di Villa Borghese,* one of the three largest parks found in the Eternal City. While it is not one of the famed Seven Hills of Rome, the elevated *Pincian Hill,* with its panoramic view, is a favorite spot for tourists and locals alike.

Truth be told, when I wrote my song, *The Spanish Steps,* I had the view of the sunset from *Il Pincio* in my mind. Both have sweeping vistas, but there is something special about the *Terrazza del Pincio* overlook with *Piazza del Popolo* just below, and the splendor of the rest of Rome on display as far as the eye can see. Crowds flock to this spot nightly to catch the rays diminishing in the west. Poetically nothing quite rhymes with *Pincio* and the Steps are both iconic and romantic. Close enough, I figured, not really imagining at the time I wrote the lyrics that I'd return to Rome so soon. I was still coming to grips with the fact that I was here.

Even at this early hour, there were dozens gathered to enjoy the view from the terrace. Later that night, the number would grow into the hundreds. I was enjoying a last gaze out over the city before retreating for the more tranquil gardens when I spotted three women trying to take a photo. They were attempting to squeeze themselves in frame, selfie-style, including some portion of the Roman skyline in the background, with limited success. They seemed pleasant and approachable, so I offered to help them.

"Would you like me to take a photo of the three of you?"

"That would nice, thank you," replied the youngest of the three, the one with the phone. I was fortunate they spoke English. I correctly guessed the slight accent to be from a Scandinavian country. Their blonde hair also gave them away.

"Where are you from?" My command of the language was less than perfect, ending a sentence with a preposition. I framed them in a nice shot that included a fair amount of Rome in the background.

"We're from Norway. Are you American?"

"Yes," I responded with detectable resignation. Our President was incredibly unpopular abroad, as he was with half of the population at home. I really didn't want to delve into politics on this trip, but rather escape them.

I took a few photos and showed them my handiwork, receiving instant approval.

"My name is Jamison. Are you enjoying your stay in Rome?"

They introduced themselves as Anita, Runa, and Anne. This was their first day of sightseeing after a neuroscience symposium. They were excited for some well-deserved leisure time.

"We rented bikes this morning and are planning on riding to most of the historic sites today," Anita explained.

"Maybe I'll run into you again, at the *Colosseum*, or somewhere."

We said our goodbyes, and I walked toward the gardens with a smile on my face. Not knowing where else I might wander the rest of the day, I hoped that our paths might cross.

I arrived at a part of *il Pincio* gardens that reminds me of a section in New York's Central Park, identifiable in several films, (one being Kramer vs. Kramer) with broad, unpaved boulevards lined with wooden park benches under a canopy formed by tall, majestic oaks. I imagined this idyllic spot looked very much the same as it had in the 19th century. I chose a secluded bench that received a small amount of filtered morning sunshine and sat, sipping from my water bottle and enjoying the tranquility.

The chirping of birds and the laughter of children playing nearby were the only sounds competing with the voices inside my head. My thoughts centered on the *pull* that I was feeling, the need for some sort of final resolution with Kate, even though we'd had a perfectly clean break in March of 2015.

I had to admit to myself that my ego seemed to need the stroking that Kate showing up on the Solstice would provide. I concluded I was in love with the idea of her still loving me, regardless of my feelings toward her. I did love her deeply at the time, and it hurt like hell when she said goodbye, even if I did see it coming. The emotions I felt then were very real, but now they had become more of a curiosity than anything. Her actions, admittedly, had a certain power over me, a fact I despised. My thoughts shifted, and I imagined her not showing up at the Steps the following evening, leaving me waiting in the dark, hours after sunset. *Is that what it would take to finally put this all to rest? I wasn't that hopeless, was I?*

I thought about her impact on me during those short, but

intense, few months. I had come to terms a long time ago as to her purpose in my life. After Anna, I honestly did not know what I had left inside me; if I'd be able to love again, to trust again. My brief time with Kate taught me I could do both; that I had so much left in my heart, despite any scar tissue that had formed.

I pulled out a small notebook and pen I always carry with me for such moments, and I began writing the verses to a song. I had some old chords in mind that I'd been playing around with before I left for Italy. I wished for a moment I had my travel guitar with me, but then thought of the hassle of lugging it to Europe and around Rome. The title came first, and the lyrics quickly followed, primarily words of immense gratitude. As I wrote the final lines of *The Long Goodbye*, I had a strong impression that this would be the final song I'd ever write for Kate.

I was quite happy with my effort, surprised that it only took about thirty minutes to write, and I felt confident that very few revisions would be needed. I reread the lines once more and tucked it away, feeling somewhat emotionally spent by the process. After this purging of sorts I'd just experienced through the writing of the song, my mind drifted to Vanessa. I missed her in this moment and wished she were beside me to see the sights of Rome together, to taste the food and drink the wine. Her schedule had been full when I was settling into Rome, and other than a text letting her know I'd arrived safely, we hadn't planned on talking right away on the phone. She was insistent on giving me plenty of space while I was here, but at this moment, space was the last thing I needed.

It was almost 1:30 a.m. in Salt Lake, not a good time to call. I sent a brief text, hoping her phone was on silent. I didn't want to wake her; I just wanted to somehow feel closer.

Thinking about you . . .

My phone rang within seconds.

"Hi, I hope I didn't wake you."

"You didn't. I was already awake and actually thinking about you, too. What time is it there?"

"It's 9:30 in the morning and my body is finally in agreement with the clock."

"Good! Where are you? It sounds so quiet."

"I'm sitting on a bench in a beautiful park near an overlook of the city. You'd love it."

"I bet I would. Someday soon, hopefully." She did her best to hide any regret. It simply wasn't in the cards for us to be together this time. The valid reasons didn't make it any easier.

I quickly changed the subject. "How was your day—yesterday?"

"It was all right. Not as exciting as yours, I'm sure. Just work and then yoga."

"Sorry for texting you in the wee hours, but it's wonderful to hear your voice."

"No, I'm so glad you did. How are you doing, is everything all right?" Her love and empathy had traveled quite a few time zones. She must have sensed from my voice that I had a lot going on inside my heart.

"I'm doing okay. Right now, I'm just missing you, a lot."

"I miss you, too, babe, but I want you to have a great time there. So, don't be thinking too much about me. Deal?"

"I can't make any promises."

"What else are you going to see today?"

"*Trevi Fountain* isn't far from here and the *Pantheon*, then *Piazza Navona* probably."

"Toss a coin in the fountain and eat some *gelato* for me. Take some nice pictures and send me a few."

"You got it. I promise, you'll see everything before I post it on *Instagram*. Well, I better let you get some sleep."

"Thanks for reaching out. It was great to hear your voice. I love you."

"I love you, too. *Ti amo, cara.*"

"*Ti amo.*"

I sat for a while, letting the echo of her voice warm my heart and fill my mind. *What the hell was I doing here?* That was quickly becoming the theme of this trip. It hit me hard, thinking of everything I stood to lose. Vanessa was graciously giving me a lengthy piece of rope. I hoped that I wouldn't end up hanging myself with it.

Before leaving, I took a picture of my lovely spot, this time not with social media in mind but to look at it down the road and recall the fond memories of the peaceful and creative feelings I experienced here. I left the shade of the trees and noticed immediately that the day had warmed up in the few hours since I left the apartment. I walked back toward the Spanish Steps but stayed on the road above the church at the top without even glancing down toward the *piazza*. I'd be back the following night. I walked the several blocks toward *Trevi Fountain*, getting turned around a bit at one point. I felt like a pathetic tourist when I had to pull out a little map to regain my bearings.

Trevi Fountain was absolutely packed with sightseers when I arrived at the fabled sculpture. It wasn't yet 11:00 a.m., but this was peak tourist season, after all. Several tour buses pulled up at the exact same time, and the lower level by the fountain looked impenetrable. A police officer was blowing her whistle at those who attempted to throw coins into the fountain from the upper terraces, so that killed my idea to fulfill Vanessa's request from that vantage point.

I did attempt to get closer but made it no further than the narrow opening that led to the edge of the fountain. I was turned away by the hordes and their annoying selfie-sticks, trying to capture the over-the-shoulder toss made famous in the film, *Three Coins in the Fountain*. I couldn't quite remember the legend and what it meant to throw one, two, or three coins into the water, and as I retreated from the masses, I seriously wondered what kind of bad karma I was inviting by not successfully parting with any coins at all. *Great, all I needed was to anger the gods of love during this visit to Rome!* I did take time to admire the breathtaking structure and snap a few nice pictures, so the visit wasn't a complete failure.

Emiliano had pointed out a good *pizzeria* and an adjoining *gelateria* nearby and in the direction of the *Pantheon* and *Piazza Navona*. Another pizza, but I figured when in Rome, and I was also craving some good, authentic *gelato*. I had lunch before dessert, opting for a couple of slices with prosciutto and sausage toppings included with a rich, tomato sauce and mozzarella cheese. I quenched my thirst with a can of *aranciata*, a more appropriate choice than the morning beer I drank the day before. I left room for a little *gelato* to complete my *pranzo*. I chose my old standbys—*stracciatella* (chocolate chip) and *fragola* (strawberry), which I took with me and enjoyed on the short stroll toward my next stop.

It would have been impossible to realize in the moment that events were conspiring to put me in the right place at just the perfect time. *Serendipity*, they call it.

Chapter 40

Make each impression a little bit stronger,
Freeze this moment a little bit longer.

Time Stand Still—Rush

I WEAVED MY WAY THROUGH THE CROWD, surprised that most people were just mingling around the exterior of the building, and there was only a single-file queue leading inside. A sense of wonder filled me as I entered the glorious *Pantheon*. Many of my fellow tourists made a futile attempt to photograph the splendor of the interior dome on their camera phones. I couldn't even capture it all in a single gaze with my God-given wide-angle lens.

I marveled at how the Romans could construct this ancient temple, still the largest freestanding concrete dome in the world, almost 2,000 years ago. I tried to fathom the architectural achievement and the inspiration for the awe-inspiring edifice, but neither my mind nor my heart was up to the task. I slipped out of one of the grandest sites in all of Rome, having spent less than five minutes inside.

A patrol of *carabinieri* parked outside the *Pantheon* offered a small amount of comfort, given the past year of terror inflicted on various parts of Europe. While the sentries seemed incredibly young, I nonetheless appreciated their show of force, automatic weapons at the ready. This is the world we now live in. I dodged several scooters and cars as I strolled the narrow, cobblestone lanes and soon arrived at my destination, *Piazza Navona*, one of my favorite sites in the Eternal City.

I found a bench to my liking that provided a nice view of *Bernini's Fontana dei Quatro Fiumi* and the *Church of Sant'Agnese in Agone*. The other two impressive fountains that graced the square were both closed and under renovation, a common reality in a city so ancient and so full of treasures.

A street entertainer was doing a decent Michael Jackson imitation, playing to the crowd through music and moonwalking. The song, *Human Nature*, filled the air, and the lyrics hit me in just the right spot, deepening my contemplation. *Why? Why? Exactly. Why was I in Rome alone? What had compelled me to find myself here, living out the lyrics to an old song?* Sitting here, it all felt ludicrous. I'd left the woman with whom I was falling very much in love back at home, for a chance meeting with an old flame. And that chance might end up being a fat one, at that.

My thoughts were broken by words spoken in English with an unmistakable Italian accent.

"How can you be so sad in such a beautiful place?"

Before I turned to respond to the woman sharing my bench, I allowed my gaze to rise from the cobblestones to the surrounding buildings rimming the *piazza*. The sun was brilliantly lending light and simultaneously casting shadows with wispy clouds splashing against the azure sky.

She was spot on. It was indeed beautiful, yet I'd hardly noticed.

"I'm guessing you are American," she said, rather confidently.

"Well, yes. But I am totally prepared to tell anyone who asks that I'm Canadian, you know, with our President and all."

"A *stronzo*, that one."

"Yep, he is pretty much a turd," I responded, proud to show some prowess with my Italian and happy to agree with her, politically speaking.

"Oh, so you *parli Italiano*? Or at least a few bad words, anyway?"

"*Si, Io parlo Italiano, un po.* The language is slowly coming back to me after many years," I continued our sequence of bi-lingual sentences.

I finally turned toward her and made eye contact. She had youthful brown eyes for a woman I guessed to be in her late sixties. Her long gray hair gave her age away, as well as wrinkles, not from a hard life but from a well-lived one, I suspected. I liked her immediately. Her hair made me imagine a free spirit I might have run into at San Francisco's Ghirardelli Square rather than Rome's *Piazza Navona*. She probably enjoyed the music of the Grateful Dead.

"You never answered my question," she broke the brief pause. "Why do you look so sad in such a beautiful place?" We settled into using my native tongue, as her English was far better than my Italian.

Fine. Her perseverance and astute observation deserved an honest answer. I boiled it down to one simple word, and I chose the more eloquent Italian translation.

"*Amore*," I shrugged.

She gently shook her head and rolled her eyes in a most nonjudgmental manner, delivering a philosophical decree rather than an indictment of my situation and me.

"*E sempre amore!*"

I had to chuckle in agreement. Yes, both the sweet joys and painful sorrows of life seem to come with love. It's always love. She'd nailed it.

"*Vero*," I said with a smile.

"*Ai un bel sorriso*! See you are already feeling much better."

"*Grazie*. So what does the woman who cheers up sad Americans in *Piazza Navona* call herself?"

"*Mi chiamo,* Daniella," she extended her hand.

"My name is Jamison."

"What brings you to Roma, Jamison?"

"I'm not completely sure how to answer that question. I might be meeting someone tomorrow night."

"Might?"

"It's a long story."

"I'm not busy the rest of the day," she offered.

"Me, neither. I basically have nothing to do until sunset tomorrow. Maybe," I added, the weight of my predicament returning to my shoulders.

The entertainer's boom box began to crank out the opening guitar riff to *Beat It,* much to the delight of the crowd.

"You could tell me your love story here on this lovely bench, but Michael Jackson is quite loud. Or, I have another idea. Are you a spontaneous and trusting man, Jamison?"

"I'd like to think so. What do you have in mind, Daniella?" *Who is this woman?*

"Would you like to see my beloved Roma while you tell me about your sunset rendezvous? I am quite adept at showing off my city. And I trust you for some reason. Sad Americans are generally harmless." She smiled warmly. "Do you trust an old, Italian woman?"

Had Daniella been several years younger, I'd have thought I was being picked up. But she seemed sincere on both propositions: Showing me her city and hearing my sordid tale of love.

"Yes, I do trust kind, Italian women." I returned her smile. "A tour sounds great. I lived here for a few months, many years ago. But I feel like I barely scratched the surface."

"If you only spent a few months here, then you truly don't know my Roma. I will show you, on my scooter, until you are no longer sad," she winked.

A giro di Roma by scooter? How could I resist?

"*Perche no?*" I shrugged. It sounded fun, and the distraction was just what the doctor ordered.

We walked to the edge of the *piazza*, and she mounted and fired up a vintage red Vespa. It was a wonderful-looking scooter and fit Daniella's style perfectly.

"We must take to the side streets and avoid *la Polizia*. It's illegal to ride without a helmet. Hop on, Jamison. Let's have you rediscover *Roma*! Where have you been so far? What have you seen?" she asked, strapping on her helmet.

"This morning, I was at *Trevi, il Pincio, Piazza di Spagna*, and the *Pantheon*."

It had been a heavy morning, full of soul-searching. I was looking forward to this spontaneous ride around Rome, for the company, and for the unexpected diversion. As I hopped on the back of the scooter, I had no way of knowing how pivotal the next several hours would be in my life.

"Then we shall ride elsewhere," she said enthusiastically, as we zoomed away from *Navona*.

We crossed *Corso Vittorio Emanuele*, keeping to the side streets. I knew we were generally headed east. We had to emerge from the smaller lanes to navigate the controlled chaos that is the massive roundabout of *Piazza Venezia*, which we miraculously survived, before making our way toward the *Colosseum*. Daniella was quite nimble on her Vespa, weaving through traffic. I held her waist and leaned into her, trying to remember my last time on a motorcycle and the proper riding technique involved as to not fight the driver's movement. She had attempted to tuck her long, gray hair inside her helmet, but I found myself dodging the stray, windblown strands, which made the experience all the more delightful.

We pulled up near the *Colosseum*, and she nodded for me to dismount. She pointed to four large stones, or bollards, rimming the exterior and explained how they were an integral part of the canvas shade system that was activated with the use of long ropes connected to the large stones. I imagined the canvas fully deployed, and the vision came to mind of a modern soccer stadium. The ancient Romans were ahead of their time. Initially the stadium was completely surrounded by the stones. All but these remaining four had been pilfered over the centuries since Emperor Vespasian commissioned the structure in 72 A.D. The magnificent stadium had been built on the site of the Emperor's private lake and had undergone several additions and modifications over the hundreds of years. Daniella spoke with such pride and called this 'her city,' that I asked if this was her birthplace.

"Yes, I was born and raised here. I have lived briefly elsewhere, even for a few years in the States, but this is my home. I'm certain I will also die here," her voice trailed off.

"We have much more to see, Jamison, let's continue our tour."

She started the Vespa, and we continued, riding past the *Arco di Costantino* and along *Circo Massimo,* now just a grassy remnant of the large stadium where chariot races were once held. I mentioned the film, *Ben Hur*. Daniella confirmed that this was indeed the historical setting for that scene. We climbed toward Aventine hill and again dismounted at the edge of a beautiful courtyard, adjacent to one of the several churches found on the hill.

"This is where I come when I need to feel peace and get away from the noise of the city," explained Daniella, who literally was breathing in the tranquility of this location.

We gazed out past the Tiber and saw the imposing dome of St. Peter's and the *Trastevere* neighborhood, just across the river. To the north, historical parts of Rome were clearly identifiable, including the church at the top of the Spanish Steps. We avoided the heavy tourist spots and their long lines but did duck into a couple of churches that graced the hill and strolled through another courtyard under the canopy of tall trees, now in their full summer splendor. Daniella offered more history lessons about the various buildings of Aventine. There was indeed a peaceful feeling to this place. The grandeur of Rome was visible, yet the city noise was almost completely muted from our lofty perch.

"Are you ready for more adventure, Jamison?"

"Yes, this has been so enjoyable. I'm grateful that you're showing me your city. I've learned more in this past hour than I did during the months I lived here.

"*Benissimo!* Let's visit a few more sites, and then we can have dinner together, if you'd like. You can tell me your love story as we dine."

"That's a deal, as long as I treat my wonderful tour guide."

"*Va bene, "*she agreed, and we began our decent from *Aventine Hill.*

We rode past the *Bocca della Verita* and the mobs of tourists lined up to test their truthfulness at the risk of losing a hand. Thankfully, Daniella didn't include a stop here on the itinerary. I was getting an authentic tour from a native Roman, and I was absolutely thrilled. We climbed again and were rewarded with a wonderful view of the *Foro Romano.* I did have a tourist moment and had someone take a picture of Daniella and me with the Forum in the background. I had social media in mind for the photo and wanted to commemorate the scene with her.

We stopped, and Daniella shared the story of *Piazza del Campidoglio* on *Capitoline Hill.* Michelangelo had designed this square in the shape of a trapezoid which now contained a museum and several Roman government buildings. An impressive statue of Marcus Aurelius stood guard over the square. I had not been to this site before, so it was a treat for me. We then proceeded down into the Jewish Ghetto district of Rome. Daniella recounted tragic tales of discrimination and confinement that were forced on its inhabitants and shared some architectural tidbits. She took us to a dead end where we saw more ancient ruins and columns. A young lady approached our vista, trying to make heads or tails of the map in her hands. Daniella offered some assistance.

"You appear lost. Can we help you find your way?"

The woman responded with a thick, French accent.

"I believe I am indeed quite lost, but I am very content to be so."

What a perfect answer, I thought. I envied her. She embraced being lost, and it gave her immense joy. I had come to Rome, in part, to find myself, and, so far, it had been a rather joyless experience except for the past two delightful hours.

We left the Ghetto and rode toward the historic district. We stopped not far from my Airbnb at *Palazzo Farnese*, the French Embassy. We rode by several of the large mansions abundant in the area, with Daniella sharing more information along the way. We passed through *Campo di Fiori*, which had morphed from the daytime open-air market into the trendy spot to experience the more touristy side of Roman nightlife.

We would not be dining there. Daniella had another spot in mind, across the river.

"We shall dine in *Trastevere*. It is my favorite part of Rome. You will see why."

"That sounds prefect," I replied.

Our time together in *Trastevere* would indeed be perfect, in every imaginable way. The next few hours would also teach me an everlasting lesson—that random human connections unexpectedly come our way in life and are to be treasured.

Chapter 41

I finally see the dawn arrivin'.
I see beyond the road I'm drivin',
Far away and left behind.

Don't Look Back—Boston

IT WAS THE EVE OF THE LONGEST DAY OF THE YEAR so the sky was still bright as we crossed the Tiber and entered the *Trastevere* district. A popular spot with the younger crowd, the mood was already vibrant, even though it was well before sundown. Daniella navigated the narrow cobblestone lanes that gave the feeling of being in a maze, where one could easily get lost, which we had just learned wasn't such a bad state of being. We parked the Vespa with other scooters in a small square that was bustling with tourists and locals alike, settling in for an evening of food and beverage.

"I suppose that if one were searching for it, the heart of *Roma* would be found here, in *Trastevere*," Daniella declared.

I was immediately smitten by what I saw and felt. There was a special energy that came from the old buildings, the peculiar asymmetry, and the variety that presented itself. One could opt for a popular and noisy cluster of bars and restaurants or a tranquil, old-fashioned atmosphere could be found just an alley away and what felt like a century ago.

Daniella chose a less crowded part of the charming neighborhood, finding a quiet restaurant where we could more easily talk. I still had a story to tell, after all, a payment of sorts for my wonderful tour of the city. We settled into a table on the patio of a quaint establishment and from the wonderful aroma spilling out of the kitchen, it promised an incredible meal. Daniella was more in the mood for beer over wine, so she ordered for us, selecting a Sardinian brew that she liked, along with an appetizer to share—fried artichoke.

"So, tell me about your love story. We have several courses before dessert."

"I suppose I should start at the beginning." And that is what I did.

I began with the first phone call I took at work from Kate, almost three years ago, and how the woman behind the voice intrigued me. I recounted the dinner with Abbey, and how her eyes lit up when she connected the two of us. I described the first kiss, along with that magical dance in her kitchen. I gave a broad overview of our whirlwind romance, the intensity, the fireworks, the passion, and the love songs. And, of course, I added that deep down, I knew it would never last, despite my initial hope that I had found exactly that for which I'd been searching. All the emotions from that time flooded back as I told her how we went our separate ways, and that I knew in my heart it was for the best, even though that organ in my chest took quite a painful hit in the process.

I shared with Daniella the lyrics to *The Spanish Steps*, and how I told Kate to take her laps around the universe, and she'd know where to find me in two years on the Summer Solstice at sunset. Just like in the song; a case of life imitating art.

"So, you write songs? Do you perform and sing them?"

"I've played the guitar and performed at some open mic events, but I have a talented partner who does the singing and writes her own music and lyrics. I'm aspiring to sell my songs and have a huge hit on the radio someday," I smiled.

"Oh, Jamison, I could tell back at *Piazza Navona* that you were a romantic, but you are also a poet! What a wonderful idea for a song and for an actual experience! *Molto romantico!* What made you choose the Spanish Steps?"

"I had the view from the *Pincio* in mind as I wrote the words, but that didn't rhyme, so *The Spanish Steps* seemed much more poetic," I confessed.

"*Piazza di Spagna* is equally lovely at sunset. You chose your setting very well. So that is where you will be tomorrow night? Will Kate be there?" Daniella seemed quite invested in the story.

"Well, that's where this story gets kind of complicated."

I rewound the videotape of the past two years to show what had transpired; how Kate had indeed taken the time to rack up the experiences that she had never truly had. Marrying her college sweetheart so young had denied her of the many experiences gained from dating.

"I've only seen Kate from afar a couple of times since March of 2015. Through social media and from what friends have told me, I've been somewhat aware of what she's been doing. She's definitely made up for lost time, shall we say."

"But you admit that she needed these experiences?"

"Of course. At first it wasn't easy to see that all play out but, yes, she needed those same experiences that I had myself after my own divorce."

I shared the pain I felt initially after we broke up, how I worked through it, wrote a couple of good songs along the way, and then finally let it go. I continued my own path, sought my own fulfillment, and did not concern myself with Kate's journey. We ordered another round of *Ichnusa*, the tasty Sardinian beer. Meanwhile, our waiter brought us some *pasta carbonara*, which was exceptional.

I then gave Daniella a quick course on American online dating. I wasn't a bit surprised that the very hip Italian lady had heard of *Tinder* and the basic concept of swiping, if not the details.

"I matched with a pretty lady named Vanessa," I began that chapter for my dinner date.

I described my relationship with Vanessa as more of a slow burn as opposed to the fireworks I'd experienced with Kate and how our first date took several months to even happen after our initial connection on the dating app. I shared that there was a great deal of hesitancy on her part, and I almost mistook her caution for aloofness. I opened the ugly box of Vanessa's secrets for Daniella that revealed the reasons why she was not a whole person and why there were so many walls built around her heart.

"So incredibly tragic to live through such events," Daniella was moved by what she'd heard. "What a resilient woman! Do you have photos on your phone of her and of Kate, too? I'd very much like to put faces to these names."

I marveled at this woman across the table from me, a perfect stranger a few hours earlier, who was so intrigued about what brought me to Rome. I couldn't believe my luck and timing in her noticing me among the hundreds gathered at *Piazza Navona* earlier; such fortuitous happenstance.

I scrolled through my photos, barely a few back, to find those of Vanessa and way back to the ones of Kate. I duplicated the pics to make it easier for Daniella to view and gave a brief history of each one. She studied the two women, the most recent in a line of lovely ladies to possess a piece of my heart.

"They are both very *bellissima*, Jamison. You have fine taste in women, I must say."

"Believe me, I just got lucky."

Daniella rolled her eyes as our *pollo con peperoni* arrived, and it smelled delicious. I'd entrusted her to choreograph our entire meal, and so far, it had exceeded all expectations.

"I detect much pain in Vanessa's eyes in the earlier photos but none in the most recent one. Please tell me more about your journey together with her."

I shared how I'd nearly given up on us a few times, and eventually, Vanessa had bravely sought help to deal with her painful and tragic past. I told her I had to helplessly stand by, without being involved in the healing process.

"In addition to that romantic you saw in me back at *Navona*, I'm afraid I've got a bit of a 'knight in shining armor complex,' something I've had to overcome. Vanessa knew about this character flaw and had me keep my distance during her therapy. I didn't even get the chance to try and fix her and make all her problems magically disappear."

"Very wise on her part, Jamison. We can only fix ourselves, and that comes through facing our challenges with very little help from others."

I detailed the gradual progress that Vanessa made and the corresponding growth in her ability to love herself and to be loved. Those steps, in turn, led her to more easily demonstrate love and affection toward others. I revealed how our relationship began to blossom, especially quite recently, peaking this past Saturday night, which now seemed like a week ago.

"That explains why you are not here with Vanessa. She wasn't ready until just recently." Daniella was putting the pieces together.

"Correct. I bought my airfare to Rome about six months ago, when things weren't very promising between us. It had been a long time since I'd visited Rome. It seemed like the romantic thing to do, to come here for the Summer Solstice, even alone. I figured, at the very least, I'd have a nice vacation, get inspiration for some new songs, and maybe, if I were lucky, get a tour of Rome on the back of a Vespa."

"You, being a hopeless romantic, just couldn't help yourself," she winked at me. The woman knew me well in a short time.

"I suppose not. But by planning this trip, I also inadvertently complicated the situation. Even though Kate wasn't even in the picture at the time, I have to admit that the song may have been in the back of my mind. I unwittingly opened up the door for her to come back into my life."

"The plot has thickened, Jamison! I was about to ask what had become of Kate in the meantime, as your romance with Vanessa flourished. Will she be at the Steps tomorrow? I assume you have been in contact with her recently."

She was quite engaged in the story, though I wondered if she judged me as a little bit crazy as the tale unfolded. Before I could answer her question, she continued connecting dots.

"Now I'm beginning to understand your mood back at *Piazza Navona*, more pensive than somber."

"A healthy dose of both emotions," I admitted.

I explained that Kate had suddenly resurfaced, first through Abbey's inquiries regarding my travel plans and her updates on Kate, and then the recent texts and phone calls from Kate, herself. Even though all these communications were rather innocuous and even cryptic, the references to the song lyrics seemed to signal she might be in the same city at this very moment.

I switched back to the Vanessa timeline, sharing how she was aware of my trip, my songs, and *The Spanish Steps* particularly. I mentioned that I didn't hide the fact I'd had some communication with Kate. I recounted her heartfelt comments on our last night together, how she felt she owed me this trip despite the possibilities that came with me traveling to Rome, and that she'd be there when I got back.

"She definitely gave me something to think about in terms of a potential future with her, more so than at any time since we began dating. She exuded confidence that my path would lead back to her, whether Kate shows up tomorrow or not. It showed me how far she's come."

"She's made incredible progress, from what you've described, Jamison. Vanessa's growth has given her increased confidence. If you love someone, set him free, so to speak. I've always believed that when we no longer concern ourselves with outcome, we open our hearts to exquisite possibilities."

I took a break from the story, as I was reliving many of the emotions involved in the telling of it, and I had to catch up on my portion of the delicious chicken. After the longest lull in the conversation since we'd taken our seats, Daniella asked a question.

"So, tell me, Jamison (I loved the way she frequently used my name), did you come this far to live out your old lyrics or to write a brand-new love song?"

I stared into Daniella's wise, brown eyes, amazed she had reduced it all down to this simple question. Was it really that straightforward? Had I greatly complicated things in typical fashion?

"That's the million-dollar question," was all I could initially muster. "I suppose that I'll know the answer to that question tomorrow at sunset—if she shows up, which isn't at all certain."

"Are you convinced that you need to see Kate to answer that question, Jamison?"

Damn, this lady and her questions! And using my name only makes these inquiries that much more personal and powerful.

"There is this part of me that can't help but wonder what Kate wants, two years later; specifically if she wants me. I'd be extremely pleased knowing she ultimately found her way back to me, even if that may not be what I want or need. It's the ego part of me, certainly not the soul. I've come to learn that my ego screams, kicks, and begs, often drowning out the soft, quiet whisperings of the soul."

"You are wise beyond your years," Daniella smiled. "What is your soul whispering to you?"

"That's what I need to figure out. At least I know which voice I need to listen to."

"I believe you will find your answers now that you know which part of you to trust."

"I admit that there is still some real fear on the Vanessa side of the equation, that my soul is possibly protecting me. There's a lot of hard work ahead for her and us. Those demons aren't quickly swept aside. The scars never go away."

"Your fears are very understandable, Jamison, but I can tell that you have much love inside of you. And while love doesn't simply fix things, it's a key ingredient in the healing process."

Daniella's kindness and wisdom truly touched me in this moment. I've always been a firm believer that certain people come into our lives for a reason and when we need them most. Her timing could not have been more perfect.

"So, Daniella, I have a question for you. Now that you've heard the entire story, what would you do if you were me?" I asked both hypothetically and jokingly. "Who would you choose?"

"Of course, I can't answer that for you; but I would ask you a question."

"Of course, you would."

"Who has come the furthest to love you?"

Once again, this wise soul had simplified things into a single question, one that I hadn't even thought to ask myself. Her words resonated deep within me, and I immediately knew the answer to her question. Looking across the table at the kindest smirk I'd ever seen, it was apparent she did, too. This was a good time to change the subject.

"I owe you a huge apology, Daniella."

"What on earth for?"

"I've made this all about me. I've been rambling on about my story, and now you know me better than I know myself; but I'd like to hear more about you."

"No apology is necessary, Jamison. I wanted to hear your love story. It was I who interrupted your somber, rather, your pensive thoughts at *Piazza Navona* and then kidnapped you on this *giro di Roma.*"

"I'm extremely grateful you did; but I would like to know more about my new, Italian friend."

From across the table, I saw a look in her eyes that I knew too well, similar to what I had first seen in Vanessa's—sadness. She, too, carried a burden and hid a painful secret.

Chapter 42

Now I see it all through different eyes;
Where I'm going, where I've gone,
All I know: I'm still surprised
That the road goes on and on.

The Road Goes On—Toto

"FINE. I'LL TELL YOU ABOUT ME. Let's finish here, get some *gelato*, and stroll the streets of *Trastevere*. I briefly lived here when I was much younger, and I'm still quite enchanted with the neighborhood."

We left the tranquility of the restaurant and joined the masses that are understandably drawn to the more vibrant parts of the district. Among the many busy *trattorias* and bars, we found a *gelateria*. I went with the usual cup of *stracciatella* and *fragola*, and Daniella opted for a *limone* and *pistaccio* combo. We took our order with us and walked the cobblestone streets while she talked, interrupting her story occasionally to point out some local history. She was also fascinated with the diverse ceilings found in the well-lit top-floor apartments that caught her eye, contrasting with the darkening sky. I was oblivious until she had me looking up as well.

Daniella had grown up in Rome and described a happy and normal childhood, including the typical rebellion against anything her parents strongly favored. Both good timing and her aptitude in school led her to be perfectly positioned for the computer boom. She worked for several tech companies as a software developer in London, Milan, Paris, and for a brief time in Silicon Valley, which explained her excellent English. She met her husband while in Milan, and they had two children. She rose to mid-management levels before becoming disenchanted with it all.

"Several years ago, I had an epiphany one day at work. I received an email from a colleague in the next office. It was nothing important. It didn't need documentation, just a simple question. I got up from my desk, poked my head into his office, and inquired why he couldn't have just come in and asked me the question instead of sending an email? He said he preferred that type of communication to face-to-face contact. It was in that moment that I knew I had to get out. I value human connection far too much, and I feared what I, and the world at large, was becoming. So, I took an early retirement."

"Wow. I definitely see you as much more of a people person than someone stuck behind a machine."

"Very true, which explains why I've been thoroughly enjoying my next chapter in life."

Initially, Daniela didn't work after her departure from the tech world but started giving tours of Rome for guests of several Airbnb properties. Many of her friends in Rome were participating in it, since that lodging option had become very popular. So, I'd been whisked around Rome by a pro!

"My husband was set to retire when he was diagnosed with lung cancer. Stubborn fool couldn't give up his damn cigarettes," her voice trailed off, the pain clearly still there.

"I'm so sorry, Daniella," was the best I could come up with.

"It's been three years now and has been difficult, but I have dear friends here in Rome and family not far away. My daughter lives in *Milano* with her husband and two children, Giulia and Luca. And my son is an administrator for the airport in *Olbia, Sardegna*. He and his wife have a son, Matteo. I need to plan a visit with them soon. We get so consumed with life."

It was Daniella's turn to be the pensive one in our unlikely pairing. We walked in silence for a bit, taking in the sights and sounds. I was beginning to understand the allure of *Trastevere*, at once frenetic and then tranquil, depending on which alley, street, or square was chosen.

"This is *Piazza Santa Maria* and the *Basilica* of the same name. It's one of the oldest churches in all of Rome." A gorgeous fountain was the centerpiece of the square, dating back to the 8th century. Bernini had a hand in one of its several restorations over the centuries.

We were making our way back in the general direction of the restaurant and Daniella's Vespa. A wave of melancholy washed over me as I realized that this wonderful day and the time with my delightful company was coming to an end. I wanted to soften the goodbye somehow.

"I assume you're savvy regarding social media?" Daniella smiled at my question.

"Yes, I'm on *Facebook*. It's an easy way to keep up with my family and friends and what they are doing."

"I'd love to stay in touch, if you'd like to. I've really enjoyed this day and your company."

"I would love to know how your story ends, although I have a feeling that I already do," her voice trailed off. "But I am not sure it will be possible for us to keep in contact."

I didn't ask why, but Daniella could see I was a bit confused and probably sensed my disappointment. She reached out and touched my arm, halting our stroll. I saw sadness in her eyes.

"Believe me, it's nothing personal at all. It's just that I won't be having much time on my hands to be online. Let's sit while I explain."

On the steps of a church, one of dozens dotting *Trastevere*, Daniella offered no history lesson on this building, nor was I interested in it. In the darkness of the ancient square, my mind raced, wondering what she was about to reveal; dreading that it was something ominous.

I had good reason for that feeling as she explained, "I have pancreatic cancer and most likely only have a few months left."

I sat in stunned silence, staring down at the cobblestones, not knowing what to say and unable to look up.

"The initial course of treatment has been unsuccessful. I've decided to forgo the next round which is a very aggressive approach and will almost kill me in order to save me and no guarantee that it will even work. I saw my husband go through hell. His quality of life was non-existent due to his treatment, and I swore I wouldn't go that route if ever faced with a similar situation. Plus, I'm too fond of my hair and can't imagine myself bald. No offense." Daniella's attempt to lighten the moment was minute, at best.

"I'm so sorry, Daniella. You look incredibly healthy. I . . .." *What a stupid thing to say,* I thought. Is there ever a good thing to say in such moments?

"So, now you see, Jamison, I won't be on *Facebook* much at all, or even online, for that matter." She managed a slight smile.

"No, I can't imagine that would be much of a priority."

"I'll be too busy spoiling my grandchildren and spending time with family and friends. I have a few goodbyes to take care of."

"That sounds like a good plan." I couldn't begin to imagine what she was facing, which severely impacted my ability to say anything even remotely eloquent.

"I was at the doctor earlier today when I received the results from the first rounds of treatment and my prognosis going forward. I went for a short ride and then found myself at my favorite *piazza*, which is apparently yours, too. You've helped me get through a very difficult day, Jamison, and I'm grateful. We may not have *Facebook* messages or emails in our future, but we shared this beautiful day together, and I will treasure that."

Emotions swelled within me and almost found their way to my tear ducts.

"So, you're telling me that in such a dark moment, you found it in your heart to be more concerned about a sad-looking American sitting on a bench in *Piazza Navona*? My little love story pales in comparison to the things you're facing. I feel ashamed and embarrassed that I've been baring my soul these past couple of hours."

"Don't be silly. Can't you see that I needed to hear your story? I was having a moment of self-pity, and your timing at *Navona* was impeccable. So, thank you! And besides, what is more uplifting than hearing about love?"

I looked at her and just shook my head, fighting tears. What an incredible soul. In this moment, I felt as if I'd known her for many years, not just a handful of hours.

"Now it all makes sense." I mustered a tiny smile. "This explains why you are so wise."

Daniella shrugged. "I suppose that when we arrive at our journey's end, we are no longer content to have more questions than answers."

We sat in silence, finally noticing the loveliness of the square and the sounds of the nightlife spilling into it. Despite the somber tone of our conversation, it was undeniably a gorgeous summer evening in a magical part of Rome.

"Well, Jamison, enough of this serious conversation. I should probably get you back to your apartment. You have a full day ahead of you tomorrow. Either way," she added, with a telling look in her eyes.

"I'd kind of forgotten about all that. Love doesn't seem so life-and-death anymore," I concluded.

"Oh, it most certainly is when you are in the middle of it all. Love has the power to breathe life back into your soul or make you feel that you won't even survive the night."

"Amen to that."

We began walking toward the restaurant.

"Have you ever considered writing a book full of Daniella-isms and words of wisdom and guidance?" We both laughed at my suggestion. "That would be a wonderful gift to leave your family."

"I doubt I will have the energy for such an endeavor, but feel free to write a song about your wise Italian friend and your *giro di Roma.*"

"I just might. This has been an incredible day, and you are an exceptional person, Daniella."

"Thank you, Jamison, and likewise. I don't just pick up random Americans, only the extraordinary ones. I could tell on that bench that you have a very good soul. Let it soar, my friend. Love should fill you with joy."

"There you go again."

The mood had lightened considerably through our banter. Perhaps there was hope that I would survive this goodbye. We arrived at our parking spot near the restaurant, which now had a long line of eager patrons waiting to enjoy a delicious meal. We climbed aboard the Vespa.

"I'm just around the corner from *Palazzo Farnese* on *Via della Barchetta*."

We crossed the Tiber in silence. I was savoring the final moments with this amazing human, my new friend. I guided Daniella to my apartment, where she stopped the scooter, and we both got off. She unstrapped her helmet, and we embraced tenderly and long enough to convey the deep emotions we both felt. She ended the hug by kissing me on both cheeks, now wet with tears.

"How can you be so sad after such a beautiful day, my friend?"

I laughed through my tears. Her eyes weren't exactly dry either.

"Thank you for everything, Daniella. I will cherish this day, and I won't forget you."

"And I will not forget you, either, Jamison; although I won't have as much time as you will to do so," she managed a smile.

I had to change the subject, to lighten our final moment.

"So, back in *Trastevere*, you mentioned that you had a pretty good idea of which path I'd choose. What is it you think I'll do?"

Daniella put her helmet back on, trying her best to tuck in her long, gray locks, and fired up the trusty red Vespa. She looked at me and gave a slight, knowing wink.

"Buon viaggio, Jamison. Have a nice flight."

And with that, she sped away into the Roman night.

Epilogue

June 21, 2017

Emiliano studied the picture on his phone for the 20th time since he'd arrived at *Piazza di Spagna*. It was still well before sunset, but he understood the importance of his mission and was accordingly punctual. He climbed his way to the top of the Steps, just as he was instructed, and waited for the sun to dip lower in the west. He knew that on this night, from this vantage point, the sun would set directly over the dome of St. Peter's *Basilica*, its northernmost point for the year.

It was a beautiful evening. After a typically hot, early summer day, the cooling *Ponentino* winds from the west offered refreshing relief. It was approaching 21:30, yet the top of the famous square was still bathed in the fading light. The fountain below and most of the steps were now in shade, as nighttime finally began to conquer the long day.

He'd been here on countless occasions at just about every time of day and night; but this visit felt quite unique. There was now a greater attachment to this date and to this place. He completely understood why this setting had been selected as a meeting place.

Well played, my American friend, he thought to himself and smiled, impressed by the romanticism of someone from the States.

Emiliano was Roman, after all, and was proud that the roots of the word *romantic* came from his beloved city. He was honored to be entrusted with this assignment, yet he was, naturally, a bit apprehensive to see how it would all play out.

Suddenly, there she was, taking the last few steps to the top terrace. He again looked at his phone and the photo he'd been sent. It had to be her. She stood about a meter and a half tall with dark brown hair. Glancing around, it was as if she were looking for someone. He was certain this was the woman he'd been asked to meet.

After a deep breath, Emiliano approached her, trying to look as far from threatening as he possibly could.

Time to turn on that Italian charm, he nearly said aloud, approaching her from the side, just as she turned away.

He tapped her gently on the shoulder, hoping to not startle her.

"Is your name Kate?" He asked timidly as she turned and faced him.

"Yes," a puzzled look filled her face.

"I'm so sorry to bother you. My name is Emiliano, and I have something to give you."

He produced a letter from his shirt pocket.

"Our mutual friend, Jamison, said that you might be here this evening, and he wanted you to have this. He also said to tell you he is very sorry he couldn't be here to meet you."

He was about to stumble on the words he'd rehearsed, so instead he kept it simple.

"I'm sure it's all in the letter."

Kate appeared stunned and said nothing, taking the letter and recognizing the handwritten 'Kate' on the envelope.

"It was nice to meet you, Kate. I hope you enjoy your stay in *Roma*."

"Thank you," she managed softly.

He felt a tinge of guilt just leaving her standing there clutching the letter, looking somewhat bewildered.

Kate watched as Emiliano descended the Spanish Steps, and disappeared into the throngs of people, all drawn here to enjoy another gorgeous Roman sunset on this, the longest day of the year. She looked up just as the sun fell below the golden horizon of the Eternal City.

The Long Goodbye

(Chorus)

We both know
It's just a long goodbye.
If we look too deep,
We'll see it in our eyes.
I'll carry your heart
'Till the day I die.
We both know
This is the long goodbye.

When you found me,
I was a broken man.
The winter tides
Had stolen all the sand.
On those barren rocks,
You retrieved my heart.
Your love gave me
A brand-new start.

(Repeat Chorus)

We both know
It's just a long goodbye.
If we look too deep,
We'll see it in our eyes.
I'll carry your heart
'Till the day I die.
We both know
This is the long goodbye.

(Bridge)

Heart to heart,
Soul to soul;
What's left of me,
I now know.

I always knew
You wouldn't stay.
We burned so bright,
I couldn't keep away.
From lofty heights,
We would soar.
When you left me,
I was so much more.

(Repeat Chorus)

Acknowledgments

Taking an idea for a story from *something in my head* to an actual published book has been a daunting process. There are several people I'd like to thank for helping me see my dream come to fruition.

Pat Parkin was my first and biggest fan, instilling in me a belief that I could pull this off. She and Joyce Ekstrand made up my mini focus group and provided me valuable feedback and even more importantly, weekly deadlines.

Thanks to Karen Christoffersen at BookWise Publishing for taking on a rookie writer and helping me become an actual author; Meagen Johnson for her marketing expertise; and Sue Robertson for her knowledge and assistance with two of the most difficult chapters.

A special thanks to Amber McRae for her amazing cover artwork and Melissa Lowe for the design.

Grazie to Emiliano Vonzin and the Norwegian ladies for the real *giro di Roma* that far exceeded the one I envisioned.

A shout-out to the Vegas Golden Knights on their astounding inaugural season. Most nights, as I wrote this book, I had vinyl records playing on the turntable with a muted hockey game on TV. The Golden Misfits were wonderful company.

Thanks to the many friends and family who gave me encouragement throughout the process. Your belief in me is greatly appreciated.

Lastly, I'd like to thank the wonderful people in my life who inspired the various characters and the original songs that are part of the story. You know who you are. You all have touched my life in some way and have taught me more about myself and about the very subject of this book, which is love.

About the Author

BRUCE BAIN IS A FIRST-TIME AUTHOR WITH HIS LOVE STORY, *The Spanish Steps*. A graduate of the University of Utah, with a degree in Mass Communication, Bruce has always enjoyed a passion for writing. His deep love for music eventually combined with his love of writing. Add to that, his newest passion: guitars. Hence, writing lyrics and composing songs on the acoustic guitar is his joy and release from the stress of life.

Bruce loves to travel, attend concerts, and his favorite activity is body surfing—typically logging more beach days in a year than time spent hiking in his nearby Utah mountains. He lives in Salt Lake City and has two wonderful daughters and two grand dogs.

Bruce Bain

Look for more tender romances to get lost in . . .
Coming in 2019, **Finding Daniella.**

Find out more about Bruce and his books and music at:
www.bruceobain.com
facebook.com/bruceobain
twitter.com/bruceobain1

Buy your copies today at Amazon.com